DEFENSELESS

#1 MYSTERY LAKE SERIES

TAMSEN SCHULTZ

Published by Devil's Gate Press, LLC

Cover Design by Melody Barber

Edited by Edited by Cameron Yeager

E-Book ISBN: 978-1-955384-23-0

Print ISBN: 978-1-955384-24-7

ALSO BY TAMSEN SCHULTZ

The Mystery Lake Series

1) Defenseless

2) Exposed (coming soon)

More to follow!

The Doctors Club Series

1) Cyn

2) Six

3) Devil

4) Nora

The Windsor Series

1) A Tainted Mind (Vivienne & Ian)

2) These Sorrows We See (Matty & Dash)

3) What Echos Render (Jesse & David)

4) The Frailty of Things (Kit & Garret)

5) An Inarticulate Sea (Carly & Drew)

6) A Darkness Black (Caleb & Cate)

7) Through The Night (Naomi & Jay)

8) Into The Dawn (Brian & Lucy)

9) The Puppeteer (Prequel)

Windsor Short Stories

Bacchara, Chimera, and The Thing About London

The Tildas Island Series

1) A Fiery Whisper (Charlotte & Damian)
2) Night Deception (Alexis & Isiah)
3) A Touch of Light and Dark (Nia & Jake)
4) This Side of Midnight (Anika & Dominic)
5) Eight Minutes to Sunrise (Beni & Cal)

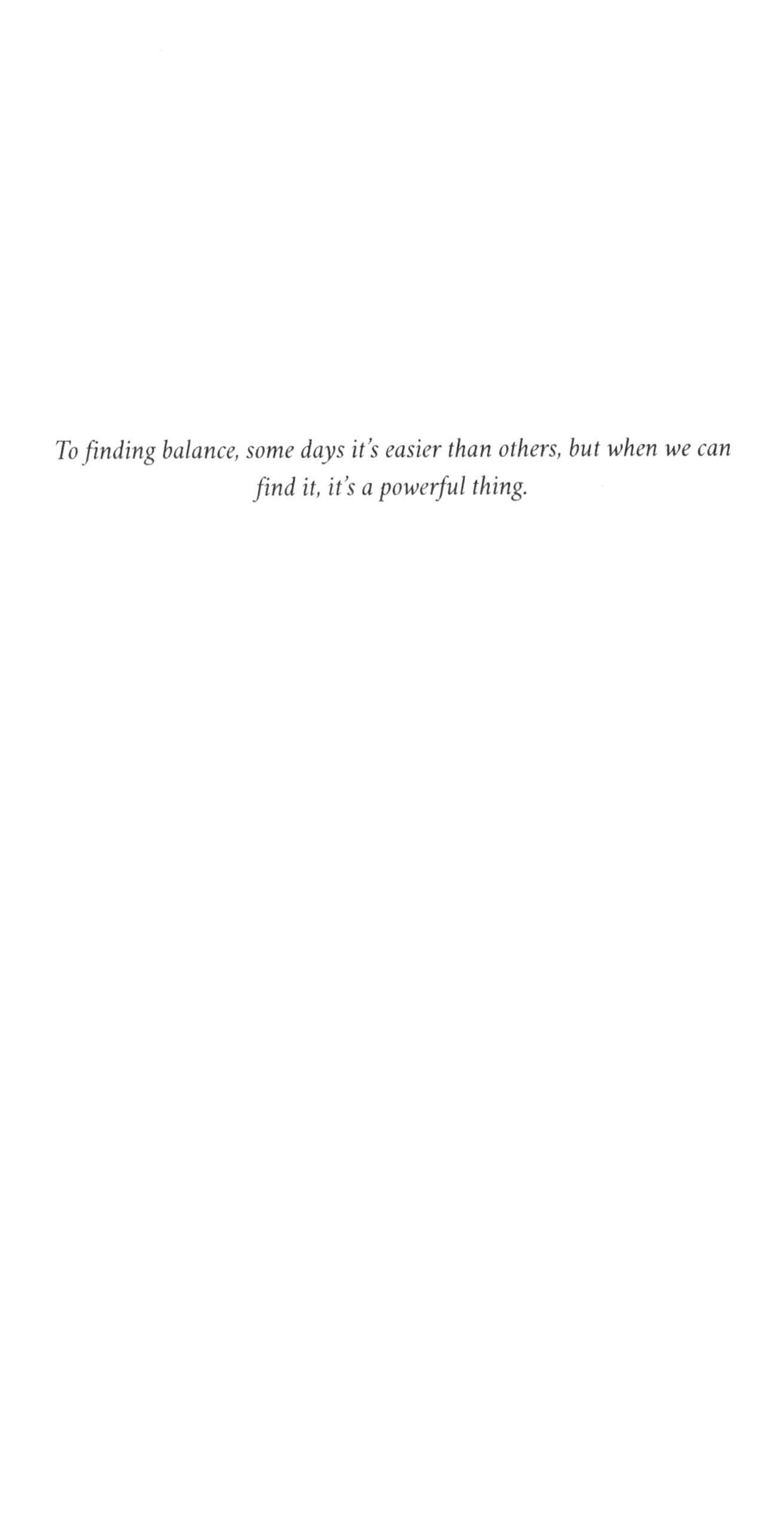

To finding balance, some days it's easier than others, but when we can find it, it's a powerful thing.

ACKNOWLEDGMENTS

This is the first time I'm bringing stories to my home state of California and I'm loving the setting I've both chosen and created. Mystery Lake is an entirely fictional place, but it has been inspired by the mountain towns of Sonora, Angels Camp, and Murphys. If you ever have a chance to visit any of those places, I'd highly recommend it. They offer a very different experience than Tahoe to the north, or San Francisco to the west, and are charming, loaded with good wine and food, and surrounded by gorgeous scenery.

This is the first book in a ten-book series that will follow the Warwick clan and I hope you enjoy getting to know the family and community. As for my community, as always, I'm grateful for my PA, Stephanie, and the whole crew at Aurora Publicity for everything they do. Eileen and Lisa—I couldn't do this without you (well, I could, but it would be *a lot* less fun). And to my family—by blood and by choice—you all are the best.

CHAPTER ONE

Bela Houseman shushed her sister as they crept through the mudroom of their house. They weren't *that* late for curfew—only twenty minutes—but it would be better if they didn't wake their mom. She was pretty cool as moms went and wasn't one to get worked up about Bela and her twin, Nala, being a little late. But if they could make it upstairs to their rooms without calling attention to their tardiness, they'd all be happier.

"Did you see Jason making cow eyes at Jess?" Nala giggle-whispered as they tiptoed through the kitchen. Jason Larson had had a crush on Jessica Blackman since kindergarten. Given that they'd all graduated from high school a few days earlier, that was a lot of years to be pining for someone. He was a good guy, and everyone knew Jessica liked him, too. No one knew why neither had ever acted on their feelings.

Unlike Nala, though, who seemed amused by the unrequited love, Bela thought it was kind of sad to see Jason so moony. Their mother often said that life was too short to live with regrets. With all of them leaving for college at the end of the summer, Jason was definitely going to be wrestling with that particular demon in the coming months. He should have bucked up and asked Jess out ages ago. Maybe he would have gotten turned down, but Bela didn't think so. Then again, did Jess want to be with a guy who wasn't willing to take a chance? Bela wouldn't have. She couldn't imagine being with a guy who was too scared to ask her out because he might get embarrassed if she said no. As if his pride was more important to him than she was.

"Shh," Bela said again, twisting her head around to faux-glare her sister. They were identical in almost every way, except Nala's strawberry blond hair had more curl to it than Bela's. Named after two archaeological sites—Nalanda and Lalibela—Bela often thought they should look more exotic than they did. But no, they were the spitting image of their Irish American mother. Straight down to the fair skin, strawberry blond hair, and blue-green eyes. They each even had a small spattering of freckles across their nose, although those seemed to be fading with time.

"Mom's not going to hear us," Nala shot back as they paused in the doorway between the kitchen and the hall. This was the tricky part. There were more than a few creaky boards between where they stood and the stairs they needed to get to. And their mother's bedroom was just down the hall to their left.

Bela lifted her foot to take a step then set it down when a grunt sounded from the living room. She frowned and turned a questioning look on her sister. Nala shrugged and shook her head. In sync, as they often were, they paused rather than continue. Was it possible their mom had someone over?

Again, another grunt and the sound of furniture scraping across the floor.

"Kevin?" Nala whispered so softly that Bela barely heard her. Six weeks ago, Kevin Jacobs had started coming around. Emer Houseman had told her daughters they weren't seeing each other in an exclusive way, but she hadn't denied that they were dating. He'd taken her to dinner a few times and out to the movies twice.

Had she brought him home, though? The sounds coming from the living room were similar to the ones Bela had heard coming from Joe and Maryann's room when they'd all gone to Maryann's lake house over spring break. Bela wasn't a virgin herself, but until that week, she'd never heard other people having sex.

But was that what was going on? Was her mother having sex with Kevin in their living room? She flashed her sister a disgusted face, and Nala stifled a snort. They were all for their mom having some fun, but did she have to do it in their living room?

"Let's try to sneak by superfast. You know, time it to when they're...most distracted," Nala said. Bela didn't want to think about her mother being that distracted, so she returned her attention to the hall. The entry to the living room was near the foot of the stairs. If they were careful about missing the loose floorboards, they might be able to make it past without being noticed.

Bela nodded and took a step forward, grateful they'd worn Converse rather than any shoe with a hard sole or heel. She stepped around the creaky boards as she tiptoed down the hall. Nala followed, clutching the back of her shirt and staying close.

Bela's foot was on the first step when they heard words for the first time. Kevin's voice.

"I'm sorry I had to do that, but if you'd given me what I asked for, I wouldn't have had to."

Bela froze, and ice shot through her system. Whatever had been happening in the living room didn't sound like it was anything good. Had Kevin forced himself on their mother? If he had, that seemed stupid for a lot of reasons. He *had* to know she and Nala would be home at some point. She also thought he was some sort of big dog in the state government, the kind of job someone wouldn't want to risk losing. Then again, people, especially adults, weren't always smart.

"Bel?" her sister said, the concern in her voice a mirror of Bela's. "We have to check on her."

Bela started shaking. First her hands, then her arms, then it traveled down to her legs. She gripped the handrail to steady herself. Nala was right, but Bela was scared. What would they find? And if Kevin had done something to their mother, what would he do to them if he realized they were there?

But Nala is right, she told herself. They couldn't leave their mother.

Reaching for her sister, she moved to Nala's side, and they entwined their fingers. As always, they'd face whatever it was together. Shoulder to shoulder.

They inched forward, closer and closer to the doorway, their feet all but sliding across the hardwood. As they closed the distance—no more than eight feet—Bela's senses sharpened. Things she'd missed before seemed to reverberate through her body. The hint of a breeze coming in from the front door that wasn't entirely closed. The smell of the lilac trees her mother had planted in the front yard before Bela was old enough to remember. And then there were the sounds of a man moving around in their home. Even if she hadn't heard him speak, his heavy tread and the unapologetic way he seemed to be moving around the room gave away his gender.

A drawer opened, then closed. Then another. The distinctive halting slide told Bela he was searching in her mother's small writing desk. She couldn't imagine what Kevin might be looking for. They didn't have anything of value, and her mother's work wasn't the kind that someone other than another archaeologist would want.

Together, she and Nala paused a foot from the doorway. One more step and they'd be inside. Nala picked up her foot, but Bela yanked her back. She had her phone! She'd left her purse in the mudroom, but her phone was in the pocket of her shorts. Letting go of her sister's hand, she pulled the device out. After making sure it was set to Silent, she pressed the numbers 9-1-1, but didn't hit the Call button. She didn't know what they'd find. If for some reason whatever had happened in the room was consensual, she didn't want to embarrass her mother.

Although in her gut, Bela knew it wasn't. In her gut, she knew that if it had been consensual, they would have heard their mother talking by now. Emer Houseman was not one to enjoy a stretch of silence.

But what worried Bela even more was that if it hadn't been consensual, why hadn't they heard their mother fighting back? She wasn't a big woman, but they'd traveled all over the world, and her mother had made sure the three of them knew how to protect themselves. Maybe not from everything, but from a lot.

Her thumb hovered over the Call button, and she nodded to Nala. Everything in her body screamed at her to run, but her heart, and her head, wouldn't let her. If their mother needed them, then she and Nala needed to be there for her. As she'd always been there for her girls.

With a deep breath, Bela took the first step. Nala might be the free spirit twin, but Bela was always the first to face the music.

Her body swayed forward as her foot touched the floor and the living room came into view. The first thing that engaged her attention was Kevin Jacobs standing in front of her mother's desk. He looked to be thumbing through old envelopes and, incongruously, he had a long, pale pink silk scarf dangling from one hand.

Her gaze fixated on the scarf. Her mother had been wearing it earlier that night when they'd left to meet their friends. It swung in a gentle rhythm as Kevin held it; whether that was from the breeze or the man's movements, Bela didn't know.

Time slowed and distantly, she wondered why she seemed

unable to pull her attention from the pale pink confection. But then Nala's hand jerked in hers and Bela's focus panned out from that singular detail to take in the room.

And her mother.

Tied to a chair in the middle of the room, Emer Houseman's body listed to the side. Her head dangled against her shoulder, and her hair fell across her face.

It would have been so much better if they'd walked in on their mom having sex.

Because this...this was so much worse. This was something her brain grasped but everything inside her rejected.

Violently.

A keening wail filled the room. Bela recognized it as her voice but not where it had come from or how she could stop it. Her mother was dead, and Kevin Jacobs had killed her. It couldn't be...but it was.

Kevin's head whipped up, the movement pulling Bela's gaze from her mother's body to the man responsible. She was wading through emotions, so many emotions, that she couldn't move. Not even when she saw the glint of calculation in Kevin's eyes.

"Run!" Nala said. Not letting go of her hand, Nala pulled her away. Bela jerked as she spun, and her phone fell to the hardwood floor and skittered off to the side. She couldn't recall if she'd hit Call or not. She didn't know if help was on the way. If someone would come to stop Kevin.

And she didn't have time to think about it, because her sister was dragging her through the house. Seconds later, they burst through the kitchen door and out into the night. Leaping down the steps, they landed in their backyard and kept going.

Behind them, Kevin's feet slapped heavily on the porch then hit the grass. He might be an adult, but she and Nala were runners. Four years of cross-country and track kicked in, and before she knew it—before she even comprehended why they were running—the two of them were flying across the yard and into the woods.

They ran and ran, leaping over roots and logs and ducking under branches. Once again, she was grateful they'd worn tennis shoes. Not exactly running shoes, but they could run in anything that didn't have a heel.

Blindly, she followed her sister as they flew past familiar landmarks and weaved on and off trails she knew like the back of her hand. By the time Nala slowed to a walk, she had no idea how much time had passed. Both were breathing hard, sucking in air, but Nala kept them moving. A few minutes later, and without question, Bela followed her into the creek that ran along the east side of town. They navigated their way upstream, staying in the middle of the flow as much as possible. In the few spots where it got too deep, they hugged the edges but remained at least calf-deep in the water.

They slogged their way north for twenty minutes before Bela stopped.

"Bela?"

Bela held up a hand to stop the questions. She and her sister had been at the diner with their friends before they'd come home. It seemed that not only was her mind rebelling against the events of the night, her body was, too. Turning away, she leaned over. Everything she'd eaten earlier that night came up, flowing away with the current.

Nala's hand came to rest on her back, slowly stroking along her spine. When there was nothing left, she remained bent, catching her breath. Then, tentatively, she dipped her hands into the cold water and brought them to her face. The thought occurred to her that she shouldn't use the creek water to rinse her mouth. But then she remembered her mother was dead—murdered—and none of it seemed to matter.

Filling her mouth, she swished the water around and spit it out. Then she did it again. Staring at the current, she had the urge to just lie down. It wasn't deep enough to carry her anywhere, but maybe, if she immersed herself, it would wash over her face and nose. Maybe it could take away the pain of the night. The pain her body, and her heart, were beginning to acknowledge.

"Don't," Nala said from beside her. "It won't solve anything, and she wouldn't want it."

Again, her sister was right. But what did it matter what their mother would want? She was no longer with them.

A sob tore from her soul, and she spun. Nala was there. Nala was always there. The sisters clung to each other in the middle of the creek and cried. They didn't have the time to give in to the grief that was swallowing them. But they could take this one moment.

When they pulled away from each other, Bela brushed her hair from her face and glanced around. "Where are we?"

"I think we're a couple of miles outside of town," Nala answered. "I've never been this way, but I think that's where we are."

Bela turned and looked at their surroundings. Dark forest hugged the creek bed, but to her right, she could see a break in the woods and a glimpse of a rolling pasture. "You have a plan." Not a question. She knew her sister did.

"We'll go to Chrissy's. This creek runs alongside the back of their property."

Bela frowned. "But Chrissy's…." And then she understood.

"Exactly," Nala said. Chrissy and her parents were in Europe for three weeks. A graduation present for their youngest daughter. Nala and Bela had grown up with her and been in and out of her house since they were old enough to walk. They knew where the spare key was and knew the family hadn't hired any house sitters. The property also had the added benefit of sitting well off the road on one hundred acres. There'd be no risk of being seen if they hid there.

Bela looked upstream, trying to calculate how far they had to go. She didn't think she'd get any sleep tonight, but exhaustion was weighing her body down.

"You don't think we should go to the police?" she asked.

Nala shook her head. "Kevin Jacobs is the state's attorney general," she responded, reminding Bela of the man's position. "And the chief of police is his brother. I'm not saying we shouldn't ever go to the police, but I think we need to understand what's going on before we do. I don't know if Chief Jacobs is corrupt or if he would cover for his brother. But I also don't know that he isn't or wouldn't. If he does, then it's their word against ours and..."

"What?"

Nala's eyes filled, and she blinked back tears. "And I don't think I'll ever forget that look in Kevin's eye when he saw us standing there. It was like I could see him calculating exactly how he'd kill us. I...we can't let that happen, Bel. I won't lose you, and I won't let you lose me."

Bela's nose crinkled as she fought back her own tears. There'd be plenty of time to cry, but Nala was right. They needed to get somewhere safe.

CHAPTER TWO

Eighteen years later

CHAD WARWICK'S gaze dropped from his boss to his loosely clasped hands resting on the tabletop. Skills honed by his years in the military and the FBI kept him from showing any sign that the bomb Stella Matthews Zatoro had just dropped had any effect on him other than the requisite mild interest that would be expected.

Lifting his gaze, he let his lips form a curious frown. "I thought it had already been decided that Jun was going to go with me to open the new office in California, and Sabina was going to stay here. Didn't they toss a coin or something?"

Stella glanced at her husband, second-in-command of HICC, the private security firm the two owned and operated. Hunter nodded as he rocked the couple's three-year-old son on his shoulder. It was Mateo's nap time, but the little boy was probably more used to being in HICC's large compound just south of Washington, DC, than his own home.

"They did," Stella confirmed. "But Jun and Sabina spoke to us yesterday and asked for the change. As you know, we initially asked Sabina to take on the role of the West Coast cyber lead. We were willing to accommodate the switch and send Jun so long as they were both happy about where they landed. Now that Sabina wants to go and Jun wants to stay, we're back on track with the original plan."

Chad fought hard to keep his carefully curious frown from turning into a real one. It wasn't that he thought Sabina O'Malley wouldn't be good at the job. The things that woman could do and find baffled the mind. There was zero doubt she was one of the smartest people he knew, if not *the* smartest person he knew.

But in the two years he'd known her, it had become obvious to him that she was hiding something. He was confident that whatever it was, it wasn't nefarious or a threat to the company. The background checks on all employees took months. They were so deep that he suspected Stella and Hunter knew everything from the age each employee lost their first tooth to their preferred color of underwear.

All the same, the muscles between his shoulder blades twitched every time Sabina was near. Kind of like they had each time he'd known one of his military ops wasn't going to go as planned. Or when, as an FBI agent, he'd known a suspect was lying to him. Not a particularly comfortable feeling. Then again, neither was the unwanted attraction he felt toward her. Or the self-loathing that came with wanting a woman he was sure was keeping something from him.

"I assume you don't have a problem with this?" Hunter asked. "We know it's last-minute, but as the office isn't set up yet and we're not running any business from it, it shouldn't be an issue."

In his mind, Chad translated Hunter's statement into what the man meant. The decision had already been made. If Chad had a problem with it, he needed to get over it. Fast.

Very fast. After six months of planning, their private flight to California was scheduled to take off in four hours.

In retrospect, he should have expected something like this to happen. From the day Stella and Hunter had approached him to lead the opening and operation of their new West Coast office, everything had fallen into place. Like well-positioned dominoes.

The unique opportunity they'd offered him had turned into a once-in-a-lifetime one when they'd agreed that Mystery Lake, Chad's hometown, would be the right spot to make their home base. Within days of reaching that decision, they'd found a 1,200-acre piece of property that suited their needs. Located high in the Sierra foothills 150 miles east of San Francisco, the varied terrain was perfect for the operatives to train on. The parcel even had a few usable outbuildings, so they hadn't needed to start the build-out from scratch.

But the property hadn't been the only deciding factor. Mystery Lake had already been in the process of upgrading and enlarging the local airfield to better serve the skiing and hiking tourist seasons. Those upgrades had finished three weeks earlier, and the new airport was now big enough to land any of the planes in the fleet owned by HICC. In addition, while housing wasn't plentiful, what could be found was generally affordable.

Best of all, though, at least for Chad, was that he was going home. As a young man, he'd needed to leave his small town and spread his wings. But now, at the age of forty-two, going home to Mystery Lake felt more right than anything had in a long while.

Yeah, everything had gone so smoothly that he'd gotten cocky and a little too comfortable. And now he was paying the price. Having Sabina switch places with Jun wasn't something he would have anticipated, but if he'd expected *something* to go wrong, maybe Stella's announcement wouldn't have been quite such a shock.

He forced himself to give a casual shrug. "Of course it's not a problem. A little bit of a surprise, but not a problem." He wanted to ask if Sabina had given them a reason for the sudden change but thought it might make him sound like a schoolyard gossip. If he wanted to know—which he did—he needed to ask her himself. And he would. The flight to Mystery Lake was six hours, and it was just the two of them. Plenty of time to poke and prod for answers.

Then again, if Sabina didn't want to tell him, it wouldn't matter if the flight was six or twenty-six hours. For someone who chattered a lot, she had a knack for not saying anything at all when she didn't want to. Not that she was vapid—she was too smart for that. Ask her about any current event and she had an informed opinion. Ask her about what was happening in a remote corner of any country and, if she didn't know off the top of her head, she'd find the answers within hours. Sometimes minutes. Ask her to opine on movies, art, and culture and she'd happily engage. But ask her about herself? Well, that was a different beast altogether.

After two years, he still had no idea where she grew up, if she had any siblings, if she was close to her parents, or where—or even if—she went to college. No one could dodge a personal question better than Sabina. Which, back to his twitching shoulder blades, made him suspicious. And wary.

"Did she need to make any changes to what we'd already agreed with Jun in terms of the equipment or setup?" Chad asked, moving the conversation to the more comfortable topic of logistics.

Stella bobbed her head. "A few minor additions to the equipment inventory, but she was happy with the setup." Sabina and Jun had been working together since before Chad had joined HICC. It came as no surprise that the two cyber experts had similar requirements. Unfortunately, the setup he and Jun had agreed to—having the cyber labs in the main building—now meant that he'd be seeing Sabina every day.

Even worse, the main building wouldn't be ready for them to occupy for another two months, and he'd offered up his own home as their base of operation. He'd now have the dubious pleasure of welcoming Sabina into his space as they—along with Colton Manning, the logistics lead—oversaw the final updating and retrofitting of the new compound.

Chad sighed inside and gave in. It would be whatever it would be. He liked Jun, but to Chad's mind, there wasn't anyone better than Sabina. At least he'd be getting the best cyber expert out of the change. Things could be worse.

"Sounds good," he said. "I assume she's all set with housing and everything, but if not, I'll help in any way I can. Now, if you don't mind, I have to run back to my apartment and pick up the last of my bags before heading to the airfield."

Stella nodded and rose. He followed suit and started toward the door.

"Warwick," Hunter said.

Chad had been about to grab the doorknob, but he dropped his hand and turned. "Yeah?"

"Thank you. HICC has been more successful than Stella or I could have ever imagined, and while there have been both bad and good times, we wouldn't change a thing. But times do change. Life changes, priorities change." Hunter tilted his head and rested it on his sleeping son's shoulder. "We don't want to pull back from the good work we're doing, but we also want to be able to spend more time as a family. And we want our employees to feel like they can do the same. Opening the California office might seem like an expansion. It might even turn out that way. But what we're really hoping is that we'll be able to split responsibility for the jobs between the offices so that neither is overloaded. For more reasons than just the skills you,

Sabina, and Colton bring to the company, you all are a dream team to lead that effort. We know you'll help us continue to build the company we want to build. So, thank you."

Chad wasn't often at a loss for words, but he struggled now. Hunter rarely said more than what was strictly needed. That he'd said what he had told Chad more about the importance of the new venture than anything discussed in the past six months. This office wasn't just about business, it was about family, too. Despite the unease he felt about Sabina now being part of his team, a sense of rightness settled inside him. He wanted the same thing they did, and he was going to do his best to make it happen.

Three hours after leaving the DC headquarters of HICC, Chad stood on the tarmac of the private airfield. Workers were loading the final pallets of equipment into the belly of the plane that would take him and Sabina to Northern California while a smaller plane idled behind it. Colton stood beside him watching the same scene, although the man would be flying to LA rather than to Mystery Lake.

"Who are you taking, Colt?" Sabina asked, coming to stand between the two men, a small aloe plant in one hand.

Colton nodded to the smaller of the two planes. "Bertha," he answered.

Sabina made a little "hmm" noise before hooking an arm in each of theirs, jostling a little dirt from around the aloe. A small shock of desire traveled through Chad as her skin brushed against his. He might believe she was hiding something from him, but that didn't mean his body had gotten the message that she was hands-off.

"Good choice," she said. "Bertha's small but fast." Before any plane made its maiden flight for HICC, it was christened with a name other than its official registration numbers. The one he and Sabina were taking was Agatha. No one seemed to recall where the name had come from, but to everyone, even Stella and Hunter, she was just Agatha.

"You're bringing that?" Chad asked, nodding to the plant.

Sabina looked down at the small, slightly sad aloe, then up at him. "I am. Roger, meet Chad," she said, holding the plant up while keeping her arm looped through his. "Chad, meet Roger. He's been with me for years," she added with a grin.

"He's a little small for being years old, don't you think?" he asked.

"Hush," she said, curling Roger closer to her belly. "You'll hurt his feelings."

Chad stared. She stared back. Then she winked and turned to Colton.

"How long will you be in LA?" she asked. A shop in the City of Angels was customizing several company cars and SUVs for them. Colton was traveling there to oversee the final modifications before bringing them north to the new facility.

"Three weeks. Maybe a month," he answered.

Chad tried to ignore the feel of her body beside his by returning his attention to Agatha and keeping it focused there. But of course, Sabina wasn't having it. Her hip bumped into his upper thigh, forcing him to turn and look at her again. "What?"

Wisps of her strawberry blond hair flew into her face thanks to a sudden gust of wind, and he fought the urge to brush them back. A storm was brewing, not unusual for DC in August, and he hoped they'd make it out before it hit. Agatha could take thunder and lighting, but the flight would be much more comfortable if they could avoid it.

"Surprised to see me?" she asked, her blue-green eyes dancing at the thought of catching him off guard. He wasn't a fan of surprises, and everyone in the office knew it.

He shrugged and swung his gaze back to the workers

loading what looked like the last pallet. "Stella and Hunter told me you and Jun switched places. I may be old, but I'm not so old as to forget a conversation from three hours ago." He wasn't old at all, but he *was* six years older than Sabina.

Colton chuckled, and from the corner of his eye, Chad saw Sabina make a face. "Try as you might, Sabina, you aren't going to get under his skin," Colton said. If he only knew.

"I don't know what you're talking about, Colt," Sabina said with so much faux innocence both men snorted. At some point shortly after he'd joined the firm, Sabina had decided he was too serious. She'd been trying for the better part of two years to get him to crack and loosen up. It wasn't going to happen. She was already under his skin—though not in the way Colton meant—and if he let go of his control even a tiny bit, he wasn't sure what would happen. And again, back to that not liking surprises thing. Not even—especially even—if he surprised himself.

"Why the last-minute switch?" Colton asked the million-dollar question. Chad didn't move, but his senses leaped to attention as he waited for her answer. Not that he thought she'd give an honest—or complete—one.

Sabina lifted a shoulder. "I decided a change of scenery would be good for me."

He fought not to slide her a look of disbelief. Sabina was not a woman who acted on whims. She might have decided a change of scenery was good for her, but there would have been a long train of logic behind that decision.

Even knowing she'd never expose her thought process, a small, masochistic part of him wanted to ask. With a deep breath, he shoved that urge down and stepped away from the pair. Her arm slid from his and he turned to face the two people with whom he'd been entrusted to head this new venture. He intended to get to the bottom of Sabina's sudden decision, but he needed a plan to break through her considerable defenses. A plan he didn't yet have, so it would have to wait.

"Ready, ladies and gentlemen?" he asked with a grin.

Sabina and Colton smiled back.

"More than," Sabina said.

"Oh yeah," Colton responded.

The sound of Agatha's loading door closing behind him echoed across the tarmac. "Bertha and Agatha aren't exactly covered wagons, but let's go forge our way to new adventures out west."

CHAPTER THREE

SABINA SAT on the couch in the private plane, her computer open and perched on her lap, Roger tucked safely at her side. Unusually, the project she was working on wasn't holding her attention. So many thoughts filled her mind, like bubbles floating in from nowhere only to pop and disappear each time she tried to examine one.

She knew the source of her distraction. A simple postcard that someone had slid under the door of her apartment three days earlier. Only there wasn't anything simple about it. The message on the back had been sparse, just two words. But those words had been enough to shake her out of the comfort zone she'd lived in for the past ten years. She'd hadn't slept more than a couple of hours a day since reading the message.

And then there was her whirlwind decision to pick up her life and move west. The choice hadn't really been hers. It was the only way to protect herself and those she loved. But the suddenness of just how quickly her life had changed still had her spinning.

In short, she was exhausted.

Chad shifted in his seat across the plane from her, drawing

her attention. He sat at the table with his own computer open. Probably working on some spreadsheet or another. Other than a mumbled "excuse me" when he'd bumped into her as he retrieved his backpack, he hadn't said a word since they'd taken off an hour ago.

With his focus on his device, she let her gaze drift over his profile. Dark hair curled over the top of his ears. Sharp cheekbones framed a pair of nearly black eyes that she knew well even if she couldn't see them at the moment. His long, strong fingers hovered over his keyboard. Her mind might be all over the place, but there was one thing she knew for certain. Chad Warwick was a good-looking man.

He sat back and raised his arms, locking his hands on the top of his head. His biceps flexed under his T-shirt, and she relaxed back in her seat, enjoying the view. On the tarmac, when she'd hooked her arm with his, she'd brushed against those biceps. His skin was warm, and the current that shimmered through her entire body at the contact was achingly familiar. Outwardly, she treated him as a friend—to the extent he'd allow. But each time they touched, something deep inside her lit up and, as much as she hated to admit it, longed for him. Sometimes it didn't even take his touch for those feelings to make themselves known. Sometimes, all he had to do was walk into the same room.

Her attention shifted to his profile when his brow furrowed and he frowned. Dropping his hands back to the keyboard, he started typing. It had come as no surprise to anyone when he'd been asked to head this new venture. Chad Warwick was far more than a pretty face. He'd earned every bit of respect that Stella, Hunter, and all the employees of the firm showed him.

As for her, well, she, too, held him in high regard. He was the consummate professional, embodying everything HICC stood for and was named after—honor, integrity, courage, and compassion. But more than that, over the past two years, the two of them had meshed so well that it wasn't uncommon for one of them to anticipate the other's needs or answer a question before being asked. They communicated seamlessly—even in the most hair-raising of situations—and he was one of her favorite operatives to work with. She understood why he'd taken the new role that would have him sitting behind a desk more often than not. But it was a shame he wouldn't be in the field anymore.

No, professionally, she had zero complaints about Chad Warwick, and she was looking forward to seeing him take on this new challenge.

Personally, well, that was another matter.

Not that she had complaints, per se. Again, he was always courteous and professional. But that was the crux of her issue. He was always so *professional* with her. She was a likable person and got on well with all of her colleagues. After-work drinks were a common occurrence, as were barbecues, hikes, and an occasional night out dancing. And while Chad often joined in, very rarely, if ever, did he engage with her during those outings. In fact, she had the sense that in some way, she disappointed him.

Of course, that could be her own guilt coloring her perspective. In his first few weeks at HICC, he'd tried to get to know her. He'd stopped by her desk to chat more than a few times and had even bought her a beer after work twice. He'd asked all the usual questions about her life, and she'd smiled and given him the same glib answers she always gave. But the answers that seemed to satisfy everyone else hadn't been enough for him. After those first few weeks, he'd simply stopped talking to her about anything other than work. She'd felt the loss more than she should have, but there was little she could do about it. Even if, at times like these when it was just the two of them, she wished she could change it. She wished she could give him more.

"Tell me about Mystery Lake," she said. In an effort to keep her thoughts from turning too maudlin, she defaulted to her usual chatter. Also, maybe to annoy him a little bit.

He glanced up and cocked an eyebrow. "You probably know more about it than I do at this point."

He had a point. She didn't tend to do things by half measures. When it became clear that she and Jun needed to switch places, she'd done her research. She knew more facts and figures about the gold rush town of fifty thousand people than probably most of the residents. But that didn't mean she *knew* the town.

"Where did the name come from?" she asked. "In everything I researched, there didn't seem to be any known origin. There is a lake, of course, but it's huge and hardly a secret." The lake, and numerous hiking trails that wound through the Sierra foothills, drew summer visitors to the area. A well-known ski resort, one owned and operated by Chad's cousin Bradley Warwick, brought the snow bunnies in the winter. The town also happened to be the location of the William Warwick Presidential Library. And no, the name wasn't a coincidence. Chad's grandfather had been a two-term, much beloved, president.

Chad shrugged at her question and returned his attention to his computer as he answered. "I don't know why it has the name it does."

That was a particularly unsatisfying answer. "There must be some reason."

"I'm sure there is. Or was at the time it was named."

She narrowed her eyes at him, although his attention remained focused on his device. She knew a nonanswer when she heard one. She was the queen of dissembling. "You may not know why the name was chosen, but you know something."

"Want to tell me the real reason you and Jun changed the plan?" he countered. He asked the question so casually that it took her a moment to digest it and then another moment to change tactics.

"What's it like living there? I know the facts, but reading about a place doesn't give you a feel for it."

He darted a look in her direction, one that was long enough to let her know that he hadn't missed her change of subject. "I haven't spent any significant time there in over twenty years. We'll practically be discovering it together."

The man could be infuriating. "But you have family there, right? How many cousins?"

"A lot. How many do you have?"

She fought the urge to throw her computer at him. She wasn't normally a violent person, but ever since he'd stopped discussing anything personal with her, this was how it had been with him. He'd give an inch if she did. He'd give her a little piece of himself if she did the same. But because she didn't have that luxury, their conversations didn't tend to go anywhere.

"Seven cousins, two brothers, two uncles, two aunts, and your grandfather," she said, reciting the number of family members he had in his hometown. When your grandfather was a former president, that kind of information wasn't hard to find.

He didn't deign to respond.

"Holding a casual conversation won't kill you, you know," she said.

At that, Chad looked up, and his dark eyes bored into hers. "You're right, it won't. But when someone wants more than just casual chitchat, it starts to feel tedious."

She drew back at that but held his gaze. A little fluttering of unease swooped through her stomach. The man sitting across from her did not look like a man who was willing to compromise. In fact, he looked like a man who knew exactly who and what he wanted and wouldn't settle for anything less. A man who would rather take nothing than bits and pieces of something.

But bits and pieces were all she'd ever be able to give. The things she'd seen and the decisions she'd made years ago had set her on a path that wasn't entirely her own. And there was too much at risk if she veered off it.

A hollow feeling washed over her at the realization that she and Chad would never be more than professional colleagues. Until this moment, this one specific moment, she'd harbored dreams that one day they'd be able to laugh and hang out and do the things friends did. But in the space of a single breath, she let that vision go, releasing it forever. She didn't have any other choice. No, that wasn't quite right. She always had a choice. She'd made hers years ago, though, and she wasn't willing to alter her course. Not even for Chad. No matter how much she wished otherwise.

Flashing a smile that she didn't feel, she nodded to his computer. "What are you working on?"

Disappointment flickered across his features, but it was gone before she could contemplate it. Then he cocked his head and grinned. "Budget forecasts. Want to see?"

She gave a shudder that wasn't altogether feigned. She might be a data geek, but she *hated* budgeting. "That one's all you, big guy," she said. "I'll stick to researching Mystery Lake."

If she couldn't have him for a friend, or more, she was going to be damn grateful to have him as a colleague.

CHAPTER FOUR

"IS THERE a different system we can put in?" Sabina asked.

Chad racked his brain at her question as he studied the documents spread across the table. Together, they were studying the architectural plans for the server room being built on the new premise.

"Maybe we can install it on the walls rather than the ceiling?" he suggested, then quickly shook his head. That wasn't a good option.

"What about putting it behind glass, like the old-school fire alarms?" she countered.

He leaned down to get a closer look at the wall depth. It wasn't a bad idea.

"What are you all doing?"

Chad straightened as Ethan, one of his cousins, sauntered into their temporary digs. In four weeks, they'd be moving into their permanent offices. But in the meantime, they'd set up shop in the prior owner's cabin rather than Chad's house. The building was a bit primitive, but he was grateful for the neutral meeting ground. Not only did it allow him to separate work from home, but it also meant he hadn't had to experience Sabina making herself comfortable in his private space.

"Ethan, good to see you," Sabina said with a bright smile. As if his arrival was a pleasant surprise. Which it wasn't. It might be pleasant, but it was hardly a surprise. The security system had let them know he was on his way up the drive five minutes earlier.

"You too, Sabina. What are you two up to?" he asked again.

Chad was certain his cousin hadn't stopped by to talk construction, but he shifted to the side and gestured to the papers. Ethan, a former naval officer and current sergeant with the Mystery Lake Police, stepped up to the table.

"We're trying to decide where to put the universal kill switch for the server room," Chad answered. "Each server has its own, of course. But in the event that something catastrophic happens, and we need to kill all servers at once, we need a way to do that."

Ethan looked down at the plans and frowned. "What's the problem?"

"The fire suppression system is the problem," Sabina answered. "We don't want the universal switch located anywhere near where that system might—or could—interfere with it."

Ethan studied the documents, his arms crossed over his chest. Dressed in jeans and a long-sleeved Henley, it was almost as if Chad were looking into a mirror. His cousin might be seven years younger, but all the Warwick men seemed to have the same look about them. Athletic builds, six feet tall—give or take an inch—dark hair, and their grandfather's sharp facial structure. The only thing that really set the eight Warwick males in his generation apart was their eye color. Chad's were dark brown, whereas Ethan's were a deep green. The rest of his cousins and brothers fell at various places on the spectrum. For as similar as they looked, it was an oddity that not a single one of them had the same eye color.

As for his female cousins, Ethan's twin sisters Joey and Charley, they shared their brother's green eyes. And although they were as athletic as their male relatives, both were petite—barely five foot five—with their mother's Mediterranean skin tone and auburn hair. A color that had more red than brown and that no one knew from where it had come.

"What if you moved this part of the wall out about six inches? If you did, you'd be able to create a small room, like an entryway, here," Ethan said, pointing to the east wall. "Then you could put in two doors—one to enter the small room and one to enter the server room—and put the kill switch in that space? With nothing in there, you wouldn't need to run fire suppression to it at all."

Chad and Sabina dropped their attention to the plans. In his mind, Chad reconfigured the wall and saw what Ethan was suggesting. To enter the server room, a person would walk through one door, which could close behind them, then a second door would open to the server room. Ethan was right. If they did that, they wouldn't need to run any suppression system into the small space and there'd be no risk of it interfering with the kill switch.

"You are a genius!" Sabina exclaimed. "What do you think, Chad?"

"I think he solved a problem in less than five minutes that we've been discussing for an hour," he responded.

Sabina grinned then started to roll up the plans. "Let's sleep on it. If we still agree in the morning, I can take the plans to Josh and go over the change."

Chad nodded. Josh was his brother, only two years younger. He owned the construction company Stella and Hunter had hired to do the work on the new facility. He was the best in the area, but he'd also done work for the DOD over the years and had the right security clearance.

Ethan and Chad remained silent as Sabina gathered the plans and the rest of her things. It was close to six, and they were done for the day. Overall, he was happy with how the facility was coming along. Barring any unforeseen issues, they'd be settling in in four short weeks.

Sabina gave them a wave before walking out the door, and Chad and Ethan nodded in response. His heart tweaked at not knowing where she was going. But he forced himself to breathe through it as she climbed into one of the company Jeeps and pulled out of her parking spot.

"You still don't have any idea where she's living?" Ethan asked.

Chad shook his head and led his cousin into a room off the kitchen that he was using for his office. "I asked, she said downtown. I left it at that. If she doesn't want to tell me, I'm not going to force the issue."

"Even though you want to?" Ethan said with a grin, taking a seat in a wooden chair. Chad shot him a look as he circled back behind his desk and took his own seat. He hoped his cousin would get the message.

But the thing about cousins is that even if they got the message, they usually didn't heed it. "All I'm saying is you two work well together. You have this seamless way of being around each other. I know that doesn't always amount to more, but in your case, I think it does."

"Next time you see her, ask her something personal," Chad said. Ethan frowned. "Ask her if she's going home for Thanksgiving, or what her favorite Halloween memories are. If you're half as smart as you think you are, you'll see why I'm keeping my distance." For now, at least. He'd been living and breathing the new facility since they'd arrived four weeks ago, and he hadn't had the time to consider what he'd do about Sabina. He knew the smart thing was to leave it—leave her—alone. If she didn't want to trust him, he couldn't make her. But something deep inside him wouldn't let it lie. Still, he had no desire to make her uncomfortable or make her feel that he was putting her back up against a wall. He needed a subtle strategy, and he hadn't had the time or energy to come up with one.

"I can't imagine you came here to talk about Sabina," Chad said. Ethan shifted in his seat and ran a hand over his face before he let out a deep sigh. "Ethan?" Chad pressed.

His cousin raised his gaze, took a breath, then asked, "Do you think HICC will be hiring once you get the facility up and running?"

That was not what Chad had expected. As far as he knew, his brother Ryan, and Ethan, liked working for Mystery Lake PD. At least they'd never said anything about *not* liking it. Like him, they'd both done time in the military—Ethan in the navy and Ryan in the air force—before settling into something a little tamer. Granted some of the ops HICC ran weren't exactly tame. And he was also sure that not every day as a police officer in their hometown was quiet. But both jobs were a far cry from the danger and near-constant stress of their first careers.

"Yes, we will be. You interested?" Chad asked. Ethan would be a great addition. Provided he was making the decision for the right reasons. HICC wasn't the military, but it did take a different level of commitment than most jobs. Including the Mystery Lake PD.

Ethan hesitated then nodded.

"I have to ask, what brought this on?"

Ethan's expression turned grim, but he straightened in his seat then answered. "Being a cop is sucking the life out of me. I know that sounds dramatic, but that's how it feels. Contrary to what most people think about police work, it's pretty routine and, even in our small town, layered with bureaucracy. I have to drag myself out of bed every day to go in, and I don't like that feeling. I need change, and I need some autonomy. I also need flexibility and think I do better, mentally and physically, if every day isn't like the next.

"I'll be honest, I'm not entirely sure of the scope of what HICC does, but I know you like it. I know you like it way more than you liked being an FBI agent. And I know you well enough to know that's probably because you've found purpose in the work you're doing. A lot of people might find that in police work, but I haven't and I'm craving it. Don't worry, I don't have any visions of sporting an HICC cape and saving the world, but I need to have some purpose. Ryan might have found it with the police—and I'm happy for him—but that's not for me."

Chad considered his cousin's words, impressed that Ethan was aware of his mental health needs and taking steps to meet them. He wasn't sure if HICC would give him the purpose he sought, but Ethan hadn't been wrong in his assessment of Chad's own happiness. HICC did good work all over the globe. Chad liked the people, the work, and the travel—it all gave him purpose. It was still a job, and some days were better than others. On the whole, though, he believed HICC was a company he'd be happy to be a part of for as long as they would have him.

Chad nodded. "I can't promise anything other than to forward your credentials and my recommendation to Stella and Hunter, the owners."

Light flickered in his cousin's eyes. "Understood. I can forward you all my details—at least those that I can—tonight." Whatever Ethan couldn't include in his CV because it was classified, Chad was certain Stella and Hunter would dig up.

"Sounds good," Chad said, shutting his computer down. "You tell Ryan?"

Ethan shook his head. "And I don't want to. Not that Ryan is one to talk out of turn, but I don't want anyone on the force to know I'm considering leaving. If it doesn't work out, I don't want them worried about my commitment to the job when I'm supposed to have their back out on patrol."

"Fair enough," Chad said, sliding his computer into his work bag. "I've been up since four this morning. First at the gym, then on-site getting all sorts of shit done. Our in-house security team is also arriving the day after tomorrow to do custom installs on the property, and we've been prepping for that. I could go for a burger and a beer before hitting the sack. Any interest in a stop at the Dirty Boom?" he asked, referring to a local favorite tavern that had been serving patrons since the gold rush days.

"You're on. I'll give Josh and Asher a call. Ryan and Mitch are on duty tonight," he responded. Out of the ten cousins, all but the two youngest lived in town. Asher was Ethan's older brother —by eleven months—and one of the local doctors. The brothers' twin sisters, Joey and Charley, had just started their last year of college. They planned to move home when the year ended, but for the next nine months, they'd be enjoying their time at UCLA. The four of them were the children of Michael and Sonya Warwick. Chad's father, William Jr., had been the oldest of William and Genevieve Warwick's three sons, but he and Chad's mother had died many years ago. Michael was the youngest, with Anthony in the middle.

Mitch, Cody, and Bradley were brothers from Anthony and his wife, Annie. Mitch was a local firefighter and Cody a country singer. Brad ran the family resort that sat on the north end of the lake. With Cody on tour and Brad already wrapped up in getting ready for the ski season, neither would be joining them.

"You think Sabina would want to meet us?" Ethan asked as they exited the cabin.

Chad paused to set the alarm and lock up. When he was done, he answered. "I don't know, but I doubt it. Josh invited her to the family barbecue a couple of weeks ago, and Ryan asked her if she wanted to come that night we went to the

Rotary Carnitas Festival. Both times, she declined. Although she did send Ryan with a donation to the Rotary Foundation. Cash of all things. Five hundred bucks."

They paused beside their respective cars, and Ethan frowned. "Who carries five hundred bucks in cash?"

Chad stifled a snort. "Usually people up to no good. But I know Sabina. Hunter and Stella know her even better. She's not up to no good. What she's up to, I don't know, but it's not anything sketchy."

Ethan opened the door to his truck and climbed in. "I'll send her a text. She's new to town—it feels wrong not to at least invite her."

Chad shrugged and set his bag down on the floor of his Jeep behind the driver's seat. "Go ahead. I'll be interested to see if you pick up on what I mentioned earlier."

"You didn't actually mention anything other than suggest I ask her a personal question."

Chad grinned. "Think of this as your first HICC test. See if you can figure out what I was talking about."

"She's your friend," Ethan said as he buckled his seat belt. "She is, isn't she? I mean, I know I said I sensed more, but you at least consider her a friend, right?"

Chad half nodded, half shook his head. "I consider her someone whose welfare I care about. Probably more than I should. And I trust her with my life. In fact, I *have* trusted her with my life on more than a few occasions. And we're friendly. But, well, if you can get her out tonight maybe you'll see why I hesitate to call her a *friend*."

"You're weird, dude," Ethan said with a shake of his head.

"It runs in the family, *dude*," he shot back before climbing into his own car. A few minutes later, he was trailing his cousin through the gates of the property and onto the road that would take them north and into town.

CHAPTER FIVE

"The middle of the country," Sabina answered Ethan's question about where she'd grown up. She also flashed him a smile that let him—a native West Coaster—know she anticipated some reaction. In her experience, those from the left or right coast couldn't help but make some sort of comment about the fly-over states.

"Oh yeah? Where? I went to college in Ohio. I love it out there. Big sky country, wide-open spaces, and all that," he answered.

Well shit, that wasn't the response she usually got. "Just a small town in Tennessee," she answered. Not the truth, but as close as she was going to get. "What was it like growing up here?" she asked, hoping he'd jump on the topic as she made a mental note never to turn her phone to silent again. If she hadn't, she would have seen Ethan's message and she would have known that the Warwick boys were in house at the Dirty Boom. And if she'd known, she would have called and placed a to-go order, instead. An order that she could have picked up from the serving window at the back of the kitchen. Or maybe chosen a different place for dinner altogether.

It wasn't that she didn't like them, because she did—more than she should. The Warwick boys were all easygoing, enjoyed one another's company, and were close in a way that she'd read about in books but never experienced. They were also easy on the eyes. Very easy. She hadn't met the youngest of the cousins yet, but she'd bet Joey and Charley were every bit as good-looking as their two brothers and six cousins.

But she couldn't let herself get close to them. The last time she'd allowed herself that luxury, bad things had happened. She wasn't willing to risk that again. Not that the Warwick cousins were in the same league as her ex-college boyfriend. Nate had been gentle and just about the sweetest person she'd ever known. The Warwicks were a bit more rough-and-tumble. Several even had extensive combat experience. But it wasn't that experience that made them different from Nate. They'd all grown up hiking, climbing, riding, hunting, skiing, camping, and generally running herd over this part of California. They might be kind and they *could* be gentle, but no one would mistake them for an easy target.

Yet no one was invincible. Not even the Warwicks. And while Sabina acknowledged that everyone was mortal, she didn't want to be the one that brought death to their door.

As she had with Nate.

Once was enough, thank you very much.

"It was good," Ethan answered her question. "There are eight of us boys only eight years apart, so we had a pretty good time growing up." Of William and Genevieve Warwick's three sons, the two eldest also had three sons each. The third and youngest had two sons, and fourteen years after Ethan's birth, the twin girls. Sabina couldn't imagine growing up in a family the size of the Warwicks. Even harder was imagining having a family of that size and liking all of them in the way the Warwicks liked one another.

"What's the story with the name of the town?" she asked.

She'd done more research than she'd admit to into her new home, but she'd yet to discover why the town was named Mystery Lake.

Ethan shrugged in much the same way his cousin had when she'd asked Chad. "I don't know why the founding fathers and mothers chose to name it that."

"So there's no actual mystery lake?" Sabina pressed.

Again, Ethan shrugged. "I don't even know what a mystery lake is. Does it hold a mystery? Did it do something mysterious back in the day? Is it, itself, a mystery? Although it's hard to see how a lake itself could be a mystery."

"Maybe there's a secret lake and they just liked the sound of 'mystery' better than 'secret'?"

"Seems to me that if you have a lake that's secret, you either keep it a secret—in which case, you don't name a town after it. Or you don't keep it a secret—in which case, it makes no sense to call it a secret. Or 'mystery' as the case may be."

Sabina frowned and took a sip of her beer. His logic was sound, but she'd grasped on to the mystery of the town's name when she made the decision to move. And no, it did not escape her notice that her interest was bordering on unhealthy. But it gave her something to obsess about when she was alone in her apartment every night. The three seconds it took to water Roger each day didn't exactly occupy her time.

"Any Halloween plans?" Ethan asked. A cheer went up from the corner of the room where Josh and Chad were in a heated game of pool. Sabina looked over to see a woman, about Chad's age, give him a high five.

She frowned. Was Chad seeing someone? The way her stomach churned at the thought didn't come as a surprise. Although if he was dating, that shouldn't come as a surprise either. Chad was a catch.

Her gaze lingered on him as he smiled and said something to the woman that made her laugh. Whoever she was, she was tall and lean, and her dark hair was the kind of wavy that looked amazing all the time. She wore black motorcycle boots, fitted jeans, a white shirt, and a red cardigan that fell to her knees. Sabina wanted to dislike her, but she wasn't really the kind of person to dislike someone on sight. And to be fair, the woman looked like someone Sabina would want to know.

Chad glanced up and caught her eye. Their gazes held for a moment that felt an eternity, then Josh said something, and Chad broke away.

"That's Jen Fisher," Ethan said. Sabina returned her attention to the man sitting across the table from her. "She and Chad dated in high school. She moved to LA after school, became some big-time lawyer."

"She back for a visit then?" Mystery Lake wasn't close enough to LA for a day trip, but it was close enough for a long weekend.

Ethan shook his head. "Her dad's health went downhill about a year ago. Right when her divorce finalized. She picked up the kids—she has two boys—and moved back. Now she and her brother run a small firm together here in town."

Great, a divorced ex. Maybe Sabina hadn't thought through this moving-to-California thing enough. When Stella and Hunter had first asked her, she'd declined. Her life in DC was stable and good and she needed that. She'd known she was giving up seeing Chad regularly, but she'd figured they'd still be working together. She'd still see him on occasion.

But then the postcard had come and, uncharacteristically, she'd panicked.

At the time, the thought of moving to California and being closer to Chad had steadied and grounded her. Clearly, she hadn't thought through all the implications of what it would be like to step into his life in his hometown.

"So, Halloween?" Ethan asked.

Sabina had lost count of the number of times in the past few weeks she'd forced a smile. It was draining, and no doubt, Chad saw through it. But hopefully Ethan wouldn't. "No plans," she answered, flashing her teeth. "Why? Should I have plans?"

Ethan grinned. "Grandad puts on a party to end all parties. Does it every year. There's a haunted house for the kids and food and decorations like you wouldn't believe. When Josh's son, Matt, and Joey and Charley hit their teenage years, he added a tent for them and their friends. Loaded it with all sorts of old-school video games, music, the works." Ethan paused. Sabina didn't know what memory was trickling through his mind, but for a moment, he was lost in the past. "Anyway, it's a blast. It was my grandmother's favorite holiday, and he's kept the tradition up."

"Isn't he in his nineties?" Sabina asked. The images Ethan's descriptions evoked were elaborate and extravagant. Not something a man in his nineties should be taking on.

"He turned ninety a few months ago. A Fourth of July baby. We had a big party then, too. He's kind of a party guy, although he prefers to host rather than attend. Are your grandparents alive?"

"How can he host such big parties?" she asked, rolling over Ethan's question. "He *must* have help."

Ethan chuckled. "He hires out the decorating and food. And also the teen tent. He'll expect us to manage the haunted house. Unless you want to get conscripted into service, I'd avoid the cousins at all costs for the next month."

"Kind of hard since I work with one of those cousins on a daily basis and another is currently building my server room."

"Then it's safe to say, your Halloween is spoken for." Ethan raised his glass and without thought, she did the same. Everyone knew it was bad luck to raise a toast then not drink, so she took a sip then set her glass down, glancing around as she did. Chad was still playing pool with Josh while Ethan's brother, Asher, was chatting with Oscar, the owner of the Dirty Boom.

Jen Fisher and the other man who'd been at the pool table earlier had moved to the bar. They looked similar enough that Sabina wondered if he was the brother Ethan had mentioned.

Mystery Lake wasn't so small that everyone knew everyone, but it was small enough that it was easy to see that these people were a *community*. She'd had a community—of sorts—in DC. She'd had her work friends, and, with the exception of Chad, they were a sociable bunch. They went out on weekends, had cookouts, and even formed a softball team. Not that she played. There were a lot of things she was good at; softball wasn't one of them. But here, she had none of that. Granted, it had only been a few weeks since she'd moved, but she had to start somewhere.

"Ethan?"

"Sabina."

She rolled her eyes and shook her head. "Can I ask for your help with something?"

He sat up immediately, and Sabina felt a rather disconcerting sensation of Ethan's attention waking up and zeroing in on her. Like a predator who's spotted its prey.

"Of course," he said.

Her gaze skittered around the room again, before landing back on Ethan's. "I want to get involved in the community. This is my home now, and I want to be a part of it. But I'm not sure where to start. Can you help me?"

"Help you with what?" Chad asked, startling her. She hadn't seen him move across the floor and yet somehow, he was standing right beside her. "Everything okay?" he pressed, taking a seat at their four-top table.

She frowned and nodded. Ethan and Chad shared a look, Ethan looking more amused than anything else.

"Everything's fine, C," Ethan responded. "Sabina was just asking for some advice on how to get involved in the community."

Chad's dark eyes remained steady on her then he blinked and looked away. Though not before he snagged Ethan's beer and took a sip. "That's a great idea," he said. "I know you're not doing it for anyone other than yourself, but Stella and Hunter hope that HICC becomes a solid member of the business community here. Having its employees engaged in the community is something I know they will support."

"Human, animal, environment...what are you interested in?" Ethan asked.

She donated money to a number of animal shelters and rehabilitation centers. But that was the extent of her involvement in that cause. She knew herself well enough to not ever set foot in a shelter unless she wanted to walk out with a litter of kittens, two dogs, and a guinea pig or two. While the thought was appealing, she didn't have the kind of life that could support so many living beings being dependent on her.

And while fighting climate change and protecting the environment was important, what really drew her in was people. She liked people—oh, not all people, of course. She wasn't the kind of person who considered everyone a friend. But she generally believed that when she met someone new, it was always *possible* that they might become a friend.

"People," she answered.

"Older people, teenagers, young kids?" Chad asked. Sabina thought of the old man she saw who came to the bakery below her apartment every day. The cashier always chatted with him as much as the morning rush would allow. Sabina had even struck up a conversation or two with him. His name was Walt and he lived in the senior housing a few blocks off Main Street. She enjoyed talking with him, but it was the thought of the kids, the teenagers, that grabbed her interest. She'd long ago given up the idea of having children of her own. Her life and work weren't conducive to it. But maybe she could be a part of a young person's life in a different way?

"Teenagers," she responded.

Chad frowned in thought, and Ethan began tapping a quiet tattoo on the tabletop. After about a minute, Ethan smacked his hand on the table. "I've got it!"

Sabina sat forward in her chair. He was so obviously excited to share his idea that his emotions were catching. "Yes?" she prompted.

"Olivia Rodriguez," he said.

"Why didn't I think of that?" Chad replied, making Sabina smile at his disgruntled tone.

"Who is Olivia Rodriguez?" she asked.

"She's the computer science teacher at the high school. The main one," Chad answered. Mystery Lake had three high schools, but only one was the "main one." One of the others was private, and the third was a highly regarded, though small, charter school that focused on trade skills.

"She started the Hedy Experience this year, a group that supports girls interested in learning about technology. I bet she'd love having you. Not only can you help teach, but you can also mentor and be a live example of how cool it can be to work with computers," Ethan said.

Sabina smiled. "Named after Hedy Lamarr?" The men nodded.

The thought of working with teenage girls was simultaneously terrifying and exciting. Sabina *loved* her work. If it hadn't been for her aunt pushing her, though, she never would have stepped into the world that now occupied her life. Maybe none of the girls in the program would ever go on to have careers in the tech industry. But if she could help open their minds to the possibility, that could be a win.

She smiled her first real smile in weeks. "That would be perfect. Can you introduce me to her?"

Chad nodded. "I'll send you email intros tomorrow." The fact that Chad knew what was going on in his hometown—even after living elsewhere for decades—was not lost on her. A flicker of disappointment threatened to overshadow her excitement. She wished she had that closeness—with family, with a place, with a community.

But she didn't. And that wasn't going to change. There were things she could change, though, and maybe, just maybe, connecting with Olivia Rodriguez would be the start of something good.

"That would be great, thanks," she said. As soon as she spoke those words, a deafening sound shot through the bar. On instinct, Sabina scrambled off her chair and ducked down. Adrenaline pulsed through her body as her eyes scanned the bar, looking for the origin.

"Sabina?"

It took her longer than it should have to recognize Chad's voice. Chad's voice that was coming from Chad's body that was still sitting in the chair he'd been in. She searched his face as he looked down at her. He held Ethan's beer, and his brow was furrowed in concern.

"It was just Angelica coming through the door," he said. "Are you okay?"

Again, it took a few seconds for the words to sink in. Angelica was Oscar's daughter, who helped her father out on occasion. It was just a door. Not a gun or someone busting into the bar.

"Sorry," she mumbled as she rose from her crouch and retook her seat. Ethan and Chad watched her. "I guess I've been hanging out in cities for too long," she said. "It sounded like a gunshot to me."

Ethan and Chad shared a look before Ethan spoke. "Angelica is getting ready to decorate for Halloween. She does it every year. She was bringing some of the boxes up from the basement."

Sabina glanced around. Sure enough, Angelica was standing

at one end of the bar, a box open in front of her and a fake skeleton in one hand.

"The town has this unwritten rule that decorations can't go up before the first of October. Angelica has a title to defend, though, so no doubt she's working on her plans," Chad added.

Sabina heard what both men were saying, but it wasn't computing. The adrenaline still pumping through her system was interfering with her logic. "What?" she asked, knowing she sounded as lost as she felt.

Chad smiled. "Halloween is huge in this town. Not sure why, but it is. My grandfather throws a big party, but the town itself goes crazy, too. In a couple of weeks, Main Street will look like a set from a movie. The chamber of commerce holds an annual decoration competition. Angelica, and the Dirty Boom, has won it the last two years. No one has ever won it three years in a row, and she wants the trifecta. I've heard that Ernie is going to give her a run for her money this year, though, and that he has something special planned."

"Ernie?" she asked.

"Ernie West," Ethan answered. "He owns the car repair shop on Main and Fourth. His daughter and granddaughter are coming to visit this year, so he wants to go all out."

"And Angelica is feeling the heat," Chad threw in.

Sabina nodded, still not processing the information completely. She was taking it in, but processing it was something else altogether. "Okay," she said, drawing out the word. "Sounds fun. Can we participate?" she asked, because it seemed like something a normal person would ask.

Chad shook his head. "Not in the business category. That's limited to businesses within the city limits. But you can participate in the residential category since you said you live in town."

Sabina considered this. It was a much more interesting idea to think about than the reason for her overreaction moments ago. "That actually sounds like fun. Maybe I will."

Chad smiled, and her heart tripped a little bit. It had been a long time since she'd seen that smile. The one that was kind of understated and a little intimate. As if she'd done or said something meaningful to him.

Oh, how she liked that smile. It felt a little like a shared secret between the two of them.

Clearing her throat, she rose from the table. Knowing that neither Ethan nor Chad would let her walk home alone if she said she was leaving, she fudged the truth a little. "I need to head to the restroom," she said. Then grabbing her purse, she made her way to the hallway at the back of the bar.

Keeping to her word, she stopped at the restroom first. But when she walked out, rather than returning to the bar, she headed out the exit and into the parking lot. It would take Chad a few minutes to realize she'd been absent from the table for an abnormal amount of time. By then, she'd be close enough to home that coming after her wouldn't make sense.

Sneaking off was more cowardly than she was comfortable with. But as she kept reminding herself, life wasn't always about being comfortable.

CHAPTER SIX

"SABINA'S BEEN GONE a long time, hasn't she?" Chad asked his cousin as he set his empty pint glass on the table.

Ethan shrugged as if to say, "who knows," but then leaned forward, resting his elbows on the table. "She doesn't answer any questions about her past."

Chad let out a long breath. "Everyone loves her and treats her like their best friend. I was beginning to wonder if it was just me who picked up on that."

Ethan shook his head. "No, I definitely noticed. If you hadn't suggested I pay attention, I don't know that I would have. Once I did, though, it was hard *not* to notice." He paused and tapped a fingertip on the table before he asked, "Why do you think that is?"

Chad lifted a shoulder. "I don't know. My first thought was Witness Protection. But her behavior doesn't align with how the marshals run the program."

Ethan nodded. "If she were in Witness Protection, she'd have a full backstory and wouldn't need to dodge questions about her past."

"Ex-CIA?" Chad posited.

"Same as Witness Protection. If she'd been an agent that the agency felt they needed to protect, they would have given her a full backstory." Ethan studied him, and Chad recognized his cousin's hesitation.

"What?" Chad pressed.

Ethan's lips thinned. "I know her past matters, but does it *really* matter? Is it possible that you're using this mystery to keep your distance from her?"

The answer to the second question was a swift "yes," but he couldn't bring himself to give voice to that response. Ethan would understand why, but Chad wasn't ready to open that wound again. The first question, though, well, that was a big one for an entirely different reason. One that Chad had given a lot of thought to. Especially after Sabina's sudden decision to move west.

"I don't care how many siblings she does or doesn't have. Or what her relationship is like with her parents, if she even has them. Or where she grew up or went to school. What I do care about, though, is the *reason* why she feels the need to keep it all a secret. What happened to her that she believes she can't talk about her past?"

"What if she can't?" Ethan countered. "I think we agree she's probably not in Witness Protection or ex-CIA. There could be another reason that prevents her from talking about it, though."

"It's possible."

"But…?"

Chad took a deep breath. If HICC hired Ethan, then Chad wouldn't hesitate to bounce ideas off him. But as he wasn't yet on board, and they didn't know if he'd be hired, Chad hesitated.

"I understand if you don't want to talk about a colleague, C. I get it. But we both know she's more than a colleague to you. Talk to me about the woman you care about. Not the woman with whom you work."

Chad looked into the steady green eyes of his cousin. Ethan

may be seven years younger, but he'd lived a life that left him far older than his years. And he cared about his family. He cared about Chad and, by extension, the woman Chad could very well be in love with.

"I think something spooked her," Chad said. The din of the bar did a good job of covering their conversation, but even so, he kept his voice low.

"When?"

"Right before we left. She wasn't supposed to be here," he responded. Then he went on to tell Ethan about the sudden change of plans that had Sabina moving rather than Jun. "I don't know what happened, but I feel in my gut that something drove her to make the rash decision." He hesitated. "And that has me worried."

"You think she's in danger?"

He didn't want to admit it, and he might be being dramatic, but he gave a small nod. "It's possible."

Ethan didn't immediately respond. Instead, he sat back and looked to be considering what Chad had told him. After a long moment, he nodded, too. "I can see it. We don't know enough to know if that's true, but it's a valid explanation for her behavior. She's running scared."

A pit opened up in Chad's stomach at the thought of Sabina in danger. He'd half hoped—hell, more than half hoped—that Ethan would tell him he was overreacting.

"It would explain the cash, too," Ethan said. Great, a piece of the puzzle Chad hadn't considered. And Ethan was right. If she was running from something, she'd want to stay off the grid. She was a cyber genius. Covering her tracks would be child's play. Including knowing she needed to use cash, rather than credit cards.

"Have you checked the HR records to see who her paycheck is made out to?" Ethan asked. Chad shook his head. He'd considered it, but then dismissed the idea. It was an invasion into her life he wasn't sure he wanted to undertake. If he were honest with himself, he wasn't sure he wanted to know the answer.

"If she's hiding from something or someone, her paycheck isn't going to be in her name," Ethan pointed out. "But I can't imagine the owners of HICC allowing her to operate under a different name."

"I'm thinking she has a company set up and Hunter and Stella pay the company. She could draw her salary from there," he said, revealing the extent to which he'd thought about this. If her paycheck didn't go to Sabina O'Malley, it would be much easier for her to hide her income. She had more than enough skill to set up shell companies, holding companies, and other entities to bury the trail of money.

Ethan was silent for a moment then asked, "Are you going to look?"

Chad hesitated. If she was in danger, then she needed to talk to someone. If not him, then Hunter and Stella. Looking into her HR files wouldn't get her to do that. It might confirm his theory. But having a theory wasn't helpful if she wasn't going to be honest about what was going on.

He shook his head. "Not yet. Where is she?" he asked, realizing it had been close to fifteen minutes since she'd left the table.

"Text her," Ethan suggested.

Chad pulled his phone out.

Chad: *Everything okay?*

Little dots popped up, followed by her response.

Sabina: *All good. Sorry to ghost on you and Ethan, but I needed to get home*

Chad: *Again, is everything okay?*

It seemed odd that she'd suddenly need to get home. It wasn't even half-past nine.

Sabina: *Yes, have some work I want to finish before tomorrow, and I also want to research Hedy Experience a little more*

Chad: *You're walking alone?*

Sabina: *A whole eight blocks. I'll be fine. I'm almost there*

He fought the urge to tell her to text him when she got home. Mystery Lake was a safe town, and she didn't need him hovering over her. If nothing else, at least he now knew approximately where she lived.

Chad: *I'll send Olivia's contact when I get home. Be safe*

It wasn't what he wanted to say. It was what he felt he could say, though. At least without feeling as though he was crossing boundaries he wasn't yet ready to cross. She sent him a little blue thumbs-up emoji that reminded him of a Smurf.

"She left," Chad said to Ethan. "Walked home."

His cousin raised one brow then shrugged. "At least you know she lives nearby."

Twenty minutes after leaving the Dirty Boom, Chad pulled into the garage of his new home. He'd bought this ten-acre piece of property with a view of the lake after he left the army. When Stella and Hunter had offered him the new job, the first call he'd made was to his brother. Josh was an architect as well as a builder and had been more than happy to take the project on. To Chad's astonishment, the house was completed in six months. He wasn't sure how his brother had managed it, what he'd needed to reschedule, or what crews he'd had to pull, but he was grateful. Gratitude Josh liked to take advantage of every time it was his turn to buy a round at the Dirty Boom. Chad doubted his little brother had charged him more than cost, so didn't mind picking up a few rounds.

As it did every time he came home, a feeling of calm settled over him. Everything about the home—from the way it blended in with its surroundings, to its exposed beams, warm hardwood floors, and views of the lake—helped him relax. His work hadn't been particularly stressful lately, but still, his home was his refuge.

Turning the engine off, he closed the garage door then headed inside. He was taking his keys and wallet out of his pocket when his phone dinged with a text. Unlocking the device, he glanced at the name on the screen and drew back.

Sabina: *Everything is fine, just wanted to let you know I'm home*

He smiled, pleased that she'd thought to let him know.

Chad: *Thanks, I appreciate it. I shouldn't say this, but I do feel better knowing*

Sabina: *Why shouldn't you say that?*

He continued into the house and headed toward his bedroom.

Chad: *Because I wouldn't worry about Colton, so it feels like maybe I shouldn't worry about you. I know you're capable of taking care of yourself and Mystery Lake is safe...*

Sabina: *Statistically, men are more likely to be victims of random violence, but since I'm not a statistic—nor do I want to be—I appreciate the concern*

He chuckled at that.

Chad: *Always*

The statement wasn't hyperbole. He'd been concerned about her for a long time, and his conversation with Ethan hadn't put his mind at ease.

He wasn't sure if the text thread with Sabina was over, so he set his phone on the bathroom counter then began stripping out of his clothes. He was brushing his teeth when another message came in.

Sabina: *Thank you for inviting me out tonight. I know I didn't get the invite until I was already there, but it was nice of you all to think of me. Your family are good people*

Chad almost snorted toothpaste foam at that. His cousins *were* good people, at heart, but that didn't mean they were *good.*

Chad: *Nah, we're not that good. Well, except for maybe Asher. He's good. But since he's a doctor, he kind of has to be*

Sabina: (gasping emoji) *I don't believe you. And being a doctor does not, inherently, make someone good*

Chad: *Ask Ethan next time you see him. He'll back me up*

A few seconds later, a new text string popped up; this time, she'd looped Ethan in.

Sabina*: Chad says I'm supposed to ask you whether you and your cousins are good people*

Ethan: (snort emoji) *No, except for maybe Asher*

Chad: *Told you*

Sabina: (huffy emoji) *I don't believe you*

Chad: *Tell her about the great camping debacle*

As he typed the text, he walked into his bedroom and climbed into his king-size bed.

Ethan: *Dude, we agreed never to discuss that*

Sabina: *Discuss, please*

Chad: *I didn't agree to never discuss. You're thinking of Cody, for, well, obvious reasons*

Sabina: *What obvious reasons???*

Ethan: *None*

Chad: *It involved ants and certain sensitive male body parts*

Ethan: *Really??? You're going there?*

Chad: *You and Cody were total shits, you got what you deserved*

Ethan: *No one deserves ants in their boxer shorts, asshole*

Sabina: (spitting out coffee emoji)

Chad: *They do when they think they are being cute by luring bears to our campground*

Sabina: *Okay, I have to give that one to Chad. I don't know much about camping, but it seems like a bad idea to invite bears into the vicinity*

Ethan: *It was just a black bear. They are super friendly*

Chad: *They are not puppies, dick*

Ethan: *I still have the video from Gramps's haunted house when you were sixteen. I'd watch yourself, C*

Sabina: *Ooo, video of a teenage Chad???*

Ethan: *Squealing like a pig when Josh came at him with a fake chainsaw*

Chad: *It looked real*

Ethan: *It was Gramps's haunted house. Nothing is real*

Chad: *I'm still sticking with my statement*

Ethan: *The best part is not only did he hide behind his girlfriend, he used her like a shield*

Sabina: *NO!!* (creepy clown emoji)(zombie emoji)(jack-o'-lantern emoji)

Chad: *I like to think I helped her define her future career path. She became a Secret Service agent. And I hate clowns. Everyone hates clowns. Don't ever send me that emoji again*

Ethan: (creepy clown emoji) (creepy clown emoji) (creepy clown emoji)

Sabina: (creepy clown emoji) (creepy clown emoji) (creepy clown emoji)

Chad: *You both are children. I'm going to bed now*

Ethan: *Sweet dreams (of clowns)*

Sabina: *I still think you're good*

Chad: *Don't worry, we'll change your mind*

Chad was smiling as he plugged in his phone and pulled his comforter up to his neck. Was he going about this Sabina thing all wrong? Maybe keeping her at a distance until she decided to trust him wasn't the way to go. Instead, should he pull her in—into his life, into his family?

He considered that option, weighing the pros and cons. If he opened up to her completely and she *still* didn't trust him, the rejection would sting. It would more than sting. If he gave her everything he had and she walked away from him, he wasn't sure what he'd do with that. Just thinking about that scenario made his chest tighten and his pulse spike.

And even if he wanted to try this new tactic, there was no guarantee she'd go along with it. He might have been holding back on her, but she wasn't exactly a font of information and sharing either. In fact, since arriving in Mystery Lake, she'd been withdrawing even more. He was pretty sure that tonight was the first night she'd been out with other people since arriving in California. And that was by accident. If she'd seen Ethan's invite before she arrived, he wasn't confident she would have shown up.

Was it worth a try, though? Holding himself back from her wasn't working. They'd spent the past two years as friends-not-friends. Yet he still knew no more about her past than he'd learned in the first two weeks after he'd met her. Yeah, if she walked away from him it would hurt like hell. But if she was in danger, wouldn't it be better to have her close than to have this distance between them?

The only answer he had for himself was an unequivocal yes. His gut told him something was very wrong in Sabina O'Malley's life. And there was no question he'd do anything to keep her safe.

Even if it meant putting his heart on the line.

CHAPTER SEVEN

Two days later, Chad walked into Bun Times Bakery just as Sabina handed over what he would swear was an envelope of cash. Bethany, the owner of the bakery, smiled and slipped it into the pocket of her apron, solving the mystery of exactly where Sabina lived. Bethany and her sister owned the four-story building that housed Bun Times. While the business occupied the lower two floors, a single two-bedroom apartment occupied the top two.

"Rent time?" he asked, coming up behind Sabina.

She gasped, spun, and lost her balance. Reaching out, he wrapped his hands around her hips and steadied her. It might have been a little harder than it should have been not to tighten his grip and pull her against him.

"You startled me," she said, one hand resting on his chest and the other over her heart.

"I can see that," he responded. He smiled when he spoke. It didn't escape his notice, though, that between her reaction at the Dirty Boom and the one just now, she was jumpier than Indiana Jones in a snake pit.

Sabina was only about five foot four, and the top of her head just reached his chin. She lifted her face and blinked up at him with her blue-green eyes. He held her gaze, and her fingers twitched against the soft cotton of his shirt.

"Am I interrupting something?" Ryan asked.

Cursing his brother, Chad dropped his hands and took a step back.

Sabina smiled at Ryan, Chad's youngest brother, and took her own step back. "I'd make some comment about a cop being in a doughnut shop, but it's a tired cliché and not worthy of me."

"Definitely beneath you," Ryan said. "I hear Chad roped you into the haunted house?"

He'd started his new campaign to gain her trust by *informing* her that she was expected at the haunted house kickoff planning meeting. He hadn't asked. She'd given him a skeptical look but hadn't outright declined.

She glanced at Chad. "I suppose I have," she answered. "I've never been part of a haunted house before."

Well, there was one new—although not earth-shattering—piece of her history. And judging by the look Ryan flickered in his direction, he'd noticed it, too. Since Chad hadn't spoken to Ryan about Sabina, he could only assume his brother had talked to Ethan.

"It's a good time. Matt and the twins have been discussing some new ideas," Ryan said. Matt, Josh's son, and the twins were so close in age, that despite being second cousins, they often had their own unholy trinity. "Something about a creepy circus," Ryan added, casting Chad a questioning look and silently asking if he'd heard anything.

Chad shrugged. "There better not be any fucking clowns," he muttered. Sabina snorted, and his brother grinned. "And don't pretend I'm the only one who doesn't like them," he continued. "Remember that time when Nana and Gramps were in DC, and they took us to that fair?"

Ryan chuckled. "Mitch and Cody screamed when the clown tried to give them a balloon animal."

Sabina laughed, a warm, husky chuckle. "I bet the press had a field day with that. A sweet innocent clown was given a photo opportunity with the president, the first lady, and their beloved grandchildren, and it all ends in tears."

"There was nothing innocent about that clown," Mitch said, joining the group. Chad hadn't heard him come in, and his gaze swept over his cousin as he came to a stop beside Ryan. He hadn't seen much of Mitch since arriving, and Chad took in his bloodshot eyes and the fatigued movements of his body. It was still peak fire season, and while they may not have had any big ones this year, the team was on constant watch. Twenty-four hours a day, seven days a week. It was taking its toll on his cousin, but Mitch and the crew wouldn't have it any other way. No one wanted another Paradise or Caldor fire.

Sabina snorted. "You all are too cliché," she said. Mitch shot her a look but said nothing. Instead, he took two steps to the coffee carafe and poured himself a big cup.

"What are you all doing here?" Mitch asked after he'd taken his first sip. Sabina had met his brothers, cousins, aunts, and uncles as they'd all stopped by the offices in the first few weeks. In fact, the only members of his family she hadn't met were the twins and his grandfather. And of course, his parents, but they'd died long ago in a car accident. Sabina had never asked about them, so he assumed that she—like the rest of the United States —knew that William Warwick's oldest son and his wife had died in a seven-car pile-up on a mountain road blanketed in fog. Gramps was only a few months into his second term when it happened. To everyone's surprise—except the family's—he and Nana had scooped up their three orphaned grandsons and moved them into the White House. In retrospect, he recognized their decision as being the right one for him and his brothers, but also a way for his grandparents to ease their grief.

"I'm paying my rent," Sabina said, answering Mitch's question and surprising Chad with her forthrightness. Then again, he already knew she'd been paying her rent, so that horse had left the barn.

Mitch glanced up. "You the one who rented the upstairs?" She nodded. "Nice place. One of our new firefighters was looking at it, but his girlfriend decided she wanted a yard. Although I might trade my yard for the views you have."

Sabina smiled. "I love it. I set my bed up to face that big slider on the top deck. I like watching the sunrise."

Ryan and Mitch shot him less-than-subtle looks when Sabina mentioned her bed. He scowled at both.

"I'm here to pick up the doughnuts Chad owes me," Ryan said.

"And here you go," Bethany said, bringing out four large pink boxes.

"Wow, all of those are for you?" Sabina asked.

"I can sense your barely leashed desire to make a snarky comment," Ryan said, taking two of the boxes. Chad reached over and took the other two. "Thanks, Bethany," he and Ryan said at the same time.

"Me?" Sabina asked, her eyes wide and her tone mocking.

"I lost the poker tournament last week," Chad said. "The cost was doughnuts for the department once a week for a month."

"You? You lost the poker tournament?" Sabina asked dramatically. Ryan and Mitch snorted.

"Shut up," he mumbled. "I'm not that bad."

Sabina snorted. "You are. We all know it. There are many things you are good at, Chad Warwick, but I think we all know poker isn't one of them."

"She's right," Ryan said with a shrug.

"Truth," Mitch said.

"Fuckers," Chad muttered. "You'll get no doughnuts today, ma'am," he said to Sabina.

Her eyes drifted to the box. "Who are those for, anyway?"

"The security team arrives in ten minutes," he reminded her. "Thought they'd appreciate a little sugar pick-me-up. Now if you ladies don't mind. Some of us have work to do."

He turned and walked away, leaving Sabina to roll her eyes at nothing and his brother and cousin debating what it would be like to be a lady.

"Sabina!" Chad called from his office at the cabin.

She turned from the picture window she'd been looking out. The team of security specialists had descended on them, devoured two dozen doughnuts, then headed out to the woods to assess how best to protect their little 1,200-acre slice of heaven. She'd been idly watching the scenery, wondering if she'd see them moving around. She had little say in how they chose to protect the land, but she was curious what they'd come up with. After all, she'd be the one to integrate their design into the main security system.

"You bellowed?" she asked, stopping in the doorway of his office.

He narrowed his eyes then gestured for her to sit. "What do you think of this?" he asked.

She took a seat and reached for the paper he held out. A résumé. An impressive résumé. She'd seen enough ex-military CVs in her time at HICC that she recognized it was also heavily redacted.

"A potential hire?" She and Chad didn't make a habit of discussing how they were building their teams, but they didn't keep it a secret, either.

"I was about to send the details to Stella and Hunter. You think it looks good, though?"

She studied him. In the past two days, he'd been subtly

different. A little more open. It was possible he was finally relaxing a little bit now that he was on his home turf. It was also possible there was some other reason driving the shift in behavior. The change hadn't been dramatic, but an easy smile here, a joke there. And he'd *invited* her to the planning meeting for the haunted house. He hadn't given her a chance to say "yes" or "no," and she still wasn't sure if she'd go. But his invitation had been the good kind of presumptuous. The kind that assumed she'd be there because she was now part of *them*.

"I think you know he's good. Whoever he is." And it was a "he." The types of positions the candidate had held were still reserved for men.

"It's Ethan," Chad said on an exhale.

Again, she studied his face. Outside of playing poker, he was pretty good at masking his thoughts. She could usually read through his neutral expression, although this time, she struggled. "Is that good or bad?"

His gaze lingered on his desktop for a moment then he looked up. "Good. He'd be a solid hire for the team Colton and I are building. But I also think it would be good for me, personally, to have him on board."

Sabina stilled. For the first time in years, Chad was talking about something that *mattered* to him. She didn't yet know how or why it mattered, but it was in every taut line of his body and in the way his lips pressed together when he stopped speaking.

"In what way?" she asked. Unease washed through her at the question. In an uncomfortable flash of clarity, she realized that she'd come to rely on the distance he put between them. If he kept her at arm's length, she didn't have to worry about her pesky attraction to him or the way her body seemed to crave his. But if he was lowering his defenses? Well, she wasn't so sure that was a good thing for her.

"You know I went straight from West Point into the army, then the FBI, then HICC?" When she nodded, he continued.

"I've always been a soldier or agent or operative. I have a business degree and this…this opportunity feels right for so many reasons. But that doesn't mean I'm 100 percent ready for it."

Oh shit. She was *not* prepared for a vulnerable Chad.

She swallowed. "In what way?"

He shrugged. "I've never run a business before. I think I'll be good at it. I *want* to be good at it. I want to be damn good at it."

She chuckled at that. "Of course you do." Like all the operatives of HICC, Chad was an overachiever.

He gifted her with a ghost of a smile. "Having Ethan here might help me. He won't shy away from telling me if I'm fucking up *or* if I'm doing something right. I know you and Colton will do the same, but…"

"Our sphere of influence in this venture is a little different than yours, though. You and Colton will need to sync on the operatives and the ops we accept. You and I will need to sync on the intelligence and all things cyber. But it might be good to have Ethan as a sounding board for the business as a whole."

He hesitated then nodded. "He does a lot of administrative work in his role with the police. That's government and we're private, so it's different, but he has a forest-for-the-trees kind of perspective that I'm still developing."

Sabina didn't take this confidence lightly. She may not know the reason why he decided to share it, but she wasn't capable of brushing it, or him, off. "Then you should tell Stella and Hunter that when you send them his details."

He shot her a wry smile. "What if voicing my concerns gives them reason to question choosing me?"

She chuckled again. "Don't underestimate them. This is new to you, and I'd be surprised if they expect you to be amazing out of the gate. Or do everything on your own. Knowing them the way I do, I think they'd value the candor. The kind of honesty you're talking about is a show of trust. A show of trust in them and a demonstration of your commitment to making this HICC office a success."

Chad stared at her for a long moment. So long, in fact, she had to fight the urge to squirm. Finally, he nodded, and the knot in her chest released.

"You're right," he said. "I'll add my personal thoughts when I send his résumé and credentials. How about you? How's your team shaping up?"

The facility wasn't ready for new employees yet, but she had two people on board who were moving to Mystery Lake in the next few weeks. All she needed was one more. It would be a small team to start, just the four of them. But she, Colton, and Chad had agreed to no more than ten new employees total in the first year. If all went well, they'd grow to twenty in the second year. After that, they planned to stabilize for at least another year before considering whether to grow more.

"Leo Gallardo and Collin Zhang will be moving up in a few weeks," she answered. "I have my eye on a potential candidate for my last hire, but I want to run it by Stella and Hunter before approaching her."

Chad arched a brow in question, urging her to continue.

Sabina made a face—half wanting to talk to Chad about it and half thinking she might jinx things if she did. "She's good," she finally said. "I've had my eye on her for a few years. She's the right kind of devious that will make a good counterpart to Collin's more straitlaced approach."

"But?"

"She's from a well-known family. Her parents are Will and Cassandra Jones."

"The director and actress?" Chad asked, both brows now raised.

She nodded. "You can understand the hesitation. She'd be a great addition."

"But you're worried about what kind of visibility she might

bring," Chad said, finishing her thought. She nodded. Will Jones was an extraordinary filmmaker and the first Black director to win an Academy Award. And with two Academy Awards to her name, one as best supporting actress and, more recently, a second as best actress, Cassandra Jones was no less impressive.

"Will she be interested in leaving LA and moving here? Assuming that's where she lives?" he asked.

Sabina shrugged. "She was in the tabloids a lot until she was about sixteen. She got into some trouble, and it seemed to shake her up—scared her straight, if you will. Now she attends an occasional event with her parents, but she's pretty much out of the limelight." The records were sealed regarding Ava Jones's criminal mischief, but Sabina knew exactly what kind of trouble she'd gotten herself into. No one other than Stella and Hunter needed to know unless Ava told them herself, though.

"You're going to talk to Stella and Hunter then?"

"I am. I have a call scheduled with them tomorrow. If they give her a pass, I'll need to go back to the drawing board."

He studied her for a moment then nodded. "It sounds like you want her, so good luck with that."

She smiled and rose. "You, too," she said, nodding to Ethan's résumé sitting on the desk.

"Sabina?"

She paused in the doorway and turned to face him. Chad's dark eyes held hers for a long moment before he spoke.

"I know something happened in your past that you don't talk about. And while I'm glad that you're here, I don't think you're here because you want to be. I think something spooked you back in DC that made you change your mind about making this jump. If you're in danger, or even if you're not and you want someone to talk things over with, I hope you know you can trust me."

With each word he spoke, her pulse kicked up. She was damn glad she'd worn a sweater with a big, high collar. The artery in her neck was currently trying to hammer its way through her skin. A reaction Chad would no doubt notice.

But as he couldn't, she forced yet another smile. "Just wanted a change of scenery and the challenge of starting something new."

Disappointment flared in his eyes, but he said nothing.

"Thank you, though," she added. "I appreciate your concern." Which she did and didn't—knowing he cared was like being wrapped in a warm down comforter on a cold night. But knowing he cared also filled her with more dread than looking down a black diamond slope and not knowing how to ski.

She held his gaze, waiting for him to acknowledge her statement in some way. A nod, a shrug, something. Thirty seconds ticked by—and yes, she counted each tick of the clock on the wall behind him. When he neither said nor did anything, she accepted the stalemate for what it was. Giving him a small nod of her own, one that she imagined admitted some sort of defeat on her part, she turned and continued to her office.

She managed to keep a steady pace as she walked to the other side of the cabin. As soon as she shut her office door, though, she slumped against it. Closing her eyes, she willed her heart rate to slow down and sucked in a deep breath. Then another. And another.

It came as no surprise that Chad had recognized her decision to move west as being out of character. That she didn't talk about her past, or that he used that fact to keep her at arm's length, was also not news. She didn't like the boundaries he'd set, but she had to respect them. Not to mention the fact that they benefited her, too.

But while they'd spent the last two years living with the repercussions of her evasiveness, he'd never explicitly called her out on it. Now, by naming it, she was very much aware that he'd changed the game. And she didn't know what to think.

Her phone jangled in her pocket, and Sabina startled at the

intrusion. Pulling it out, she read a number she didn't recognize on the screen and her heart skipped a beat. In her experience, unknown numbers didn't tend to bring good news. Bracing herself for the worst, she hit the button to connect the call just as she recognized the area code as local to Mystery Lake. It could still be one she didn't want to receive, but perhaps not.

"Hello?" Sabina answered, hating the tentative question in her voice. She was a badass behind her computer, but in the real world, she didn't feel quite so untouchable.

"Sabina O'Malley?" a woman asked.

"May I ask who's calling?"

The woman huffed a laugh. "Sorry, I should have started with that. This is Olivia Rodriguez, from the high school. And a friend of Chad's. You sent me an email yesterday about the Hedy Experience program."

Sabina let out a relieved breath and moved toward her desk. "I did, and thank you for calling."

"No, thank you for reaching out. Ryan Warwick told me a little bit about you. Never in my wildest imagination would I have thought I'd have access to such talent."

"Um, thanks?" Sabina said, booting up her computer.

Olivia laughed again. "So, without turning this into any more of an awkward fangirl moment than it is, the answer to the question in your email is 'yes.' We are definitely looking for volunteers. I will take as much or as little time as you are willing to give."

Sabina smiled. "Great. I have to tell you, I don't have much, or really any, experience with kids, but I'm willing to learn."

"That's a great start. Do you want to stop by sometime in the next few days? I can show you the setup and we can go over my plans for the program?"

Sabina agreed and after setting an appointment for the next day, she hung up. Excitement coursed through her body at the possibility of using her skills to help the community. She still wasn't sure about working with teenage girls, or any teenagers for that matter. But she loved her job, and she loved working with computers. If she could share that with even one interested student, then it would be worth it.

Her mind was conjuring images of a roomful of girls who were interested in technology but not sure whether they could make it a career when she thought of Ava. Sabina had no idea if Stella and Hunter would give her the green light to make the young woman an offer. Or if Ava would accept if she did. But she had no problem picturing the two of them at the front of the classroom together.

With a smile, she pulled up Ava's information, drafted an email to Stella and Hunter, and shot it off.

She'd never know unless she tried.

CHAPTER EIGHT

Sabina stood in her living room, looking out the picture window onto Main Street. Roger, her aloe, was perched happily on the frame, observing the same scene. Ethan hadn't been exaggerating when he'd told her the town went all out for Halloween. Not a single store was bare. The decorations ranged from scarecrows to witches to hay bales with jack-o'-lanterns. Her favorite, though, was a mini Headless Horseman display.

A month had passed since that night at the Dirty Boom. That night that seemed to change so much. She was volunteering twice a week with the Hedy Experience, and Olivia was slowly becoming someone Sabina would consider a friend. And Chad continued to sweep her into his life on a near-daily basis. She didn't agree every time he invited her to join in some activity or another, but she found herself saying yes more often than not. It was hard to resist the loud, boisterous, and loving Warwick clan.

The only drawback to the gatherings was that at least once during each, Chad would ask if she needed help and assure her that she could trust him. He didn't understand it wasn't him she didn't trust. There were many nights she wanted to tell him this, but it was a discussion she couldn't start. It would crack open a door she had no intention of opening.

The biggest change of all, though, was that the West Coast office of HICC was officially open. Stella, Hunter, and Mateo had flown out that morning and cut the figurative ribbon. Colton had six operatives—Ethan, Killian, Teague, Tucker, Ryder, and Eli—on the books and Sabina's three hires rounded out their staff.

She smiled thinking of her team. Ava Jones had joined Leo and Collin in Mystery Lake a few weeks ago. When Sabina had called to feel her out, she'd been so enthusiastic about the opportunity that she'd flown up in her father's helicopter that afternoon. She was now restoring a 1920s-built lakeside cabin she'd bought that same day.

Two teenagers burst from an alley across the street, drawing her attention. Their skateboards rumbled on the asphalt as their laughter echoed between the buildings. She followed their progress until they were out of sight, then shifted her attention to the display in front of the bookstore across the street. A dragon sat on a pile of books as it read a history of firefighting. She'd seen it dozens of times since the owners had installed it, but it never ceased to pull a laugh from her.

Her chuckle trailed off when her phone vibrated in her hand and she pulled her gaze from the dragon and glanced at the message.

Chad: *Leaving in five minutes, be there in 15(ish)*

She sent him a thumbs-up emoji although, in truth, she was less than thrilled about his picking her up. It wasn't the celebration at the Dirty Boom she had reservations about. She was looking forward to spending some downtime with the whole team. But any time alone with Chad in an enclosed space did things to her body that left her feeling a little out of control. He elicited too many reactions—too many emotions—from her that it wasn't a comfortable place to be.

She had no one to blame but herself, though. Sure, Stella and Hunter had been in the room when he'd offered her the ride. But it was Mateo who'd crumbled her defenses. He'd been climbing all over Chad as though he was a human jungle gym, and the pair had been more adorable than any man and toddler had the right to be. She hadn't been able to deny him.

She sighed, thinking about how easy Chad was with Mateo. How easy he was with most everyone. It was one of the things that made him so good at what he did. His chameleon-like talents were something she both admired and didn't understand. Give her a computer and she could work magic. Ask her to do anything else—like play softball, paint, sing, negotiate a contract, or babysit—and she struggled. She even had some trepidation about managing her new team, despite it being only three people.

With a sigh, she stepped away from the window and closed the curtain. At least the Boom was only eight blocks away. The ride wouldn't be long enough for Chad to dig into her life.

Her phone vibrated again as she selected a pair of boots from her shoe rack. There was no way Chad had already arrived, and she frowned as she glanced at the screen. She didn't recognize the number, but she knew the name.

Kara: *It's me. We need to talk*

Sabina shoved her foot into a boot then braced herself against the wall as she responded.

Sabina: *Phone or in person?*

Kara: *In person*

Sabina: *Is it safe?*

Kara: *Will it ever be?*

And that was the crux of every problem in her life. No, it wouldn't ever be safe. It wasn't like Sabina, or Kara, to be so defeated, but they'd lost enough in their lives to know it was never safe.

Sabina: *When and where?*

Kara: *There's a park in Tulare. Meet tomorrow at noon?*

Sabina: *Send me the name and I'll be there*

Kara: *Will do. Love you and be safe*

Sabina: *You, too*

Sabina closed her eyes and considered texting Chad to cancel. Maybe she could say she came down with the flu? No, that wouldn't help. Then she'd be alone in her apartment with too much time to come up with dozens of disaster scenarios. No, it would be better to be out. If she were out with Stella, Hunter, and the team, then maybe, just maybe, it would be enough to distract her for at least a little while.

"Are you okay?" Chad asked Sabina.

She blinked at him then shifted her body so that she faced him. They were standing in the nook to the side of the bar watching Ava and Ethan play a game of pool. A tournament of sorts had started not long after they'd arrived, and now his cousin and Ava were the final bracket.

"Yes, I'm fine," she answered.

"Are you sure?" he pressed, because he was pretty sure she wasn't. She might have joined in all the night's activities—eating, drinking, laughing, and even dancing a time or two. But she'd also jerked her head toward the door every time it opened and startled at every loud noise.

"I'm pretty sure I know whether I'm fine or not," she shot back.

He tried to stay relaxed, approachable, but his jaw ticked. For four weeks, he'd been pursuing his new strategy to get her to open up. In some ways, it worked. He'd learned a few small details of her life, such as the fact that as a child, she'd opened presents Christmas Eve rather than Christmas morning. But overall, it hadn't resulted in any significant progress. He still didn't know what she was hiding or why. And he still didn't know if she was in danger, although his gut told him she was.

"Who's got the betting book?" he asked, nodding to the table.

Sabina quirked a smile. "Colton. But since Ava is about to sweep the floor with your cousin, I'm not sure he'll be taking any more bets."

"I concede she's winning this match. But Ethan is a sneaky bastard. If he loses, he'll suggest best two out of three or three out of five," he replied with a matching smile.

"Are you saying your cousin is a hustler?"

"I'm saying I'd watch your back with him. There are only two things I've seen him lose at—running and skiing."

She chuckled. "Who beats him at those?"

"I'm a better skier. Cody is a better runner. Do you ski?" Assuming they got good snow, the season would start soon. He was looking forward to having the slopes just minutes away again.

"Not for years," she said, revealing another small part of herself.

"We'll have to get you out this winter. The lodge has a good mix of runs," he replied, keeping his response casual, aware that she likely regarded her response as a slip.

"Hmm, maybe," she said, then yawned.

"Are you ready to head out?"

"In a little bit, but Leo is going to give me a ride. I meant to tell you earlier," she answered. His jaw ticked again. It was one step forward and two steps back. Maybe he'd be better off taking the multiple hints and letting it go. Letting her go. She enjoyed his company and that of his family, but she couldn't be any clearer about not wanting to get any closer than they currently were.

Only that wasn't entirely true. He'd seen the way she looked at him when he and Mateo were roughhousing earlier that day. Her unguarded expression was filled with a mix of warmth, longing, and an intimate amusement. And it hadn't been the only time he'd seen such emotions reflected on her face. More than once over the past four weeks, he'd caught her watching him wearing the same look. There had even been a time or two she'd started to reach for him before abruptly pulling back.

He took a controlled breath and nodded in response to her comment. "Sounds good. I'm going to go say goodbye to Stella and Hunter then ghost." He had to have faith his strategy was working. All he needed was more time.

She nodded and looked about to say something, then shook her head and smiled. "Drive safe, and thanks for picking me up." That hadn't been what she'd intended to say, that was obvious, but he didn't call her on it. Instead, he flashed her a smile then turned and walked away. Again.

"How's the test going?" Chad asked, poking his head into the cyber lab the day after the opening celebrations. Ava, Leo, and Collin were all huddled around their computers. With the operatives on a training exercise somewhere on the property, they were putting the comms and tech equipment through its paces.

"Good," Collin answered. The trio was an odd group and not one that would have formed on its own. Collin was short, no more than five foot five, and skinny as a rail. He wore glasses and was often unable to look people in the eye when he spoke. But his demeanor hid a sharp wit. If you were lucky enough to be close enough to hear him—his voice was rarely more than a decibel above a whisper—he'd usually leave you chuckling, or outright laughing.

Leo was also on the quiet side, but not as quiet as Collin. Coming in at a hair over six feet, he had the build of a runner and, as Ava and Sabina liked to point out, the face of an angel. Chad wasn't so sure about the comparison, but did agree that

Leo's face, which was usually hidden by his shaggy black hair, was rather...arresting.

As for Ava, she wasn't quite as tall as Leo, but she towered over Collin. She was also, hands down, the most glamorous person Chad had ever met. She wore her long black hair in braids. Sometimes they hung down her back. But other times they were displayed in elaborate styles that drew the eye in a way that was almost uncomfortable. It wasn't sexual, but more like the styles hinted at magic and history and power in a way he couldn't explain but felt. He had also yet to see her without four-inch heels, nail extensions, and flawless makeup. As for her skills, well, within a week of starting, Sabina had designated her as her second-in-command. Despite Ava being the youngest of the three teammates, he'd seen no reason to second-guess Sabina's decision.

Yes, definitely an odd trio. But within hours of meeting, they'd bonded over the work they'd been hired to do. And so far, a few weeks in, they seemed to have slipped into a dynamic that boded well for the team.

"Where's Sabina?" he asked. He'd noticed that she wasn't in the room, but that didn't necessarily mean anything. She could have popped out to the restroom or gone to the kitchen.

"She called me this morning and told me to take over the test run," Ava said, her eyes not leaving her computer screen. "Something about an errand she had to run. More house stuff, maybe? Said she'd check in by the end of the day."

Not that Sabina had to run her schedule by him, but Chad's spidey senses tingled. "Did she seem okay when you dropped her off last night, Leo?"

Leo flashed him a quick frown before returning his attention to his computer. "I think she walked home. I didn't drop her."

Chad's stomach plummeted, and his body tensed. She'd lied to him. Probably to avoid him. Warring emotions churned inside him, but he smiled at the team. Not that they noticed as not a one was looking anywhere other than their computer.

"Guess I misunderstood her last night then. I'll check in later to see how it's going." Not expecting any response, he left the lab and made his way back to the office, picking apart the threads of his emotions as he walked. He was angry that she'd gone somewhere without telling someone. Hurt that she'd felt the need to hide it from him rather than tell him. And last, but definitely not least, worried.

It was possible she *did* have some innocuous errand. Maybe she *was* picking up some new home goods for her apartment. Or even buying herself a new car, since she'd been using a company one for the past few months.

But he doubted it. Not on the day of their first big test run. She'd lied to him, and that didn't sit well.

With zero hesitation, he sat down at his desk and pulled up the tracking app for her phone and the car. The car was parked at the high school, which gave him some measure of comfort. He didn't yet know why it was there, but at least it—she—wasn't somewhere dangerous. When he brought up her phone data, though, whatever calm he'd felt fled, and his blood pressure spiked.

There was nothing.

Which meant she'd either turned it off or someone had turned it off for her. Yes, it was possible it had run out of battery. But in more than two years of working with Sabina, that had never happened before. He didn't place good odds on that being the case now.

Drumming his fingers on his desk, he considered his next move. It was almost noon. If today was Sabina's day to volunteer at the high school, then maybe she stopped by during lunch to chat with Olivia? But was today her day? It was Wednesday, and he thought her days were Tuesdays and Thursdays.

Picking up his phone, he sent Ava a message.

Chad: *Can you check to see the movements of this GPS chip today?*

He added the tag data from the device on the car.

Ava: *Busy*

He frowned.

Ava: *Shit, sorry. Still getting used to not being my own boss. Give me two mins, boss*

That was better. Less than ninety seconds later, he had his response.

Ava: *At seven this morning it drove from Sabina's place to the high school, and it hasn't moved since. Anything else I can help with, boss?*

Despite the unease unfurling in his stomach, Chad smiled.

Chad: *Thanks, and good recovery*

Ava: (Wink emoji) *I try*

He was closing his texting app when another idea came to him. Sending a quick message to his brother, Ryan, he asked for Olivia's number. A few seconds later, her contact popped up in the thread.

Rising from his seat as he hit the Call button, he started to pace. One ring, then another. When it rang for the third time, he braced himself to leave a message. He wanted answers now, but he couldn't force Olivia to answer her phone. Especially not in the last few minutes before the lunch break started.

In the middle of the fourth ring, it wasn't her voice mail that answered, though.

"Hello?" she said.

"Olivia, this is Chad Warwick."

She paused. He and Olivia were friends in the way those who'd grown up together were. But they weren't close friends.

"Hi, Chad. Is everything okay?"

"Have you seen Sabina today by any chance?"

"I saw her this morning, but not since. Is she okay?"

"When did you see her?" he asked, ignoring her question a second time.

"She dropped her car off and borrowed mine. She said she had some errands somewhere south and wanted a more comfortable car for the highways. She's also considering getting the same make and model I have so may have wanted to test drive. We'd been talking about that."

"And she didn't say where she was going?"

"Should I be worried? Oh, hell. Never mind. I'm worried."

Chad inhaled a slow, deep breath. "I didn't mean to worry you, Olivia. I'm sure she's doing exactly what she said she was going to do. But she hasn't checked in with her team today, which is unusual. It's possible that she's out of cell range, though, or busy with something else. Did she tell you when she'd bring your car back?"

"She said she'd be back by five. She left me the keys to the Jeep and said she'd meet me at my place to return my car and pick hers up. She promised me a full tank of gas and a detail job as a thank-you, although I told her not to bother."

Chad glanced at the clock on his wall. Five o'clock was four and a half hours away. He stopped his pacing and sank onto the leather couch that lined a wall of his office. He had no clue where Sabina was, and now he'd have to spend the next 270 minutes thinking about all the possibilities. "Let's wait until five. If she doesn't show up, call me. If she does, can you ask her to call me herself?"

"Of course," Olivia replied. He made sure she saved his number, then the two hung up. He debated whether to call Stella and Hunter. On one hand, he was certain *something* was going on with Sabina. On the other, running to the bosses seemed extreme.

His eyes flitted to the clock again. Four and a half hours.

Sabina had no idea what was waiting for her when she returned. Wherever she was, doing whatever she was doing, he hoped she was enjoying her short-lived reprieve.

CHAPTER NINE

SABINA PARKED the Honda CRV she'd borrowed from Olivia in the shade of an oak tree and scanned the park. Tulare was just a little bigger than Mystery Lake, but as a Central Valley town, it had a much different feel to it. The land was flat and relatively sparse. She suspected there was a historic downtown core somewhere, but the park was located in the middle of a newer sprawling development.

Spotting a lone figure on one of the swings, a woman Sabina knew almost as well as she knew herself, her heart dipped. How much had they lost, how much had they missed and given up because of the decisions they'd made so many years ago?

Pushing aside the maudlin thought, she exited the car and started toward the playset. Taking a seat on the swing beside the occupied one, she finally looked at the woman's face. A face identical to hers in so many ways.

"I missed you," Sabina managed to choke out. And then both women were up and hugging. A tear or two might have appeared as well. But if there was one person in the world Sabina trusted with her pain, it was this woman.

Her sister.

When the moment quieted, Kara stepped back and retook her seat on the swing. But as when they were little, she took Sabina's hand and the two swayed together, staying at the same pace. Staying connected.

"You look good," Sabina finally said.

Kara cast her a wan smile. "I look like you, of course I look amazing." Kara was the younger twin. By two minutes.

Sabina smiled back. "Not with your hair and colored contacts, you don't." Sabina's hair fell to below her shoulders and was their natural light strawberry blond. Years ago, Kara had chosen to color hers a rich mahogany and cut it short, somewhere between a pixie cut and a bob. Kara also sported contacts that turned her blue-green eyes—eyes the same shade as Sabina's—more of a green-gold.

A crow flew overhead and cawed, drawing Sabina's gaze away from her sister. When she dropped it again, it was no surprise to find Kara still looking at her, drinking in the sight.

"Did something happen?" Sabina finally forced the question from her lips. She didn't want to ask. She wanted to sit on the swings and enjoy the fall sunshine and forget, if even for a few hours, why they were there in the first place.

Frustration and sadness flashed in Kara's eyes before she gave a jerky nod. "I don't know if it means anything, but someone was asking about me at a conference I was at last week. He wasn't a participant."

Kara was a physician who managed to stay hidden from their past by working for an international aid agency. She was out of the country more than nine months a year. Usually in places most people in the United States wouldn't be able to locate on a map. On the rare occasions she was stateside, her employer often asked her to attend conferences on their behalf. Privately, Sabina thought Kara should decompress from her work when she was home, not work more. What she saw and did while out in the field was not for the faint of heart, and everyone needed time to heal.

"Did you get a picture of him?" Sabina asked.

Kara let go of her hand and dug into her purse. Pulling an image out, she handed it over. "I downloaded this from the conference website after the event. It's not very good, but he was in the background of a couple of shots. I wrote the name of the conference on the back as I'm sure you'll be able to find more. Or do more with what's on the site."

Sabina looked at the picture that Kara had enlarged to center on a man. The image was too grainy to make out details, but Sabina could see enough to get a general idea. Everything about him was nondescript, from his build to his hair color to his clothes.

"I'll look into it," Sabina said, slipping the picture into her own bag. She reached for her sister's hand again and in sync, they started to swing.

After a long moment passed, Kara turned to her. "You're different. Something is different this time." Whether it was because they were sisters or twins, or perhaps it was only because of their shared experiences, they'd always been able to read each other's moods.

Whether one wanted the other to or not.

Sabina shook her head. "It's nothing."

Kara smiled. "Now I *know* it's something. We don't get much time to talk, but I get the feeling this is something you need to talk about."

It was. But Sabina wasn't sure if she was ready. Chad, and his persistent campaign to get her to open up, had her wondering if the decisions she and Kara had made were the right ones. He and his family had folded her into their lives with no question, no judgment, and nothing but open arms. They weren't the first people to offer that to her over the years. But they were the first people—especially Chad—that it bothered her that she couldn't give that back to them. To him.

If Chad had continued keeping her at a distance, she wouldn't be thinking the things she was thinking or questioning the things she was questioning. But he hadn't. The sneaky bastard had shifted tactics and completely thrown her off-balance.

"Spill it," Kara pressed. "There's nothing out of bounds for us. You know that."

She did know. But still, she hesitated. If she gave voice to her thoughts, she'd be questioning everything they'd done, every decision they'd made, for years.

"Sabina?" Kara pressed, shifting on her swing to get a better look at her sister.

Sabina looked up at the endless blue sky. A single puff of a cloud hovered in the distance, and two crows flew west. "Do you ever wonder if we made the right decision? If we're still making the right choices?"

She couldn't look at Kara as she voiced the question that she felt she had no right to ask. The plan had been Sabina's, and Kara had gone along with it. It had been no small thing what they'd done, and to question it now had Sabina's stomach churning and her palms sweating.

"What happened?" Kara asked gently.

Sabina shook her head, surprised to realize a single tear tracked down her cheek. Brushing it away, she took a deep breath and tried to center herself.

"And don't even think of trying to brush over this by telling me to never mind and that you're being silly," Kara admonished. That drew a look from Sabina. Mostly because her sister had called it exactly right. "We made the decisions we did because that seemed like the best plan at the time. It set things in motion in a certain way, but that doesn't mean we can't question it," Kara said.

"Do you think we made a mistake?" Sabina asked.

Kara shook her head. "At the time, no. We did what we felt we needed to. Has it been easy? No. Have we been hurt and hurt others? Yes. But we're alive, and I'd argue that we're leading good lives."

Sabina felt the moment her sister caught the thread that had led to Sabina asking the question. "You want more, don't you? Something has happened, and you're not sure that our lives are enough anymore. Tell me about him."

Sabina jerked her head around and stared at Kara. "Maybe it's not a 'him.' Maybe I'm just tired of the secrets."

Kara arched an eyebrow.

Sabina scowled. Then huffed. "Fine, there's a him. But there's more than a *him.* It's the whole freakin' family. They're warm and funny and welcoming and..."

"And it feels good to be around them. And then you remember how much you're keeping from them. And you remember what happened the last time you got close to someone. And you want to pull away. Even though, in your heart, you don't."

Sabina studied her sister's eyes, hating that she wore contacts. She hated that they hid her away and she hated what they stood for. "You sound like someone who might know a thing or two about what you're talking about."

Kara's gaze drifted left then met hers again. "There was a man, a few years ago. We met while working in Haiti. He was... special. Different. I *felt* different when I was with him. I wanted more. More of him and more of who I was when I was with him."

Sabina clutched her sister's hand. "What happened? Why didn't you talk to me?"

Kara sniffed and shook her head. "Because there was no need. We were together for four months, but then he was sent to Africa. He couldn't even tell me where. And yes, before you ask, he was military."

"What happened?" she asked again.

"What happens so often in a war zone. He was killed. Caught by a sniper as he tried to pull one of his injured men to safety after an ambush. One of his friends was kind enough to track me down and give me the news."

Her sister's pain lanced through her as if it were her own, and she fought back tears for a man she'd never known. "You never said anything."

Kara gave her a sad smile. "What would I have said?"

Sabina considered that. It wasn't as if she could have rushed off to her sister's side if she'd known of her heartbreak. This meeting was the first time they'd seen each other in three years. There were reasons they stayed apart. But even so...

"I would have liked knowing about your happiness even if there was nothing I could do to help with your pain," Sabina said.

Kara shrugged. "I don't know that things would have ended differently if my life—if *our* lives—were different. His job was dangerous, and his death had nothing to do with me."

"But you wonder if it would have been different when you *were* together. If you'd been able to give him everything of yourself."

Kara looked off to the horizon then nodded. "If anyone would have made me question our decisions, it would have been him." She took a few deep breaths then turned and smiled at Sabina.

"And you? Who is this man?"

Sabina felt a flush creep up her cheeks. She wasn't much for blushing, not at her age, but this day was nothing if not filled with surprises. "I've known him for a couple of years, and there's always been something between us. But he's not a halfway kind of guy. And it's all or nothing with him. For a while, I was okay." She paused. "I was okay with *nothing*. But lately, he's changed and...it's making it hard not to want more," she answered. Then she proceeded to tell Kara all about Chad Warwick and his extended family. As the words flowed, the awkwardness of admitting her feelings for him out loud, and the terror that came along with admitting those feelings, diminished. It almost felt as if they were back in high school, gossiping about boys.

Almost.

"He's not Nate," Kara said softly when Sabina had talked herself out.

"Not yet, he's not," Sabina said, voicing her biggest fear.

Kara shook her head. "Don't be stubborn. You know what I mean. This man you've fallen for has lived, and survived, combat. He knows how to fight, and he knows how to protect himself." Kara hesitated, then took a deep breath before pressing on. "Please don't think I'm second-guessing your decision not to tell Nate the truth—I know in my heart it wouldn't have made a difference. But with Chad, maybe telling him is the best way to protect him. He can't protect himself, or you, from things he doesn't know."

Sabina's heart squeezed in her chest. "I agree, it wouldn't have made a difference with Nate. He didn't die because of what he knew or didn't. He died because he was close to me."

"Then isn't it already too late for Chad? Whether you admit it or not, it sounds like you're already close."

Suddenly, Sabina found it hard to breathe as the truth of the situation hit her. She'd been fooling herself for months. Years, even. The distance she kept between them, the distance *Chad* kept between them, was flimsy at best. They might not share family secrets or swap childhood stories, but they *were* close. Other than her sister, there was no one more important to her than him. And once again, she'd put someone at risk simply by being a part of their life.

Her sister was right. She *had* to tell him the truth. It would be the only way to protect him.

"It's been a long time that we've been living like this, Sabina," her sister said. "I know we could go on for years. We're both happy in a way. But if we're given a chance for more, maybe it's time to stop running. Maybe it's time to consider the possibility of putting an end to it altogether."

Sabina's gaze shot to Kara. "What do you mean?"

Kara lifted a shoulder. "I don't know much about investigating crime, but I do know that medicine has changed a lot in past fifteen years. Maybe there's a chance, with new technology, that we could prove what we know happened that night. But even if we can't, we're older, more experienced, and we have friends in high places. Hell, you work for the sister of the vice president, a man who is all but the anointed next president. We're not those scared little girls anymore.

"I'd like to see that man rot in hell for what he did. But even if we can't prove it, surely there's a way to safeguard ourselves? A way to give ourselves a chance to reach for what we want?" Kara's question reached deep inside Sabina. With her sister giving voice to the possibility of going after the man who'd killed their mother, Sabina realized that subconsciously, she'd already considered it. Not the how or when, but what it would be like if they succeeded. And how their lives would be different. Maybe it *was* worth considering. Maybe it was worth more than considering. As Kara had said, they weren't scared young girls anymore. They had resources now. And connections.

"Are you leaving again?" Sabina asked instead. She needed time to think about what Kara was suggesting. She wanted to believe it would work. But after years of keeping so many secrets, she didn't want to act without considering all the potential consequences.

Kara nodded. "I was going to stay in LA for a month or two. After the thing at the conference, though, I signed up to go to Bangladesh and help after the latest cyclone." When Kara wasn't traveling, she lived in a small apartment in Malibu. The proximity between Mystery Lake and Malibu was one of the reasons Sabina had originally opted to stay on the East Coast. The closer they were, the harder it would be to stay apart. But what if they could change things? What if they could find a way to make themselves safe? If so, being five hours away from her sister would be a godsend.

Sabina acknowledged Kara's decision with a nod. As she did, a little grain of hope took root. Could this be the last time one or the other of them had to run off? Sabina wasn't prepared to commit to that path yet. She was even less ready to consider where that path might take them. But their conversation had given her permission to at least think about it.

"You'll keep me posted on what you decide?" Kara asked, letting go of Sabina's hand and rising from the swing.

"I'm not deciding anything on my own, Kara. *We* make this decision, or it doesn't get made."

"Which is a decision in and of itself," Kara pointed out. She paused, and the two stared at each other for a long moment. "I love you," Kara said, wrapping her in a big hug. Sabina hugged her sister back, committing the feel of her to her heart. "I understand we make decisions together," Kara continued. "But if you can't reach me and you need to do something, know that I trust you. I always have and I always will."

Sabina squeezed her a little harder then stepped back. "Take care of yourself, and if anything happens, I'll use email." Years ago, they'd set up dummy accounts with a free public service. They rarely used them, but when Kara was traveling, it was sometimes the only way they could reach each other. It was how

Sabina had let her sister know she was relocating to the West Coast.

Kara nodded, her reluctance to leave mirroring Sabina's. Then finally, she straightened her spine, set her shoulders, and walked away. Sabina remained where she was until her sister's car was no longer in sight. Never once did Kara look back.

CHAPTER TEN

"CHAD CALLED. You should call him and let him know you're back," Olivia said as Sabina dropped her friend's keys into her hand. She'd stopped off to get the car washed and detailed. She'd even taken the long road home. Despite all that, she still wasn't sure what she'd do with the permission Kara had given her. She and her sister had been living in the shadows for as long as not, and that was a hard habit to break.

She smiled at Olivia. "I'm not surprised. Sorry about that. I hope it didn't put you in an awkward position."

Olivia shook her head. "I've known all the Warwick boys my whole life. It's hard to feel awkward around people who pretty much lived those uncomfortable teen years with you. His call did worry me a little, though."

"I'm sorry," Sabina said again. She should have planned for Chad checking in on her. "I promise I won't go haring off again without telling anyone unless I have to."

Olivia shrugged. "You don't answer to me. I just want the people I like to stay safe, so if there's anything I can do, please know you can always call on me."

Because that was how it was in Mystery Lake. Not that

everyone loved everyone else, but when push came to shove, they were there for one another. Or at least that's how it seemed to Sabina and her two months of experience with the town.

"I will, thank you."

"Are you sure you don't want to stay for dinner?" Olivia asked, gesturing to her kitchen that lay at the back of the house. Sabina hadn't eaten anything all day. Her stomach grumbled at the scent of spices emanating from the room, but she shook her head. She still had some thinking to do.

"Maybe tomorrow after the session with the girls?" she suggested. "I know I got your car detailed, but I feel like I owe you more than that. How about dinner and drinks at Dirty Boom?"

Olivia waggled her eyebrows. "I'm never one to turn down dinner and drinks at the Boom. It's a date."

They finalized their plans as they walked to the HICC Jeep Olivia had driven home. A few minutes later, Sabina was inside it and, not yet ready to head home, driving north. She didn't have a destination in mind, but the gentle curves of the mountain road soothed her.

She didn't bother to call or text Chad. She wasn't ready to talk to him yet, and when she'd checked in with Ava earlier, Sabina had asked her to let him know she was home so that he didn't worry. Unfortunately, she learned that Chad had asked Leo about taking her home the night before. That little fudging of the truth—fine, that lie—was one more thing she'd eventually have to apologize for.

After forty-five minutes of aimless driving, her stomach began to protest in earnest. There was a town fifteen minutes farther north. Or she could head back to Mystery Lake. If she did, she'd reach the diner on the outskirts of town in thirty minutes, and she could eat before heading home. Decision made, she found a safe spot to turn around and started making her way south.

Not paying attention to much of anything, before she knew it, she was finishing her BLT and asking for a second cup of coffee. She didn't need the caffeine, but since she wasn't counting on getting much sleep that night anyway, she took comfort in the warmth and familiarity of the hot drink.

She was lifting the mug to take a sip when Chad slid onto the seat across from her. Startled by his appearance, she dropped her hands, and the mug landed with a loud *thunk* on the tabletop.

"Chad," she said, hating how surprised she sounded. Like the phone call to Olivia, she should have known he'd track her down.

"Sabina," he responded, his gaze sweeping over her, taking her in.

"I'm fine," she said.

His eyes met hers and although normally, they were nearly dark as pitch, they seemed to darken even more. "I see that."

She held his gaze, but then a scuffling at the counter pulled her attention away. Ryan, Mitch, and Ethan were each propped on a stool. She spared a moment's thought wondering why Chad thought he needed their backup. But then she saw their empty plates and glasses and realized they'd been there a while. Chad could have tracked the Jeep, but she'd bet one of those men had called him.

She took a deep breath and faced her colleague—her friend—again. "I'm sorry I lied to you last night about Leo. I had a lot on my mind and needed the short walk to my apartment."

Disappointment flashed in his eyes. She should be used to it by now, but she hated it. The worst part was, she knew how to make it go away. She'd spent the afternoon debating whether to tell him everything, and she'd almost decided she would.

But she wasn't quite there yet.

"I need time," she said, knowing he'd know what she was talking about.

"You've had years, Sabina," he countered. "You hide your past. You fled across the country. You out-and-out lied to me *and* your team. And you abused your friend's trust by borrowing her car specifically so that you could skulk away without anyone knowing. All that simply because you're not willing to talk to someone. Everyone is entitled to their secrets, but yours are starting to impact the people around you. The people who care about you."

She flinched at the honest assessment. He was right. Trying to slip away from Chad was one thing. She wasn't proud of it. For right or wrong, though, she had her reasons. But lying to her team about where she was today? That wasn't good.

"I'm worried about you, Sabina," Chad said, reaching across the table and taking her hand in his. It was the first time he'd ever done something like that, and she stared at his fingers wrapped around her palm. His suntanned skin against her pale Irish tone.

In that moment, she wanted to tell him everything. But after eighteen years of silence, the words wouldn't come out. Nor was the diner the right place.

"Talk to me, Sabina. You know I can help."

Her eyes searched his, and she hesitated. A small whirlwind of doubt started swirling in her mind, pulling her different directions. She didn't want to carry this on her own anymore, but she didn't want anyone else to get hurt.

Her gaze strayed to the waiter approaching the table behind Chad. In his hand, he carried a plate with a small chocolate cake on it. Her stomach churned at the thought of eating something so decadent. Then it dropped when the waiter brandished a match, waved it over the dessert, and the whole thing caught fire. It was ten feet away, but still she drew back. Away from the imagined heat, away from the dancing blue flames curling around the cake.

Memories she tried not to think about slammed to the forefront of her mind, and suddenly she was back in her college apartment. Nate was lying dead at her feet, and fire was licking the walls. Waiting to consume them both.

They were memories. Only memories. They couldn't hurt her anymore. Not physically. But even so, she felt the heat, she felt the sparks landing on her skin. She felt the sweat dripping down her body as she tried to pull Nate's body from the building.

"Sabina?" Chad squeezed her hand. Her gaze jerked to his. "Talk to me," he said.

Before she even had a chance to think, she was shaking her head. "I can't." *At least not right now.* But she couldn't bring herself to say that. If she did, Chad would never let it go.

"You can and you will. Sabina, you're shaking." He reached up and uncurled the hand she had still gripping the mug. With both of his hands now holding hers, she should have felt comforted; she should have been leaning into him. Leaning *on* him. But she couldn't do it. Not right then and not right there.

She yanked her hands away from his. She'd needed to sever the connection, but even so, she immediately missed it. She'd go home, get her head on straight, pull her files together, then talk to Chad tomorrow.

"Stop hiding and talk to me," Chad said.

"I can't." Again, she didn't add that she would. She didn't tell him she needed to be in a better headspace first.

"You can. But you're choosing not to. Is someone after you? Did you do something that put you on the wrong side of the law? Did you see something you shouldn't have? *What happened,* Sabina?"

"Stop!" she said, pushing against the back of the booth, her heart beating a rapid tattoo. "Please stop, Chad. This is making me uncomfortable. *You're* making me uncomfortable."

The color drained from his face, and he yanked his own hands back. Her brow dropped in confusion. That was hardly the reaction she'd expected. She wasn't sure what she'd expected, but it hadn't been the look of stunned surprise on his face. Surprise tinged with what she thought might be panic, or possibly fear.

He straightened away from her, and holding his palms out in surrender, he pressed even further into his seat.

"I'm making you uncomfortable?" he asked, his voice strained and barely above a whisper.

She sensed there was more to the question than the question itself, but because she didn't understand what it might be, she gave a shaky nod.

He blinked and looked out the window. He took a few breaths as if trying to center himself, but if anything, he lost even more color.

Then suddenly he was sliding from his seat.

"Chad?" she asked, not knowing what she was really asking.

He shoved his hands into his pockets and rocked back on his heels. "I apologize for making you uncomfortable. It wasn't my intention at all, and it won't happen again. I can promise you that."

And with that, he turned and stalked away.

CHAPTER ELEVEN

CHAD LEFT Sabina at the table and considered walking straight out the door. At the last minute, though, he swung right and headed to where his brother and cousins sat.

"Everything okay over there?" Ryan asked, not even pretending he hadn't watched the scene.

Chad shook his head. "It's not, but I'm out," he said.

Ethan frowned. Ryan and Mitch shared a look that Chad didn't have the mental space to decipher.

"Out?" Ethan asked.

A band was tightening around Chad's chest, squeezing his heart, squeezing the breath out of him. But he managed a sharp nod. "I need to get out of here for a few days. Maybe go hiking and camping. I'll be back Monday." *Maybe*, he amended in his head.

"What was that about?" Mitch pressed, jerking his head in Sabina's direction. Chad didn't turn around.

"A lot of things," Chad answered. "I can't…I can't talk about it right now, though. Whatever is going on in her life, it's not my business. I'm not going to pursue it anymore, and it would be best if we stop inviting her out. We can find someone else to take her place at Gramps's haunted house." Again, his relatives shared a look. "I'm also going to ask Colton and Ava to make a few changes at the office. Don't be surprised when those start happening," he added, looking at Ethan.

"You don't look so good, C," Ethan said. There was a reason for that. Every breath he took felt more and more difficult, and he could feel his head starting to swim.

"I've got to get out of here. When I decide where I'm going, I'll let you know," he said. He knew they had questions, he could see it on their faces, but he couldn't be in the diner anymore. He couldn't be inside, around people.

The minute he walked through the door he gulped in huge breaths of the cold October night air. He ran his fingers through his hair and wasn't surprised to notice his hands were shaking. Shoving one into his pocket, he walked toward his car and unlocked the door.

He made it two miles from his home before he had to pull over and throw up. Standing beside the passenger door, with one hand on the handle, he leaned over the shoulder of the road and emptied his stomach. PTSD could be a bitch that way.

When there was nothing left inside him, he grabbed his water bottle and rinsed his mouth out. Then taking a few deep breaths, he walked back to the driver's side and climbed in. He sat for a few moments in the stillness until he felt grounded enough to drive the rest of the way. As soon as he arrived home, he walked straight to his room and changed into a pair of cargo pants, a lightweight performance hoodie, and his hiking boots. He wasn't leaving for the camping trip yet, but he knew himself well enough to know that he needed to be outdoors. He needed to feel the fresh air against his skin, the stretch of his muscles, and the timelessness of nature.

Even distracted by the events of the past forty minutes, he

couldn't forget the rules his parents and grandparents had drilled into him. Grabbing a backpack, he stuffed a water bottle, snacks, a shock blanket, a can of bear spray, a headlamp, and a beacon inside. His phone he kept in his pocket and his firearm at his side. He had no intention of using any of the items, but habit and training wouldn't let him leave without any of them.

After resetting the alarm and locking up his house, he headed out into the night. Picking a trail that he'd discovered a week after moving in, he headed south, walking parallel to the lake below him. The night was cold, but his body warmed up as he moved. Eventually, he was able to tune out everything he was thinking and feeling and simply exist in the woods.

A full moon lit the way, casting shadows among the tall pines. A gentle breeze rustled the top of the trees, but it wasn't strong enough to reach him on the forest floor. Scents of evergreen and that unique dusty dirt smell of a dry mountain forest wrapped around him. A smell as familiar to him as his own heartbeat.

He walked and walked. Time didn't matter. He dropped down to the lake at some point, but only stopped long enough to admire the moon reflecting on the still waters. When the sound of someone canoeing—no doubt a resident taking one last full-moon paddle around the lake before the winter set in—interrupted his reverie, he turned and headed back up the mountain.

About halfway home, his phone vibrated in his pocket. He should have shut it off, but he couldn't bring himself to be *that* cut off from his family. He didn't have to answer it, though. If it was important, whoever it was would call back again, and he'd consider answering then.

To his dismay, ten seconds after it stopped buzzing, it started again. With a sigh, he pulled the device from his pocket and saw Ethan's name on the screen.

"Yeah?" he answered.

"Sabina called; she's got a flat tire. Can you go out and help her?"

"Not a good idea," he answered as all the peace he'd found on his hike bled from his body. "Besides, she's capable of changing a flat." Stella and Hunter made sure all their employees knew the basics of a lot of things, including how to change tires. "Wait, aren't those run-flat tires?" he asked before he could stop himself.

"They are, which is why you should go check on her," Ethan answered. Run-flat tires were designed to stay sound enough to drive on for at least thirty miles.

Chad faced the lake and let his gaze skate over the inky blue. "I give you it's odd that it went flat so fast that she had to pull over, but there's still a spare." Cars with run-flat tires didn't typically carry spares, but again, Stella and Hunter insisted.

"She's close by, C. Just head over and give her a hand."

"I'm not home, how can you know she's close?"

"Because I'm tracking your phone, moron. Why are you being so difficult?"

Given that Ethan had no clue what Sabina had said to him, he kind of deserved that comment. His tune would change if Chad told him, though. But he couldn't bring himself to talk about it yet. Just thinking about it still had the power to suck the air from his lungs.

"You might regret this," Chad said, accepting that unless he wanted to bare his scars right there in the middle of the woods, he'd have to do as Ethan asked.

"I don't even know what that means," Ethan retorted. "I'm sending you her coordinates. If you head up the mountain and hit the roadside trail, it shouldn't take you more than fifteen minutes."

He was already walking, but he kept the line open. "Why call me? Why not head over yourself? If there's a problem, we're still going to have to call for a ride."

"Because I'm home already, and I'm thirty minutes away. If you have a problem, call and I'll come get you. But call me crazy, I don't like the idea of her—or anyone—sitting on the side of a mountain road any longer than they have to."

"What the hell is she doing out this way anyway?" Based on the coordinates Ethan had sent, she'd gone the opposite direction from her home when she'd left the diner.

"Have no idea. The only thing in that direction is you. And the lodge. But probably you."

"She was definitely not coming to see me," he grumbled as he hit the roadside trail. The name was a bit of a misnomer. The trail itself didn't run alongside the road but rather ran parallel to it, about thirty yards down a steep hill.

"Are you going to tell me what happened at the diner?"

He was leaving his cousin hanging, he knew that. But he wasn't ready to. "I'm going to head out on that camping trip tomorrow for a few days. I'll be back Sunday and I'll fill you in then. In the meantime, I think it's better for everyone if she and I are not in each other's company unless we have to be."

There was a long pause on the other end of the line. Long enough that he could now see a faint glow, either from the interior light of Sabina's Jeep or maybe her phone.

Finally, Ethan spoke. "I wish you'd give me more than that, but I understand you don't want to right now. Get her tire changed, go camping. We'll talk Sunday."

And that, right there, was one of the reasons he was glad to be home. His family was nosy and pushy and embodied every aspect of the cliché big family. But when the chips were down, they knew when to back off and how to be there for one another.

"Deal. I can see her car. I need to hang up now as it's a bit of a climb to the road. And if you make an old man joke right now you will not live to see tomorrow."

Ethan snorted. "Right, old man, what are you gonna do about it? You're going camping."

Despite himself, Chad smiled. "Asshole," he groused before hanging up and starting up the hill.

"Sabina?" he called, pausing a few yards off the trail. He wasn't sure what she was doing, but the sound of her moving around stopped.

"Chad?"

"Yeah, it's me." *Unfortunately*, he almost added.

"Where are you?" At least she sounded confused and not worried.

"Down the hill. Ethan called me, but I didn't want to just walk up and startle you."

A few seconds later, he saw her form appear at the lip of the shoulder. She swept a flashlight down the hill until the beam landed in front of his feet. "What are you doing out here?"

"I was hiking. Like I said, Ethan called me after you called him. I was only fifteen minutes away, so he thought it would be faster to ask me than to come himself." She kept the light pointed on the ground in front of him.

"I would have called you, but you seemed like, well…when you left the diner, you didn't seem very happy."

There was no way he was touching that comment with a ten-foot pole. "Can I come up and help?"

She paused then quickly gestured him up. "Of course. Do you need a hand?"

He declined and started making his way up the steep slope. As Sabina usually did, she filled the silence.

"I'm capable of changing a tire, and normally I wouldn't have called Ethan, but the problem is, there are two flats."

He paused and looked up. "Two?"

"Yeah, weird. But yes, two."

The hairs on his neck started to come to attention. Having one run-flat tire bunk out completely was unusual enough. But having two go out at the same time and so completely was almost unheard of. Unless she'd driven across something that would have torn them completely apart. If that had been the case, though, it would have impacted all four.

"Well, let's see what we can do," he said, starting up the hill again. He reached her a few minutes later and assessed the damage to the back tire closest to the shoulder. Sure enough, it looked shredded. Only it was shredded on the tire wall, not the tread.

"You have any enemies?" he asked, keeping his voice light, wanting to downplay the oddity of what he was seeing. The second the words were out, he regretted them, though. "Forget I said that," he said before she could answer. "What about the other one?"

"The other rear tire," she answered. "And again, yes, I know this is weird. Of course, it's less weird when you consider both tires look slashed." She paused, then clarified. "What I meant is that it's not weird that if someone was going to slash my tires, they'd slash two. But it's still weird that someone would slash my tires in the first place."

He'd walked around the car as she chatted and sure enough, the other back tire looked exactly like the first one. He thought about everything she hadn't told him and wondered if it had anything to do with the vandalism. It was hard to make a guess on that, or at least an educated one, since he had no idea what skeletons she had in her closet.

"Why two?" Sabina asked, bringing him back from his musings.

"What?" he asked, turning to face her.

"Why two?" she repeated. "Why two tires and not four? Or three?"

Pausing, he mentally switched gears from thinking about the

skeletons in her closet to her question. Two was an odd number.

Unless…

His heart seized and adrenaline shot through his system like a cannon as the answer came to him in a blinding flash.

And as it did, a red dot from a sniper rifle began dancing on her forehead.

CHAPTER TWELVE

A BULLET GRAZED Chad's upper arm, but he was so focused on getting Sabina down and out of the line of fire, he barely registered it. The back window shattered above them, and he positioned his elbows to take the impact of their fall. His arms were wrapped around Sabina, and he didn't want to turn and take the brunt of their landing on his back as that would expose her to the shooter.

As planned, his elbows were the first to collide with the road, and the gravelly asphalt dug into his skin through his hoodie. Immediately after that, his knees made contact. His cargo pants were sturdier, but he'd bet a pitcher of his favorite beer that he'd be black and blue tomorrow.

Beneath him, Sabina grunted in pain and burrowed against his chest as her hands gripped the material of his shirt. At least he'd managed to get his hand behind her head so that she hadn't slammed it against the hard surface.

They might not be in the best shape in a few hours, but right now, they were alive. Still, he wasn't going to take any time to linger on that small triumph. One shot had been fired, and his training had him assuming that it wouldn't be the last. Dropping a hand to Sabina's waist, he urged her to flip over.

"Go!" he ordered. "Crawl to the other side and don't stop until you get to the shelter of the tire." The shooter was across the road and up the hill. Taking cover on the side of the car by the shoulder would give them a few moments to collect themselves.

She responded to his order without hesitation, and a few seconds later, she was army-crawling away from him. He followed behind, half his body shielding hers, doing his best to give her cover.

Another shot pierced the night, and his left thigh caught fire with the sting of the contact. As bullet wounds went, it was minor, but it still stung like a mofo, and he couldn't stop the sharp inhale or muttered curse.

"Chad!" Sabina cried out, obviously having heard him.

"Don't stop, just keep moving," he ground out, grateful that whoever the shooter was, he wasn't very good. He seemed to sight a target pretty well, but he didn't appear to have the skills needed to anticipate and account for movement. And Chad was just fine with that.

When they finally rounded the car and reached the back tire, Chad didn't think. He just set his back against the car and pulled Sabina to sit between his legs with her back to his front. There was very little chance the shooter would be able to spot them from his current position. Even so, Chad wanted his body between whoever was out there and Sabina.

"Chad?"

He wanted to reassure her, but he didn't have that luxury. Instead of answering, he pulled out his phone and hit Ethan's number. He should be calling Colton, but Ethan's number was easier to reach since it was the last call he'd made. He figured Colton would have called Ethan—and Ryan—anyway. He was good, but he didn't know these mountains and these trails the way Ethan and Ryan did.

"You got her?" Ethan said by way of answering.

"There's a shooter on the hill behind us. Her tires were slashed. It was an ambush. Two shots fired."

The sound of Ethan scrambling for his gear filtered through the line. A sense of calm washed over Chad. His cousin, Colton, and any of the others those two decided to call in would handle the shooter. Leaving him to focus on Sabina's safety.

"Anyone hit?" Ethan asked.

"Call Colton and Ryan. We'll want police involvement," he said, ignoring the question. "I think he's on the old logging road. We can figure out how he got here later. I'm going to leave him to you and get Sabina back to HICC. We'll head down the hill to the trail then jog home for my car."

"Good, we'll meet you there when we know anything."

And with that promise, Chad ended the call and slipped the phone back into his pocket.

"We're going down that?" Sabina asked, pointing down the side of the mountain. It wasn't quite a cliff, but it wasn't far off.

"I came up that way," he reminded her. "There's a trail about thirty yards down. We're a little less than two miles from my house, by foot. We'll grab my car and head into HICC." He started to push her forward toward the edge of the road, but her hand came down, landing on the road beside his thigh, stopping his movements.

"I know this sounds crazy, but I need my bag," she said.

He hesitated. It *did* seem crazy to take that chance. The minute they opened the door to the Jeep the light would go on, giving the shooter their location. On the other hand...

"Is your computer in it?" he asked. He trusted that the device was as encrypted as it could possibly be. But still, the thought of it getting into the hands of someone they didn't know—someone who was currently trying to kill them—didn't sit well.

Ethan and the others would arrive soon. But if the shooter was after something on the device, he'd have plenty of time to grab it and run before they showed up.

She gave a jerky nod.

He bit back a grunt then continued to inch her forward, pressing her lower back with his hand. Biting his lip against the pain in his arm as he, too, shuffled forward, he pointed down. "You head down, I'll get the bag. I want you at least ten yards down before I open the door of the Jeep."

"Chad."

"Don't argue, Sabina. We don't have time. Just go and wait. I'll be down in a second."

She hesitated then acquiesced. He pulled his gun from its holster as she started scuttling on her behind down the hill. Sabina was trying to stay quiet, but stealth wasn't her strong suit. If the person hunting them had any sort of experience in the woods, he'd know exactly what direction they were heading.

He watched until she was far enough away to give him some comfort, then made his way to the passenger door. He should have confirmed with her where her bag was before sending her down the hill. If history was anything to go by, though, it would be on the floor in front of the passenger seat. At least he hoped so. It would be a cluster if she'd dumped it in the rear. Crawling into the back of the Jeep to retrieve it was not high on the list of things he wanted to do in the next few minutes.

Taking a deep breath, he decided there was no time like the present and without hesitation, he yanked the door open. A moment of relief filled his body when he saw her bag right where he'd hoped it would be. The moment was short-lived, though. A bullet tore through the driver's side window and embedded itself in the passenger seat six inches from Chad's head.

Ducking behind the safety of the car, blindly he reached in, his hand quickly moving across the floor mat. His palm brushed her bag as another shot went off. This one hitting the open door less than a foot away. Wrapping his fingers around the canvas, he yanked as he rolled away from the glow of the interior light.

The bag snagged on something, but with one more hard pull, it came free. Not wasting any time, he scrambled down the mountain to meet Sabina.

"Are you okay?" she asked the second he reached her. Her voice shook, and he glanced in her direction as he gestured her farther down the hill.

"What the hell?!" he asked, jerking her to a stop. He'd only caught a glimpse of her face, and it had taken a moment for him to process what he'd seen. She turned and faced him fully. "What happened?" he asked, raising his hand. He wanted to turn her head to better see what was starting to look like a pretty good black eye. But remembering their conversation at the diner, he dropped his hand and moved back a few feet.

She grimaced. "I think your elbow hit it when you pulled me down."

His eyes searched hers, looking for any signs of accusation. She must have read his mind, because she gave him a soft smile. "I know it was an accident, and I'd rather take an elbow to the face than a bullet to the forehead any day."

He thought she shouldn't ever have to take either, but he bit back any comment. He was certain this ambush had something to do with her past and her secrets, and he'd promised he wouldn't push the matter.

He grunted some unintelligible response and gestured for her to continue down the hill. He scrambled behind her, ignoring the burning wounds on his body and focusing on the feel of the ground beneath him.

A few minutes later, they hit the trail, and he pointed north. Without a word, she started walking. They proceeded in silence until they hit a fork, where he directed her to take the left branch.

They stayed quiet the entire walk. He was a little worried about her state of mind but didn't know what to say or how to check in with her while still keeping his promise to back off. So instead of offering any sort of comfort, he, too, remained quiet.

When they reached the edge of the forest near his house, he asked her to wait. Without a word, she moved to the side of the trail and stopped. Stepping around her, he eyed the small clearing of land. His security system would have let him know if anyone had been on his property, but still, he wanted to confirm with his own eyes.

When he was confident they were alone, he led her toward the house, bypassing the back door and heading straight to his garage.

"Are we going in?" Sabina asked.

He shook his head and keyed in a code to his garage. The door started rolling up as he turned to answer. "We'll go to HICC. You can wait in the car while I grab an ice pack for your eye."

Light from the garage began to illuminate them and, feeling exposed and wanting to move quickly, he gestured for her to follow him inside. Reaching his car, he opened the passenger door, but she didn't climb in.

"Your arm, Chad. You've been hit." The pitch of her voice told him she was close to losing it. Not that he thought she would, but she was fighting hard not to. She reached up to touch him, but he jerked away, not wanting to feel her fingers on his skin. She frowned. "You're hurt. You need to see to that. Or let me. Please," she added.

He shook his head. "Go on and get in. I'll get the ice pack, and then we'll be on our way. I'll get Ethan or Colton to look at it once we're at HICC."

She hesitated then climbed in. He let out an exhale of relief as she shut the door, putting a barrier between them. Of course, once he got in the car, that would go away, but for now, he'd take the respite distance gave him. It was hell not being able to comfort her. Or himself.

Entering his house through the mudroom, he turned the alarm off, holstered his gun, then pulled out his phone. As he dialed Ethan's number, he made his way to the freezer.

"What have you got for me?" he asked when Ethan answered.

"Tire tracks and some shells," Ethan answered. But no shooter. Chad wasn't surprised, but he'd be lying if he said he wasn't disappointed.

"We just got to the house," he said as he pulled an ice pack out then started back to the garage. "I'll bring Sabina in right away. We'll be there in twenty minutes."

"Ryan's going to stay out here for a bit, but Colton and I will meet you there. Are you okay?"

"I'd be better if Sabina hadn't been shot at, but other than that, I'm fine." He wasn't. He was pretty far from fine. He had a flesh wound on his arm, one on his leg, and a woman he loved who didn't like being around him. Not to mention the fact that it was probably all her damn secrets behind the events of the past hour.

Ethan grumbled something that conveyed nothing coherent other than that he'd seen his cousin's lie for what it was. "We'll see you at HICC," he said before hanging up.

Chad reset the alarm then stepped into the garage, closing the door behind him. Climbing into the driver's seat of his SUV, he handed Sabina the ice pack.

"Thanks," she mumbled, lifting it to her face.

They were ten minutes away from HICC when she spoke again. "What's wrong?" she asked.

His eyebrows shot up and he jerked his head around in surprise. She was studying him, the ice pack resting over her right eye.

"You're kidding, right?" he shot back, returning his attention to the road.

"No, I'm not. There's something wrong that has nothing to do with the shooting," she said.

Anger flooded his system, replacing the adrenaline. He gripped the steering wheel and clenched his jaw. It wasn't a productive emotion, but it was hard to quell. He'd wager his new house on the possibility that if she'd talked to someone about her past, the events of the last hour—and the fact that someone had tried to *kill her*—wouldn't have happened.

Communication was vital in the field they worked in, and he was furious that her pride, or whatever it was, kept her from seeing that. Fortunately, he was smart enough to recognize that a fair bit of his anger came from fear, and that alone kept him from responding. Things would go better for them if he kept his mouth shut.

"You're not going to talk to me?" she pushed when he remained silent.

He cocked his head and opted for honesty. "I think it's best if I hold my own counsel. We'll be at HICC in five minutes, and Ethan and Colton are meeting us there. There will be plenty of talk then." He wouldn't be a part of it, he'd already decided that, but she didn't need to know that right now.

He felt her eyes on him for a long moment, then she shifted in her seat and looked out the window. And remained silent, thank god.

On schedule, they pulled up to HICC five minutes later. Chad keyed in his code and submitted to the retina scan before the wide iron gates swung open. The guard posted in the nearby cabin must have been alerted to the goings-on, because he stood at the edge of the woods and raised a hand to them as they passed.

Parking close to the main building, Chad was glad to see not just Ethan's and Colton's cars, but also Tucker's and Teague's. The two operatives—brothers—that Colton had brought on a month before were good men. Both were former marines, and both had enough history with Colton to slide into the HICC culture.

In the glare of the parking lot security lights, Sabina's soon-to-be black eye was bright red with hints of purple. He winced at the sight. "Keep the ice on it," he directed as they entered the office. It would help, but there was no way she was going to escape a shiner.

Opting to take the stairs to the situation room, he opened the door and let Sabina precede him. Ethan and Colton were waiting when they walked out of the stairwell on the third floor. Ethan's eyes flashed in surprise at the sight of Sabina with the ice bag, then his gaze jerked to Chad in question. Chad gave a little shake of his head and walked straight to his office. Colton seemed to understand that Chad needed a moment, and he stepped forward, ushering Sabina to one of the conference rooms.

"What the fuck happened to her?" Ethan demanded, following him.

The anger in his voice had Chad spinning to face his cousin. Ethan's gaze narrowed as he studied him. The sudden certainty that his cousin thought that he could have done that to Sabina *on purpose* hit him like a sledgehammer to the gut, and Chad stumbled back.

But there was no emotion quite so strong as anger driven by betrayal. Forcing himself to stand his ground, Chad straightened and met his cousin's gaze. "You think I did that to her? That I'm capable of *that*?"

His cousin drew back, but Chad was too mired in his own head to notice Ethan's look of confusion. "I'm out of here," Chad said, swiping up the keys he'd just set down on his desk. "Whatever is going on with her, you figure it out."

He moved toward the door, but Ethan stepped in front of him. Chad had a few more years of experience than his cousin. He could probably take him. But the truth was, he was exhausted. Body and soul. And he just wanted to go home and tend to his wounds. All of them.

"What?" he asked on an exhale.

"What's going on, C?"

Chad raised a brow at the use of his nickname but answered all the same. Only because he was too tired to not answer. "What's going on is that my cousin thinks I have it in me to hit Sabina, and Sabina doesn't want me around because I make her uncomfortable. She's in danger, though—tonight proved that—and she needs help. But since no one trusts me, it can't be me. And if it can't be me, it needs to be you. Or Colton."

Ethan blinked. "What the fuck? She said that to you? She said that you make her uncomfortable?"

"No, I made it up. Now if you don't mind. I'd like to head home, tend to my two bullet wounds, and pack for a camping trip. You know, get far away from Sabina so I'm not tempted to hit her."

"That's not what I meant, C, and you know it."

Chad stared at him.

Ethan's eyes traveled over his body, lingering on the tear in the fabric at his biceps and again at the injury to his leg. His cargo pants were light brown, and the blood was obvious. The black fabric of his shirt was different, though, and it hid most of the staining.

Ethan huffed. "You would never hit her, or anyone who didn't deserve it. If anyone knows that, it's me. I apologize if that's how my question came across, I was just caught off guard. You didn't tell me either of you were injured when we spoke on the phone. For the record, it's not awesome to see your cousin, and the woman he cares about, walk into a room looking like they'd been on the losing end of a fight."

Chad studied his cousin, feeling a little of the fight drain out of him. The longer they stood there, the more he realized that his reaction to Ethan's comment wasn't fair. The rational part of his brain, the part that was still being overridden by the emotional part, *knew* Ethan wouldn't ever think that about him. But with the adrenaline from the shooting compounding his earlier conversation with Sabina, Chad wasn't thinking clearly.

Yet another sign he needed to step away.

"I'm sorry," he said. Ethan's shoulders relaxed at his words. "I know you know me better. Still, it's been a rough night, and it would be best for me to step away."

"No one will protect her like you will," Ethan said.

Chad snorted at that. The way his mind had made a muddle of Ethan's comment was proof enough that he wasn't the best person for the job. But that was a minor issue compared to the elephant in the room.

"You heard what I said. I make her uncomfortable," he repeated.

Ethan frowned. "She really said that to you? Those exact words?"

"She said that I make her uncomfortable. Those were her exact words. As you can imagine, given my history, that's a statement I want to stay far away from. Not to mention the fact that she needs someone she can trust to see her through this. That obviously isn't me." He ignored the stab of pain that lanced through his chest at the words.

"She didn't mean it," Ethan said.

Chad shrugged, a gesture that was more nonchalant than he felt. "Doesn't matter. She said it."

Ethan studied him again. This time Chad couldn't stand the pity he saw in his cousin's eyes, and he looked away.

"It's killing you, isn't it?" he asked softly.

Chad's lips thinned before he answered. "That's a bit dramatic, but no, it doesn't feel good."

"Bring back memories?"

"Hard not to."

"You going to be okay?"

Chad exhaled. Those five words told him all he needed to know. Ethan would take care of Sabina and understood why Chad couldn't. "I'll figure it out," he said. "I'll call and make some arrangements tomorrow then head out for a few days as planned. I think it would be best if I had a little break."

Ethan hesitated then nodded. "I still don't believe she meant it that way, but it doesn't matter. Not now. Go and do what you need to. You're a good man, someone I respect and look up to. I know that might not mean much coming from your little cousin, but it's the truth."

Not willing to say anything other than "thank you," Chad stepped forward and hugged him.

"Let me know if you need anything," Ethan said, moving away from the door.

Chad nodded but didn't speak.

Less than five minutes later, he was pulling through the gates of HICC. Headed away from where he most wanted to be.

CHAPTER THIRTEEN

SABINA SAT on a couch in the small conference room that Colton had shuffled her off to after she'd arrived with Chad. He'd brought her coffee and a glass of water and was now chatting with her about, of all things, the weather. Colton was her colleague, a man she considered a friend. And yet a small part of her felt as if he was playing good cop. That he was making her comfortable not because he wanted her comfortable, but because he wanted something from her.

"Would you like some more coffee?" he asked, nodding to the empty mug in her hand.

She shook her head. "Where's Chad? Is he getting his arm and leg cleaned up?"

"He's gone," Ethan answered, entering the room. If Colton was the good cop, there was no question Ethan was the bad one. His eyes met and held hers with a cold glint she'd never seen before, and a chill raced down her spine. Hostility radiated from his body as he leaned against the opposite wall, crossed his arms, and stared—glared—at her.

She drew back but refused to be cowed. She might be

confused as to why Ethan was so angry, but she wasn't afraid of him. "Gone? Where? Did he get his wounds cleaned up?"

Ethan looked at Colton, and the two shared some sort of silent communication. Only Ethan's ever so slight tip of his head toward the door wasn't hidden from her. Colton nodded, rose, and slipped from the room.

"What's going on, Ethan?" Sabina asked, her mind instantly conjuring images of Chad being more injured than he'd let on or an infection setting in.

"That's exactly what I want to know, Sabina. You've lied to your colleagues, hidden secrets from your past, and now you've put my cousin in the line of fire." She flinched, but he wasn't done. "Let's be very clear about this, Sabina. Unless you can convince me that the attack tonight wasn't because of whatever *you've been hiding*, everything that happened is your responsibility. My cousin was almost killed trying to save you. He's one of the best men I know and because of you, he could have died tonight. Whatever your secrets are, they end now."

Sabina wasn't much to cry, but Ethan's words had her eyes filling. He was right. She *was* responsible for Chad being shot. She hadn't pulled the trigger, but if not for her, Chad wouldn't have been there. If not for her, the *shooter* wouldn't have been there.

She should have told Chad the truth. Or run away altogether. But she hadn't. She'd selfishly tried to have both—him in her life and her secrets.

The thought of losing him had her stomach cramping, and she looked away from Ethan.

"Where is he?" she asked, her voice quiet.

"Gone." One word. One cold word.

"I want to talk to him."

Ethan cocked his head. "Too bad. He's not willing to be in the same room with you anymore."

His words sucked the breath from her lungs. She rubbed her

hand across her chest, her heart beating furiously beneath her palm. "I guess he has every right to hate me."

At that, Ethan scoffed. "That's the thing, Sabina. He doesn't hate you. That's why he can't be around you."

Her brows dropped. "I don't understand."

"I'm sure you don't." He paused, but she felt he had more to say, so she held her tongue. After a long, tense moment, he spoke again. "When Chad was in college a young woman—a classmate of his—accused him of sexual assault."

Sabina's heart skipped a dozen beats, and she was shaking her head before Ethan even finished speaking. "He wouldn't do that. I know that's what everyone says, or what a lot of people say, about perpetrators, but in Chad's case, he wouldn't. I know that."

Ethan studied her for a long moment. She saw the moment he decided to speak again, and his chest rose on a small inhale. Whatever he was going to say wasn't easy for him, either. "You're right," he said. "Of course you are. But it was, quite possibly, the worst two weeks of his life. There was an investigation, and although the school managed to keep it quiet, it divided the class. For two weeks, he walked around campus with half his classmates thinking he'd assaulted a woman and having no way to prove he hadn't. It...had an impact on him."

Sabina couldn't imagine what that must have been like for him. To be innocent of a crime and unable to prove it. "What happened?"

"It turned out that the young woman *had* been assaulted. But not by Chad, of course. She'd been a victim of her uncle's predation. She needed help. She *wanted* help. But her uncle was high up in the administration of the academy, and she didn't think anyone would believe her if she spoke the truth. She also struggled with naming him knowing what it would do to the rest of her family."

"And so she named *Chad*?" Sabina asked, horrified for both

of them. She wasn't about to forgive the woman for putting Chad in that position. Good god, it must have made his life a living hell. But her heart also ached for his classmate. She couldn't imagine what the young woman must have been going through.

Ethan nodded.

There was more, still, that Ethan wanted to say, but he seemed to be looking for something from her. "I didn't know," she said, then she frowned. "Why are you telling me this now? Surely it doesn't have anything to do with what happened tonight? You made your opinion very clear on the matter that what happened was my…responsibility."

"I'm telling you because you brought that all back for him tonight. The fear, the panic, the *helplessness*. When he left here a few minutes ago, he was as close to breaking as I've ever seen him, Sabina. And maybe I can forgive you your secrets, depending on what they are. But I can't, I won't, forgive you for what you did to him tonight."

Panic clawed inside her, like a hundred birds fluttering to get free. "I swear, Ethan, I have no idea what I did. What did I do? I know I didn't tell him things I should have told him. Things I shouldn't have kept secret—"

"But why would you tell him anything when he makes you uncomfortable?" Ethan cut her off.

She blinked at him, the words sounding vaguely familiar. "What?"

"Tonight, at the diner," Ethan said. And just like that, she knew. She held up her hand to stop Ethan, but he paid her no mind and continued to tear through her. "He was holding your hand, giving you comfort and encouragement. He was trying to convince you to trust him so he could *help* you. That's all he's ever wanted, Sabina, for you to trust him so that he could *love* you. But you couldn't do that. You *wouldn't* do that." Ethan paused, his chest rising and falling in a rapid beat. "I'm not saying you have to trust people or like people just because they want you to. But why did you have to make him feel so unwanted, so dirty? So evil?"

The words she'd tossed out at the diner danced in her head, taunting her. They'd been meaningless words. Well, not exactly meaningless. She *had* been uncomfortable with the questioning. But not because *Chad* made her uncomfortable, not in that way. It was unfathomable to her that he would ever even consider preying on a woman, much less act on it.

But still, she'd said those words. They were not meant in the way he'd heard them, but that hardly mattered.

And now they couldn't be taken back.

She could own that mistake, at least. She didn't know how or if she could fix it, but she could at least own it.

Raising her eyes, she met Ethan's gaze. "I didn't mean it the way he interpreted it." She held up a hand to stop Ethan from interrupting her. When he closed his mouth and nodded, she continued. "But I did say those words and know full well the power words can have. I was uncomfortable with the conversation because I knew I was in the wrong. I knew I needed to talk to him. I *wanted* to talk to him. But for reasons we can get into later, I couldn't bring myself to do it right then. And because of my own issues, I lashed out. I didn't mean to hurt him or imply what I did, but that doesn't matter, because I *did* hurt him. I don't know if I'll ever be able to rectify the damage I've already done, but I can try to not do any more."

She paused and watched Ethan. The hard glint in his eye wasn't quite as sharp, but he still didn't look very forgiving. She suspected it wasn't just her relationship with Chad that she'd damaged tonight.

"Will you please go get Colton, and maybe bring Ava in, too? Once everyone is here, I'll tell you everything I know about Kevin Jacobs."

Ethan frowned. "The senator from Kentucky?"

She nodded. “And the man who got away with killing my mother.”

CHAPTER FOURTEEN

CHAD STEPPED out of the shower, dried off, then wrapped the towel around his waist. Two hours in his home gym should have tired him out after the night he'd had, but he suspected sleep would still elude him.

Not bothering to get dressed, he walked straight to his bed, dropped the towel on the floor, and climbed under the covers. Lying on his back, he stared at the ceiling. How had everything gone so sideways? He'd been making progress with Sabina, or so he'd thought. Funny how that had turned out. Not that it was funny at all. More pathetic. He was still struggling to accept that he hadn't figured out her aversion to him was deeper than just not wanting to talk about her past.

All those looks he'd been so sure he'd seen…

As he thought back over the past few months, images flashed through his mind. Sabina sharing a smile with him as Ryan relayed yet another "let's embarrass Chad" story. The gentle touch of her hand on his arm as she leaned in to say something to him during a meeting with Stella and Hunter. Those moments, and so many others like them, had led him to believe there was, or could be, more between them. Well, suffice it to say, he definitely needed to brush up on his people-reading skills.

Forcing his thoughts away from reinterpreting every interaction he'd ever had with Sabina, he started to think about office logistics. Tomorrow, he'd ask Colton to move his office from the third floor to the first. Sabina shouldn't have to work on the same floor as he did if his presence made her uncomfortable, and he didn't have a problem being the one to move. He was working through which of the small conference rooms would make the best office when his phone vibrated on the bedside table.

Grabbing the device, he opened the app for his security system then frowned. Hitting a button, he dialed Ethan's number.

"Why is Sabina driving up my driveway?" he asked.

"Because she wanted to see you, and you need to see her," he answered.

"She's alone. Weren't you supposed to protect her?"

"Teague and I escorted her here in our own vehicles. We're waiting at the end of your drive until you tell us to leave, or she comes back out."

"Since I'm not going to answer the door, your wait won't be long."

Ethan grumbled something Chad couldn't quite catch. "You should let her in," he said instead.

"As I said to you earlier tonight, it's not a good idea for the two of us to be alone, and now you know why."

"And as I said to you earlier tonight, I don't think she meant what she said when she said what she did. In fact, I know she didn't."

A tiny weight lifted from Chad's chest, but his brain wasn't ready to latch onto that yet. "That's nice. And yet I still don't think it's a good idea for her to come here."

"Why? Is your pity party getting a little too wild and crazy?"

Chad was glad his cousin wasn't in the room with him. It would have taken more effort than he had not to deck him. "I'm being smart," Chad bit out.

"You're being stubborn. Trust me on this. You need to give her a chance to talk to you. No, wait, more to the point, you need to *listen* to her."

"Why are you so Team Sabina now?" Chad muttered as his doorbell rang.

"I'm team Chad-Sabina, and you'll figure that out if you listen to her. Now stop acting like a three-year-old and go answer your door." And with that, Ethan ended the call.

Chad tossed the phone onto the duvet and debated whether to wait Sabina out. He was nice and cozy, tucked up in bed. She was standing out in the cold October night. Outlasting her persistence, if she had any, wouldn't be hard.

The bell rang again.

He reached for his phone and pulled up the security app. Standing at his door, Sabina was hunched against the cold with her arms crossed over her stomach. She was wearing little more than a lightweight jacket and a look of determination. A look that would have been fierce had her teeth not been chattering.

When she reached for the bell again, he threw his blankets off. Sometimes he really hated being a good guy.

Chad: *Getting dressed, be right down*

He saw her look at the text on her phone and didn't miss the visible exhale as her shoulders relaxed and her eyes closed. Before tonight, he'd swear her body language screamed relief, but he wasn't ready to trust himself—or her—yet.

Three minutes later, he jogged down the stairs in a pair of jeans and a long-sleeved shirt. Turning on the gas fireplace as he passed, he walked to the door and opened it. Sabina must have been looking out into the night, because she whipped around at the sound. Then she froze. Not like a deer in headlights who didn't know which way to run. But as if she couldn't believe he'd answered. In some ways, he couldn't either.

Stepping aside, he gestured her in. She studied him closely then darted in. "Thank you," she said, rubbing her hands up and down her arms.

He turned and walked back to the large family room. The fireplace wasn't quite circulating heat yet, but it was on its way.

"Have a seat," he said, pointing to the couch that also had a throw blanket rumpled in the corner. Not surprisingly, as soon as she sat, she reached for it and pulled it over her lap, tucking her hands underneath. He took a seat on a recliner toward the opposite end from where she'd curled up.

Her hands twisted under the blanket, and several seconds ticked by before she spoke. "I'm so sorry, Chad. When I said those things in the diner, I didn't mean them the way you think I did. Never, not once, has your presence made me uncomfortable in that way. You're one of the best men I know. Maybe even *the* best. I just..." She hesitated. "I've known for a long time that you deserved to have more from me than I ever gave you. Not because you asked, but because I wanted to give that to you. But my past isn't just about me, and telling you wasn't a decision I could make on my own." She paused again and turned her gaze to the fire. She no longer held her body so tight, nor were her hands fidgeting under the blanket.

"When you came to me at the diner, I'd just been given permission by the other person involved to tell you. I'd made the decision that I *would* tell you, and I hoped we could figure out the consequences together. But after living with my secrets for eighteen years, silence is not an easy habit to break. And the diner wasn't the right place to try to break it. I also wanted to show you some of the files I have at home. My tentative plan was to gather all those files tonight and talk to you tomorrow in the privacy of your office."

She started to twist her hands again. "You kept pushing,

though, and I...I panicked. I *was* uncomfortable, and the conversation was making me uncomfortable. But only because I knew what I needed to do—knew what I wanted to do—but you were asking me to do it in a way I wasn't prepared for. Like a child who hasn't gotten her way, I lashed out, and you will never know how much I regret it."

"Ethan told you?" He'd been listening, as Ethan had suggested. His mind even recognized that her words could be true, but his heart wasn't as certain. Being hurled back to those days all those years ago was a horrifying place to be. And truth be told, he hadn't recovered from it. Even if he believed her, which he was leaning toward doing, that didn't mean he wasn't bruised from the experience.

She nodded in response to his question. "I can't imagine the pain my words must have caused, and I don't blame you if this is something I can't fix. But at the very least, I wanted to tell you that not in a million years would I think of you like that."

There was nothing but raw honesty in her eyes, and yet he wasn't ready to respond to her explanation. That didn't mean he couldn't get some answers, though. He still believed that it was best for Ethan and the others to take over. But if he knew her truths, it might help his—and probably, her—bruises heal a little faster.

"Would you like some tea?" he asked.

Her eyes searched his face. Then hesitantly, she nodded. She started to shift the blanket off her lap, but he stayed her with a gesture.

"I'll get it. This time of night, I assume you want mint?"

She hesitated again then smiled. "That would be great, please."

While the water heated in the electric kettle, he sorted through her words and his feelings about them. He didn't think he'd overreacted at the diner. In that kind of situation, it was better to react the way he had and be wrong than to remain and keep pushing. But to Ethan's point, perhaps his own history—and his own fears—had blinded him to any other explanation. And in letting his past experiences taint his present, it had been easy to slide into that pity party his cousin had called him on.

"Here," he said a few minutes later as he handed Sabina a cup. Retaking his seat, he wrapped his hands around his own mug.

"I owe you the rest of the story," she said after taking a tentative sip.

"You don't owe me anything, Sabina," he said. He *wanted* answers, but not because she felt she owed them to him.

She looked up at him. "You're wrong, Chad. I do owe you. Not because you've asked, but because you're my friend and someone I trust. And because you're someone who cares about me. Maybe a little less now than earlier today," she added with a self-deprecating smile. "I think you still care, though. And even if you don't, HICC will be helping me so, at the very least, as the director of the West Coast operations, you should know."

He nodded, not willing to comment on whether he still cared or not. He did. His pity party proved that—if he didn't care, the events of the evening wouldn't have bothered him much. But he wasn't ready to voice that reality.

"Are you familiar with Kevin Jacobs?" she asked.

"The senator from Kentucky?"

She nodded. "Rumor has it he's going to make a run for president, but we'll see." She fidgeted with her mug then turned her attention to the fire. "Eighteen years ago, when he was the attorney general, he murdered my mother. My sister and I walked into the room just after he'd finished strangling her."

Chad sucked in a breath. "Your sister?" he asked, wanting to clarify that point before she moved on to the rest of what he was guessing would be a long story.

She glanced at him and nodded. "My twin. Kara's a doctor. She lives in Malibu but travels for work most of the year."

If someone was after Sabina because of what had happened eighteen years ago, then her sister was likely in danger, too. "Did Ethan...?"

She nodded, knowing what he asked. "Yes, Colton has a couple of buddies down there who were going to check on her. She leaves for Bangladesh tomorrow so should be safe."

He nodded then waited for her to continue. And when she did, a tale as heartbreaking—and as surprising—as any he'd ever heard emerged. He'd always thought her a strong woman, and now knew just how strong she was. He'd also long suspected she was in danger and unfortunately, her story proved his suspicions right.

She paused after telling him about the moment she and her sister stood together in the middle of the creek, in the middle of the night, and first made the decision to go into hiding. Her gaze took on a vacant look, and he sensed she was reliving those minutes over and over. Chad cleared his throat, and her eyes lifted. "You did the right thing. Running. Hiding," he clarified.

She gave him a wayward smile. "Most days I think so. Some days, I wonder."

"You didn't end up going to the police, did you?"

She shook her head then fought a yawn. She'd already told this story once, probably in more detail than what she was relaying now. After not talking about it for years, Chad recognized it was taking a lot out of her.

"It's late and you've already told Ethan and the others everything. Why don't you give me the CliffsNotes?" he suggested.

She futzed with her mug then let out a soft laugh. "Thank you. It's...weird talking about it after so long. But as I said before. It's time. We can't keep running forever. There were good reasons for it at the time, but as Kara recently pointed out, we're not those scared little girls anymore. And science has changed a lot since that night. If anyone can help us find the evidence we need to end this, it's you and everyone at HICC. I know that."

He still had more of her story to hear, but the certainty in her voice—both regarding her decision to talk and her decision to work with HICC—gave him some relief.

"Whenever you're ready," he prompted.

She gave a sharp nod but turned away from him as she answered. "By the next day, Kevin Jacobs had spun a story to the media. Over and over, the news reported that he'd been dating my mother for a few months. He said he'd stopped by to say a quick good-night only to arrive at the same time as the first responders. I don't know how he managed to convince people of that version of the events. The only thing Kara and I could come up with was that when he realized he wasn't going to catch us, he returned to the house, saw that my phone had connected the 9-1-1 call, and somehow managed to get the first responders to *witness* his supposed arrival. Our house was at the end of a dead-end lane. There was no way he would have been able to drive away without the incoming responders seeing him."

"Did you have a long driveway?" Chad asked. Sabina nodded. "He probably parked somewhere along the way and waited until he heard the sirens. Then when they were close enough, started back toward the house, making it look like he'd just arrived, and they were following him in."

"That's what Kara and I figured, too. But the really big red flag was how, within hours of her death, Kevin Jacobs had put a whole big spin machine into play to protect himself. We didn't know what it might mean or what we could do about it, but it scared us. Even more than we already were. And so instead of going to the police, we called my mom's stepbrother, our uncle Mike. Aside from our father, who, at that point, we hadn't seen in six years, he was the only family we had.

"By the time we called, he'd already been notified of her

death. Kevin Jacobs had even stopped by to see if either Kara or I had been in touch with him. Uncle Mike was former CIA and had a pretty good bullshit meter. He didn't believe a word of Jacobs's *concern.* He said that the only reason an AG from Kentucky might have to come to his home in Tennessee wouldn't be a good one."

Chad let out a soft chuckle at that, and Sabina shared a smile. There was nothing quite like a grizzled, experienced intelligence agent to run circles around a politician.

"What did he do when you called him?" Chad asked.

"He told us to hang tight, stay out of sight, and that he'd come pick us up. A day later, he made good on his promise and managed to sneak us out and back to his place. It got...complicated after that."

"Even more complicated, you mean?"

She tilted her head in acknowledgment. "With each passing day, more evidence appeared pointing to either a vagrant, or at one point, human traffickers, being responsible for my mom's murder."

"Traffickers?"

Sabina nodded. "Another Jacobs spin—traffickers had killed our mom and kidnapped us to sell us off. It was a headline-catching story. But after two weeks of subtly promoting the theory, Jacobs started seeding doubts that we were still alive. A few days after that, he had the authorities call off the search. He did, however, keep in touch with Uncle Mike. In the four months after the murder, he called several times to see if we'd been in touch."

"What kept you from stepping forward? I'm not passing judgment, I'm curious," he clarified.

"That was Uncle Mike's call," Sabina answered. "The evidence continued to support Jacobs's version of the story. We were the only two witnesses who could dispute it, but if we did, it would be our word against all that evidence. We debated it. For weeks, we debated it. But then the police found the body of a vagrant, ostensibly a man who'd OD'd, in the next county over. He had one of my mom's rings in his pocket, so they pretty much closed the case."

"Did your Uncle Mike think Jacobs, or someone in his camp, killed the vagrant to frame him?" Chad asked. Sabina nodded. "He was worried about what might happen to you and your sister if you came forward," he said, finishing his thought. Had he been in Uncle Mike's place, he would have been worried, too.

Sabina nodded again. "We agreed not to go to the police, but he did reach out to one of his former colleagues for help. She managed to get all the case files for us so that we could at least understand the scope of Jacobs's efforts. More importantly, though, she also set my sister and me up with new identities and full background covers. It wasn't ideal, especially at our age. But until we could prove something, until we had some way of poking holes in Jacobs's story, it was the safest way."

Chad agreed. Despite everything that had happened that night, he grieved for the girls Sabina and her sister had been and everything they'd lost. "And one year turned into another, then another?"

She nodded again. "We went to college under our new names. We'd originally planned to attend the University of Kentucky together, but Uncle Mike and I thought it would be best to split up. I ended up in Boston while Kara went to LA." She paused, and a small smile teased her lips. "And if you're wondering, Gina took care of that, too."

"Gina?"

"Uncle Mike's CIA friend. Not only did she give us new identities, but she also altered some college records to ensure that our new personas were enrolled. Including fake applications, records of the acceptance letter, housing letters. Everything. She was the first person to show me the magic of computers."

He chuckled at that. It wasn't hard to picture a young Sabina leaning over this woman's shoulder and taking everything in. Then he frowned. "It's not really relevant, but how did you pay for it?"

She huffed a small laugh at that. "Uncle Mike set up a fake scholarship through a bank in Bermuda. He funded it with his own money. The plan was always to reimburse him once it was safe enough for us to come forward. Or until Lalibela and Nalanda Houseman were declared dead, and my mom's estate came to him."

"Is there a 'but' I hear?"

Sabina set her mug down on the side table and tugged the blanket higher against her chest. He had a feeling what was coming next was the heart of the matter, the real reason behind her secrecy.

Sabina cleared her throat then answered. "While Kara and I were in school, Uncle Mike and Gina kept working on the case. One evening, in May of my senior year, my uncle called to say he might have found something. By then, Jacobs was making a bid for the governorship. I think Uncle Mike was feeling a little desperate and wanted to bring the truth out before Jacobs gained any more power."

"Understandable."

Again, Sabina's eyes took on a vacant look as she recounted what happened. "But the next day, his car went over a cliff," she said, her voice quiet in the night. "Ruled an accident, of course. But Kara and I have our doubts." She paused. "And our guilt. We have a lot of that. All he was trying to do was help us. All he wanted was to bring a murderer to justice and keep us safe. And because of that, he lost his life."

Chad studied her. Her hair was pulled back into her usual ponytail, giving him a view of her delicate profile. She was watching the flames dance in the fireplace. No doubt remembering those few days so many years ago. After a long pause, she took a deep breath and continued.

"It wasn't just Uncle Mike, though. I was living with a guy at the time. Nate was everything my life was not. He was gentle and quiet and so kind. I know that sounds dull, but he was also funny in a quirky kind of way and a brilliant artist. He was the first person I let myself get close to after my mother's death. I wasn't passionately in love with him, but he was hard not to love, if you know what I mean? He was just so *good* without being too sweet."

"What happened?" Chad prompted gently. He had a pretty good idea what had happened, but he wanted Sabina to have the chance to tell him.

"I have no idea how Jacobs or his people found out that Mike was still looking into the case. They did discover his involvement, though. And along with his involvement, they somehow managed to discover where I lived. Probably from the phone records of the call he made to me. Thankfully, he'd only called me. And not Kara, too."

"And once they had the phone number, it wasn't hard to figure out who, or where, you were," Chad said.

"It wasn't," she agreed. "Nate and I…we were home that night. We'd been play-arguing about who'd take the garbage out. I lost the bet and popped down to the bins in the basement. When I got back…it was like a repeat of the night my mom died. I walked in and…and there was a man, not Jacobs, standing over Nate." She wiped a tear from her cheek. Grabbing the tissue box from the side table, Chad leaned over and handed it to her. She took it with a wan smile.

"He'd shot Nate and was obviously looking for me. Like that night with my mom, I ran. The man was standing between me and the front door, so I ran back to the kitchen, hoping to reach the door to the service stairs. I was almost there when he hit me on the head with the butt of his gun and knocked me out. Or at least that's what the doctors surmised happened based on my injuries. Whoever he was wasn't done yet, though. Before he left, he set fire to the apartment." She dabbed her eyes then traced the side of her mug with her fingertip.

He wanted to ask what happened next but held back. She'd tell him in her time. Half a minute passed before she took a deep breath and continued.

"Rather than kill me, though, he dragged me close to Nate, left the gun in my hand, then lit the place on fire. I can't say for certain that making it look like a murder-suicide was his plan, but over the years of thinking about it, that's what Gina and I came up with."

"It would have kept the police from looking into it too much," Chad concurred. "But you woke up."

She gave a jerky nod. "I did. And I tried to save Nate. I mean, not *save* him. He was already dead, and I knew it. But I tried to save his body. I latched onto this idea that he'd died because of me and the least I could do was give his family a body to bury." She choked on a sob then, and he couldn't stay away any longer. He was still bruised, but she was bleeding from her scars.

Only he didn't get far across the room before his phone vibrated with another alarm. Halting midway to Sabina's side, he reached for the device. A few swipes later, he accepted that his night had taken yet another grim turn.

"Sabina? Honey?"

She blinked and looked up.

"I need to know if what you said earlier today—here in the house, not at the diner—was true. Do you trust me? Are you okay with me?"

She frowned. "Yes," she answered without hesitation. "In case you haven't figured it out, I love you. I'm *in* love with you. But I didn't want you to turn into another Nate. I wouldn't be able to live with myself if that happened. That's why I kept my distance."

There was a lot in that statement he'd tuck away and process later, but for now, he held out his hand. "I need you to come with me then."

Shifting the blanket off her lap, she reached for him. Then, curling her fingers around his, she rose. "What's going on, Chad?"

"I'll tell you in a minute. Can you go wait by my office door?"

He saw the questioning look on her face, but he'd already let go of her hand. After shutting the fireplace off, he hurried to the mudroom and grabbed his boots. As he pulled them on, he dialed a number. He was on his way back to Sabina, who was waiting where he'd asked, when it started ringing.

Ethan answered as Chad reached for a small spot alongside the doorframe into his office.

"Did you make nice?" Ethan asked.

"There are three figures making their way across the back part of my property. They may have come up from the lake," he said. Beside him, Sabina sucked in a breath. He cast her a reassuring look as he pressed his fingers onto the four hidden sensors that would read his fingerprints and pulse.

"I'm taking Sabina out the back way. I need you and Teague to deal with the intruders," he said.

"You focus on her. We got this," his cousin replied.

"See you at the cabin," Chad replied before hanging up and sliding his phone into his pocket. "Don't be startled," he said to Sabina as a three-by-three section of the floor popped up.

She didn't gasp or startle, but she did inch closer to him. "Chad?"

The opening was cleverly aligned with the natural breaks of the hardwood floor and impossible to detect with the naked eye. And even though he'd been the one to design it, he couldn't help but admire the results.

Reaching down, he lifted one side, angling it up and

revealing a steep staircase. "A light will go on as soon as you set foot on the first step," he said.

Her hesitation lasted less than two seconds, and then she was scrambling down with him hot on her heels.

"What is this?" she asked when the door above them started closing and they stood on solid ground. Solid ground fifteen feet below the foundation of his house. "A safe room?"

"It can be," he answered, taking her hand and leading her down a short hall and into a room. Once inside, he hit a few buttons and brought two monitors to life.

Sabina leaned forward and studied the screens. There wasn't much to see at this point. The figures weren't in range of the video cameras he had positioned closer to the house. But they could make out three human heat signatures moving through the woods toward his home.

Sabina sucked in a breath. "It's happening again," she said. "I brought this on you. Just like Uncle Mike. Just like Nate. This is exactly what I didn't want to happen, Chad. Exactly why I tried to stay away from you."

"I'm not Nate," Chad said, reaching under his desk and pulling out a small gun case. He'd left his own weapon beside his bed, but he had plenty in storage.

"Chad." The look she turned on him was so wary, so sad, and so scared that he paused. Slowly, he raised a hand and traced the fine line of her jaw.

"I'm not Nate, Sabina. Not only do I know *how* to protect us, I also now know what I'm protecting us from. I know it's hard, but you need to trust me on this. You need to trust Ethan and Teague and the others, too."

He saw the moment she accepted that she had two choices: keep running, or trust her team and stay and fight. Her eyes cleared, and the lost look that had filled them for the past hour disappeared, replaced with the sharp focus he was used to. Her lips firmed and her shoulders straightened. It wasn't going to be easy to stand and fight, but she made her decision.

"I do. I want this to end. I want Jacobs brought to justice, and I want Kara and me to be free to live our lives. And...and I'm trusting you and Ethan and Colton and Teague and everyone else to help me do that."

He smiled at her statement and nodded. Then hitting a few buttons on the computer, he powered down the screens. Lowering his hand, he wrapped his fingers around hers and pulled her into another room.

"Here," he said, grabbing a thick fleece from a small closet. The first room they'd entered was what he referred to as the ops room, or command station. But in addition to that, there was a bedroom with four bunks—and extra clothes—a kitchen, and a bathroom. They wouldn't be staying long enough to use any of those, though.

"Where are we going and what is this place?" she asked again as she tugged the sweatshirt over her head.

"To HICC. But the back way," he answered. Pausing at the door to the hall, he sent a quick text. Then hitting a few buttons on his phone, he checked the progress of the three intruders. This time, five figures showed on his screen with two of them moving toward the original three. Ethan and Teague doing exactly what they promised.

"Back way?" she asked.

He nodded and started down the hall. Passing through a thick door, he shut it behind them then waited a beat for the security lights to come on. Once the dim lights flickered on, he locked the door then continued forward.

"It is a safe room of sorts," he answered her prior question. "You saw that. But there's also a tunnel to a neighbor's property. Jack was part of my grandfather's Secret Service detail, both during his presidency and after. When he retired, he decided that he'd lived here long enough that he should buy a place and stay. We'll follow this tunnel for about thirty minutes to an exit that will take us into his barn. I texted him to let him know we're coming."

"Okay." Sabina drew out the word. "So you've known him a long time and can trust him? Is this kind of thing—all these secret tunnels—normal for a presidential family?"

He chuckled at the last question. "I've known Jack pretty much my whole life. As to your other question, no, it's not normal. I shouldn't laugh, because the reason we have them isn't a happy one. But you sounded so…not confused, but like you'd just been let in on a secret."

"Because I have. Even if it's not a secret about all presidential families, it's a secret about the Warwick presidential family. Isn't it?"

He inclined his head. "Yes, it is, actually."

"Can I ask why? I don't feel like I deserve an answer given everything I've kept from you. But if you're willing to tell me, I'd like to know."

He hesitated. Not because he didn't trust her, though. It was obvious she wasn't sure if the two of them were on steady ground. Honestly, he wasn't sure either. But in this moment, he could choose to either answer or not. Both decisions would have repercussions on any future he and Sabina might have.

Unsure if he was making the right decision, Chad braced himself and picked a path. "During Gramps's tenure at the White House, there were two kidnapping attempts on us grandkids," he answered baldly. "Everyone in the family took extra precautions after that."

Behind him, Sabina gasped. "Two?!" she exclaimed. "I don't even remember hearing about one. That seems like something I would hear about."

"Not if it's in the interest of national security to keep it quiet," Chad answered. He rarely thought about those years of his life. Aside from the death of his parents, he'd had a good childhood. It had been different from most kids, but it was just the way he'd grown up.

Sabina put a hand on his arm, staying him. "Who was it?"

Chad turned and met her gaze. This wasn't something he talked about outside the family. Hell, it was so long ago that the family never even talked about it anymore. And yet he found himself wanting to tell her.

"The first was me," he said, his voice so soft it didn't echo in the tunnel. "I was in fifth grade. It was after my parents died and we were living with my grandparents in DC. Ryan and Josh started classes later than I did, so I was on my way to school on my own. Well, with my Secret Service detail. As a kid, I didn't really understand what was going on when it happened. There was some commotion outside the car, then a loud bang. I learned later that it was a small bomb meant to disable the vehicle, but it misfired and barely damaged the car. To this day the people who lived on that street would tell you it was a gas leak."

"Were you hurt? Was anyone hurt?"

He didn't want to talk about any more violence. Not after everything she'd been through, everything she'd shared that night. But he couldn't *not* answer. Not when she was looking at him, her expression filled with concern. "A shot was fired," he answered. "It hit the agent riding in the front passenger seat in the arm, but he was okay. It was…a weird experience," he continued. "It seems like I should have figured out what was going on, but I didn't. It seemed to me like we'd been in a car accident or something."

"Only it wasn't an accident of any sort," she said.

He shook his head. "A few days after that morning, my grandparents sat me down and explained everything. They were careful to keep it age-appropriate, of course. And it helped that by then, the four men responsible had already been caught. Knowing they weren't still out there made it all a little less scary. Even so, learning that someone had come after me, and hurt the people who looked after me, was...it was a little bit of a shock. Despite everything I'd already gone through with the death of my parents, I grew up a lot that day." More than any kid should, but it was what it was.

Sabina's eyes searched his. "What about the second? That wasn't you, too, was it?"

He shook his head. "That was Cody. Right here in Mystery Lake actually. It was a different group of people behind that attempt. But between the two perpetrators, they targeted the oldest and the youngest of the grandkids. Or at least the youngest who was alive at the time. The twins came along a few years after my grandparents left DC."

"What happened?" she pressed. Standing in the tunnel while his cousin and Teague dealt with the three intruders on his property probably wasn't the right time for this conversation. The irony of the situation wasn't lost on him, though. Hours earlier, Sabina had been making the same kind of decision—when would be the right time and place to talk to him, to tell him her secrets? She'd made a decision that hadn't been good for either of them. He wasn't keen on going into this part of his family's history, but he wasn't going to make the same mistake. Not when they were already on shaky ground.

"It was less organized," he said. "All Cody remembers is walking into the woods to help find some guy's puppy. Again, Secret Service did their job as efficiently as they do, and he wasn't harmed. The men involved were in custody within a week." He paused and noticed that the cool air of the tunnel had started seeping through his shirt. "Needless to say," he continued, with a wry smile, "the family started taking security a little more seriously."

"Including building safe rooms?"

He smiled. "And escape tunnels. I'm not the only one who has one. The cousins who live in town don't. But those of us who live out, who have any property, do."

She seemed to consider this then nodded. "Got it. Okay, so what next?"

Grateful for the change of subject, he checked his phone then turned and continued down the corridor as he answered. "Next, we get to Jack's. Then we use his pickup to drive to HICC. I do want to hear what happened after Nate was killed. But if you want to wait until we're somewhere less, well, less on the run, I understand. I just want you to know that I do want to hear the rest of your story if you're willing to share it with me."

A few minutes passed before she responded. "I do want to tell you, but before that, I have a question."

They paused at a sturdy metal door and Chad put his left palm on a reader as he leaned forward for a retina scan. "Ask away," he said as the massive door swung open silently.

"I'm working on the assumption that it's Jacobs's men coming after me. Probably because he is planning to make a bid for president and wants to clean up any loose ends. If that's the case, then it means they tracked me to you, which also means they know about HICC. Do we need to worry about my team? I assume the other operatives can take care of one another. But Ava, Leo, and Collin aren't exactly set up to defend themselves if someone comes after them in any way other than electronically."

"On it already. Ethan let me know that Ava stayed at HICC after you left to come see me. She'll be bunking there tonight. As for Leo and Collin, Ryan called in some favors and has a couple of colleagues watching their places. They live in town, so are harder to sneak up on, which works to our advantage. We'll update them tomorrow when they come in."

Behind him, she let out a long exhale. "Thank you. For right or for wrong, one of my reasons for keeping my past a secret was to protect the people around me. I don't want anyone else to get hurt because of me."

Chad stopped and turned. "Let's get one thing straight. You

are not responsible for this. Kevin Jacobs is. I understand that might be hard to accept, but all you've done is what you've needed to do to survive. Kevin Jacobs, and whoever is behind him, is responsible."

"Intellectually, I know that," she said with a huff. "Emotionally, it isn't so easy to set aside the fear and anxiety. The conflict between the two isn't something I'm going to resolve tonight, though, so which do you want to hear first? The rest of the Nate story or the reason why I ended up on the West Coast with you and Colton?"

One of his eyebrows winged up and his lips quirked. Rather than comment on her confession, though, he spun around and continued down the tunnel. "Tell me about Nate."

CHAPTER FIFTEEN

THE GROUND they walked on was dirt but compact enough that Sabina wasn't worried about watching her step. She did notice they were walking down a gentle slope, though, and wondered how deep they were. She'd never been claustrophobic before, but she'd also never been under this much earth. She shivered at the thought of it all coming down on the two of them. Wrapping her arms around her middle, she hugged the fleece against her body as they walked.

"I managed to get Nate out of the apartment," she said. "But I wasn't strong enough to get him any farther. After a while, I blacked out from the smoke. There were two other apartments on our floor. But one was unoccupied, and the couple who lived in the other were at work. There was no one to help, or even see us."

The path dipped again, and Chad gestured to the ground. "Careful. We got most of this cleared out, but a few spots were harder than others." As he spoke, he pointed out a handful of rocks jutting up from the ground. She nodded and stepped around one as they continued.

"The next thing I knew, I woke up in the hospital with a few burns, a concussion, and some smoke damage to my lungs," she said. "At the time, the authorities weren't sure if I was the one who'd shot Nate, so they had me under police guard. I was grateful for it even if it wasn't for the reason they thought."

"How long did it take for them to clear you?" Chad asked.

"Only a couple of days. When they interviewed me, I told them what I saw and about the man in the apartment. Both CCTV footage and another resident confirmed that such a man existed. The cameras didn't get an image of his face, but his clothes matched the description I gave them." They rounded a gentle bend, and she drew to a halt as the ground all but dropped away ahead of them.

Chad cast a look over his shoulder at her but kept going. "It's not much farther. About five minutes down, then another five up. Then we'll be to Jack's."

The lights illuminated the path, but they were dim enough that within twenty feet, the tunnel receded into darkness. Still, Chad was carrying on, so she hurried after him and continued her narrative.

"The day after they cleared me, Gina showed up. She breezed in like she owned the place, claimed I was her niece, and swept me away. All under an assumed name, of course. Three days later, at her townhouse in DC, Sabina O'Malley was born. That was fourteen years ago."

Chad glanced over his shoulder at her again. "You had to change your name twice?"

She nodded, though he'd turned back around and couldn't see. "Right after my mother died, I changed my name to Bella Wright, from Lalibela Houseman, my given name. My sister was born Nalanda but changed her name to Sakara. Her cover hadn't been compromised, so she's been able to keep that name."

"The names sound like they have meaning?"

They reached the bottom of the hill, and Chad hadn't exactly been truthful when he'd said it was a few minutes up. It was up, but it was *up* a staircase so steep that a rope, anchored somewhere above them, lay along its length. It reminded her of the pyramids in Mexico and the ropes designed to give the tourists something to hold onto as they clambered up and down.

"Ready?" he asked.

She eyed the stairs but nodded. "Ready."

"Ladies first." He stood aside, picked up the rope, and held it out to her.

"This isn't one of those things that if I go first, I'm going to be clearing the way of spiders and things like that, is it?" she asked, taking the thick rope in her hand. It was coarse and rough against her palm. She hoped she didn't need to use it much. Then again, a few blisters here and there wouldn't kill her.

He chuckled. "After everything you've told me, you're going to run from a few spiders?"

"I don't mind spiders. It's when they skitter out of nowhere or land on me that I have a heart attack."

He chuckled. "If I go first, I won't be able to help you much if you need a hand. The stairs aren't wide enough to turn or move around each other."

She gazed up the tunnel again. She wasn't a particularly clumsy person, but her luck hadn't been so hot lately. Giving herself a nod of encouragement, she grabbed the rope and started up. Hopefully, she'd stay on her feet and not go tumbling backward into Chad.

"Tell me about the names," he prompted as they started to climb.

"Lalibela and Nalanda are archaeological sites that our mother named us after. I went by Bela and my sister by Nala. When we first went into hiding, I officially changed my name to Bella—with two *L*s—and Nala changed hers to Sakara."

"Like the funerary site in Egypt?"

"Exactly, but with a *K* instead of two *Q*s."

"And Sabina?"

"Sibinacocha is a lake in Peru that holds Inca artifacts. Again, similar in pronunciation to the first part of the word but spelled a little different." She was starting to huff a little. She'd been so busy getting HICC up and running that she'd been neglecting her runs and workouts. Something she'd have to change once they sorted everything out.

At that thought, she drew to a stop. Then jumped when Chad's hand landed on the back of her thigh.

"Sorry," he said when she looked over her shoulder. "You stopped so quickly, I figured it was better to steady myself with my hand than ram your behind with my head."

Her gaze dropped to the top of his head and his thick dark hair. Inappropriate though it was, the thought of his head anywhere near her upper thighs didn't sound so bad.

"Everything okay?" he asked.

Shaking herself from those thoughts, she nodded. "I was thinking that I needed to get back to my workouts once we settle everything."

He smiled. "Your mind has finally made the jump to believing that we *will* sort this out?" he asked, picking up on her train of thought.

She smiled back. "I guess so."

"Good," he said with a sharp nod. "Now why don't you lead us the rest of the way out of here and while we climb, you can tell me why you picked the names you did."

It was a good plan. If only she hadn't been so out of shape. It wasn't until they were seated in the cab of a pickup that must have been twenty years old that she caught her breath enough to answer. "There's not much to say about the names," she said.

"They have a story, though," Chad pressed as he turned onto the rural highway that would take them into town. "But even if the names aren't important in the grand scheme of things, the fact that you are now free to talk about them is," he added.

He had a point. Several, actually. She *was* free to talk about her past and prior identities. She didn't have to hold everything so close to the vest anymore. Perhaps more important, though, was that Chad had *asked* and she could tell *him.*

The magnitude of the change that the last several hours had brought to her life unfurled with the subtlety of a tsunami. Every question he'd ever asked she could now answer. She wasn't fooling herself that everything was magically fine between them, but she'd be damned if she was going to pass up the opportunity to try to make it so.

"They do," she responded. "I told you where they came from, and you know my mom was an archaeologist. Kara and I decided that if we had to change our names, we wanted to honor our mom. I did it by staying as close to my original name as possible—at least the first time. Kara did it by picking the name she did which, as you know, is a huge archaeological site." In the dim light of the cab, his smile was little more than a shadow, but she did get a glimpse of it.

"And the second time?" he asked.

She couldn't help it, she snorted. "Sorry, it's just that the second time around wasn't so easy. I'm sure you'll be shocked to hear that some locations, like Bryce or Devon, also make good names. However, most do not. It took me several days to find a name I wanted."

"I'm sorry you had to change your name at all, but Sabina suits you," he said. "I haven't known you as anything else, but still, it suits. It's a strong name but also unique and pretty." He paused then added, "No, it's more than pretty, it's elegant."

Sabina wasn't sure she was those things. She'd been told before that she was attractive, and she had a mirror to see for herself. But no one had ever put those characteristics together to describe her. That it was Chad who'd done so caused a hint of heat to creep up her neck. She didn't think he could see her reaction, but she turned and looked out the window just in case.

Groves of tall pines bumped up against the asphalt, lining their way even as they cast the road into shadow. With every passing mile, she was acutely aware of every way she'd failed Chad. Failed them. Only a few hours earlier, she'd nearly destroyed the man she loved with her careless words in the diner. And that was just the beginning of a long list of her transgressions.

And yet he'd allowed her into his home and listened to her story. He'd spoken to her about his family, shared the secret of the tunnel, and asked more questions about her. His character and strength humbled her. She wanted to believe his openness meant she hadn't irreparably harmed their friendship. Even if she didn't deserve it.

"You're awfully quiet over there," Chad said.

Not wanting to share her train of thought—not yet, anyway—she asked, "What's next? Once we get to HICC?"

It turned out there was not a lot that was "next" when they arrived at HICC. Ava had left a bag of clothes for her in the upstairs apartment at the cabin. She'd also left a note telling Sabina that she was sleeping in the guest room in Colton's downstairs apartment and that they had a lot to cover in the morning.

Ethan had also texted Chad to let him know they'd be tied up long into the night. One of the men who'd come onto the property had escaped. One had been shot in the leg and taken to the hospital. The third was dead. Sabina had no idea who the men were, but since they were likely there on Kevin Jacobs's orders, she didn't feel bad about the two who hadn't walked away.

Settling into one of the guest rooms—alone—Sabina wasn't sure sleep would come easily. But human bodies were funny that way. Much to her surprise, when she woke, the October sun was streaming into the room and she remembered nothing after crawling into bed.

But it wasn't her bed or her room. A moment's disorientation, like a touch of vertigo, swirled in her head as she remained burrowed under the covers. After several moments, she forced her eyelids open and looked around. When her gaze landed on the curtainless window, with its views of the tall pines, everything came flooding back. Throwing off the blankets, she quickly changed into a pair of jeans and a lightweight sweater. As soon as she opened the door of her room, she smelled coffee and heard the low, comforting rumble of Chad's voice. She hadn't thought he'd leave her—at least not without saying goodbye or leaving a note—but her shoulders slumped with relief that he was still nearby.

He looked up when she entered the kitchen and smiled. He was leaning against the old slab wood counter, coffee in hand and phone to his ear. He jerked his head in the direction of the coffeepot. She flashed him a grateful smile before grabbing a mug and pouring herself a cup.

"Nothing yet, though?" Chad asked whoever he was talking to. "No, I get it. Just anxious. I know we all are." He paused to listen then spoke again. "Sabina is up now. We'll head over to the office in a few minutes. We can continue this then." He murmured something else then ended the call.

"Everything okay?" she asked, mirroring his position but on the other side of the kitchen.

"Ethan and Teague were cleared to leave the scene late last night. Officially, the shooting was ruled self-defense."

Sabina raised her brows. "Officially?"

Chad inclined his head. "It was self-defense. We have the cameras to show that the three men fired first. They might have been a little provoked, but they definitely shot first."

Sabina had an image of Ethan in the forest, taunting the intruders like the French knights from *Monty Python and the Holy Grail.* She smiled. She doubted it had gone down quite like that, but she liked the idea of it so didn't ask any further questions.

"Glad to hear that. What about the one who got away?"

Chad shrugged. "Intentional. We wanted to let one go to make sure the message got back to Jacobs."

She frowned as she raised her cup for another sip of coffee. "What message?"

"That you aren't alone anymore," he answered. "That you have powerful people protecting you."

His eyes had met and held hers as he'd spoken the words. As if it was as important to him that *she* believed them as it was for Jacobs to. Slowly, she nodded.

"You forgot one thing," she said.

"Yeah? What's that?"

"*I'm* one of those powerful people." A pleased smile broke across his features at her statement. She set her empty mug in the sink then turned to him. "I'm going to grab some food to go and then we can head to the office. We have a few things to sort out today."

CHAPTER SIXTEEN

Chad reached for a file on the conference room table as Ava wrapped Sabina in a hug. The younger woman towered over her boss, but neither seemed to find the height difference uncomfortable.

"You get any sleep last night?" Ethan asked, taking a seat to Chad's right.

"Enough. You?"

Ethan lifted a shoulder. "Enough," he echoed.

Teague, Tucker, and Colton made their way to seats, then the rest of Sabina's team filed in. Leo and Collin were the only ones in the room unaware of the prior evening's events. Both looked more curious than concerned about the early-morning company meeting, though.

When everyone was finally seated, Colton turned to Sabina. "Why don't you give Leo and Collin the quick rundown. Then we can jump to why we're all here now and what our plan is going to be."

Sabina's body drew back. Chad suspected that her hesitation, and the flash of fear in her eyes, stemmed from habit.

Having someone so bluntly tell her to reveal secrets she'd kept for years had caught her off guard.

As if sensing her need to gather herself together, the room stayed quiet. Her attention swept over everyone before finally landing on him. Sitting across from her, he held her gaze and hoped she saw the support that he offered. Support that was hers to take or not.

After a beat, she nodded then turned to speak to her two colleagues. In less than eight minutes, she gave them the facts of her past and her assumptions about the present. When she finished, she turned to Ethan and asked him to step in. "I know what we *think* about the ambush and intruders, but you three might have some actual facts."

"We have the shell casings from the ambush, and Mystery Lake PD is running a comparison," Ethan said. "We think they'll be a match for a sniper rifle we lifted off one of the intruders last night. It was the right kind of ammo for that weapon, but we'll let the tests confirm."

Sabina nodded and he continued.

"We have prints from two of the intruders that the police lab is running through IAFIS. I forwarded them to Ava, too, and she'll start looking in our systems. There's overlap, of course, between HICC and Mystery Lake PD, but HICC has more resources. We may have better—or if not better, faster—luck."

Chad cast a glance at Ava. "I put them into the computer just before this meeting," she answered his unasked question. "We may have something by the time we're done here."

"Good," Colton said, stepping into the fray. "Hopefully we get a hit or two, but in the meantime, we need the three of you to start picking apart Kevin Jacobs's life." He pointed to Sabina's team as he spoke. "I want to know everything from his travel schedule to his credit card expenses to where he likes to eat for breakfast. You name it, we want it."

"Four of us," Sabina interjected. When everyone looked at her, she clarified. "You said 'the three of you.' There are four of us on the cyber intelligence team."

Colton paused then nodded. "There are, of course. But there's something else we thought you might want to do."

Sabina's gaze skittered to Chad before returning to Colton. "What's that?"

"You said you thought your uncle might have found something just before he was killed," Colton said.

"I did say that, and I do think that," Sabina replied.

"Gina O'Rourke had everything in his house boxed and put into storage within hours of his death," Colton said. "She pulled some spook-strings and claimed it was best for national security. Locked them up tight enough that Jacobs couldn't get to them."

Sabina blinked. "You talked to Gina? When did you do that? I don't recall her ever telling me that. Why wouldn't she tell me that?"

Colton shrugged. "She says she did. Maybe you were still in shock from his death. Or from the subsequent attempt on your life and murder of your boyfriend. But she said she did tell you. And yes, we called her last night after you left here. Had a nice long chat. She's retired now and was even talking about coming out to visit."

Sabina frowned in thought. "We should keep her out of this. Especially if she's retired," she said. "I do vaguely remember her telling me about a storage unit. I guess I blocked it out, or maybe it just didn't fully register at the time."

"Shock can do that," Chad said, drawing her attention to him. He wanted to reach out and take her hand but stopped himself. Not only was she sitting across a four-foot table, but the two of them still had a few things to work out between them.

"What's the plan with the storage unit, then?" she asked, swinging her gaze back to Colton.

"I want you and Chad to go pick up the contents," he answered. "It's in a place a few miles outside Memphis. You can take Bertha. She's small, but also the fastest plane we have. Based on what Gina told us last night, everything you'd want to bring back should fit."

Again, her gaze slid to his, as if checking to see if he was okay with the decision. He gave her a tiny nod, and she turned back to Colton. "Fine. When do we leave?"

"We've got the pilot getting the plane ready. Before you go, though, I want to follow up with you on something you told us last night."

To her credit, she didn't hesitate. "Anything."

A hint of a smile flashed across Ethan's lips, and he turned toward Chad and discreetly wiggled an eyebrow. Chad wasn't the only one who noticed Sabina's about-face. Now that she was committed to this new path, it didn't surprise him that she was *fully* committed.

"You said that Jacobs was muttering something about if your mother had only given him what he'd asked for. And then, when you walked into the room, he was going through her desk. Do you have any idea what he wanted from her or what he thought he might be able to find?" Colton asked.

Sabina stilled and held Colton's gaze. When she spoke, though, it wasn't to answer. "I know the solution to that puzzle is somewhere in the past. And I promise you, I will give it thought. But before I get to that, I want to talk about two recent events. I wasn't intending to hide them last night. With everything else going on, they honestly slipped my mind." She paused and waited for Colton to gesture for her to continue. "There was a reason for my sudden change of plans to move here. On that topic, Chad was right." She reached into her canvas bag, the same one he'd rescued from her Jeep last night, and pulled out a ziplock bag. She glanced at it then slid it over to Chad.

He picked up what looked like one of those free postcards that shops give away. This one was from a distillery in Kentucky, and it listed the name, website, and phone number. Turning it over, his body jolted.

Found you

That's all it said.

Chad looked to Sabina as he handed the bag to Colton. "When did that arrive? And how?"

"The day before we left for Mystery Lake. Someone slid it under the door of my apartment while I was out on my morning run," she answered. "I've been carrying it around ever since."

His nerves prickled and crawled. No wonder she'd changed her plans and hightailed it off the East Coast. "Any idea how he found you?" he asked. There was no question the card was from Kevin Jacobs. The front image, with its ties to Kentucky, ensured Sabina would have no doubt.

She inclined her head. "You remember that fundraiser a couple of months ago? The one when HICC provided extra security for Stella, Hunter, Beni, Cal, and all the kids?"

Chad nodded. Stella's brother, Calvin, and his wife, Benita Ricci, had twins who were a few months younger than Mateo. Beni had been an FBI agent prior to marrying the vice president and was the reason HICC had recruited him.

"What fundraiser?" Teague asked. Chad glanced at the man, somewhat surprised. Not at the question per se, but that he'd asked anything. He and his brother, Tucker, tended to be on the quiet side. Then again, when you were built like Teague and Tucker, Chad imagined their mere presence said quite enough.

"It was the opening of a new children's garden and play park," Sabina answered. "The couples wanted to bring the kids. It was a good day, but the event was out in the open, and Cal wanted more security." She glanced at Chad, no doubt remembering the kidnapping attempts on him and his cousin. "He hired us to supplement his team."

"But you're not a field operative. If the senator was there, how would he have even seen you?" Chad asked. He hadn't been there that day, as he'd been on a job down in Savannah.

"I was in the van, but after everyone left, I got out to gather my equipment," Sabina answered. "It's the only thing I can think of." The surveillance van was her portable command center back in DC. She hadn't taken it out often, but when she had, the things she could see and hear were astonishing.

"Providing additional visuals?" Ethan asked.

Sabina nodded. "We had some extra cameras and things like that in place. A few silent drones as well. Once everyone was gone, I left the van to collect it all. I also chatted with a couple of the operatives. If Jacobs was there, and I assume he was since it was such a big political event, he could have seen me then. It's probably also how he connected me to HICC and found me here," she added.

Chad agreed. In fact, he was kind of amazed she hadn't run into Jacobs before that event. Sabina had lived in DC for over a decade, and Jacobs was a second-term senator. She might not be in the field often, but over the six years she'd been at HICC, he had to believe it was more than once or twice.

"We need an evidence person," Chad said to Colton.

Colton studied the postcard that had made its way to him. "I agree. In the meantime, I can send this to the DC office. We can have the pilot drop you off in Memphis, hop up to DC, then come back and get you."

It would be a lot of flying, but doable. And the DC office had a full lab staffed by four scientists. "Sounds good, thanks," Chad said. "Now what was the second thing?" he asked Sabina.

"This," she said, handing him a piece of folded-up paper.

He took it, unfolded it, and scanned the grainy image of a

brown-haired man. Raising his gaze, he looked to Sabina in question.

"I went to see my sister yesterday. It was the first time I've seen her in three years, but she wanted to meet because of that man," she said.

Chad looked at the picture again. The pixelation on the enlarged photo made it hard to see anything but the vaguest of features.

"Who is he?" he asked.

"I don't know," Sabina answered. "But he was at a conference with Kara and was asking around about her. The company who hosted the meeting uploaded several images to their website and she found him in the background of one."

"I can take that," Ava said, leaning across the table to take the picture. Chad handed it over. There was no point in showing it to Colton, Ethan, or the others since it wouldn't tell them anything.

"The name of the conference is on the back," Sabina said to her team. "Kara thought I might be able to get a better picture. And an ID."

"We can," Leo and Collin said at the same time. Ava had handed them the paper, and they were both looking at it.

"We can also look through the hotel CCTV," Collin said. Or at least that's what Chad thought he said. He was sitting across the table and down a few people, so it was a stretch to hear him.

Ava nodded. "Leave this and the fingerprints with us, we'll take care of it. We'll also start taking apart Jacobs's life. And of course, let us know if there's more that we can do."

Colton's phone dinged and he hit the Answer button. "Yeah...great, send them in," he said, then hung up.

"Who else is coming?" Sabina asked, glancing around the table. There were six operatives in total, but only three of them were in the room. Chad didn't think the other three were the subject of the call, though. If it had been them at the gate, the guard wouldn't have needed to check with Colton.

"Give me a few minutes and you'll see. Gina O'Rourke sent all the files she collected over the years. We'll go over those," Colton said, gesturing to himself, Ethan, Tucker, and Teague. "Ava, Leo, and Collin will work the cyber angle while you and Chad head to Memphis. Between those leads, and anything Ryan and his team get from the guy in the hospital, we have enough to keep us busy for today."

"And tomorrow? What about tomorrow?" Sabina asked.

"Tomorrow we start to bring Jacobs down," Chad answered.

Sabina looked at him, her expression inscrutable, and yet he recognized the look. She wanted what he said to be true. She *hoped* it would be. But it would be devastating if they failed. He didn't know what failure would look like, but he knew she was worried about it. "How about we get back to Colton's original question," he said. Having her mind spiral down the path it looked to be going wouldn't be helpful to anyone, let alone Sabina. "Do you have any idea what your mom had that Jacobs wanted?"

She frowned and opened her mouth to answer, but a commotion outside the conference room drew everyone's attention. On instinct, all the operatives rose and reached for their weapons. Chad moved between the door and Sabina. Four seconds ticked by before he realized the sounds weren't threatening ones. No, a woman was laughing and there was the rumble of a man's voice, but it wasn't loud enough for Chad to make out.

"At ease, gentlemen," Colton said. "It's just my little surprise."

Chad glanced over his shoulder at his colleague then whipped around again when the door flew open. Standing in the opening was a woman, presumably the one he'd heard laughing. She was petitely built, like Sabina, but had short mahogany hair. Her brown/hazel eyes scanned the room then landed on Sabina.

The recognition in her expression needed no explanation. Chad stepped out of the way as Sabina and Kara rushed toward each other, throwing their arms around each other.

"What are you doing here?" Sabina demanded. She'd finally pulled back from her sister, although she kept hold of her hands.

The other woman smiled. "This guy told me what was going on up here," she said, waving to the man standing behind her. He wasn't an HICC operative, but Chad figured he was one of the local guys that Colton had put on Kara last night. Time had been of the essence, and sending someone from HICC would have taken too long. The man grinned, looking as though he hadn't minded doing Colton the favor.

"You have to know, I'd never let you face Jacobs alone," Kara said. "But more important, if we're going to end this, we're going to end it together."

Sabina blinked away tears then threw her arms around her sister again. The two women held each other for several seconds, then Sabina sniffed and stepped back again. "Well," she said with a watery smile. "Welcome to my world." She gestured to the people in the room.

As Kara turned, her eyes swept the room. Then they landed on Chad. He had no idea if Sabina had told her anything about him or, if she had, what it was. He returned her study and as he did, he was amazed he hadn't seen the resemblance more quickly. Other than her hair and eye color, which he'd wager were modified, she and Sabina were the spitting image of each other.

"Kara, I presume?" he said, stepping forward, his hand outstretched.

She nodded, ignored the hand, and wrapped him in a hug.

Then whispered to him, too quietly for anyone to hear, "Thank you. She's worth it."

He cleared his throat. "I know," he replied.

She gave him another squeeze then released him and stepped back. Glancing around the room again, her gaze landed on the files sitting on the desk. It lingered there for a moment then drifted to her sister. "Why don't you introduce me to everyone and tell me what the plan is."

CHAPTER SEVENTEEN

SABINA PACED THE CYBER LAB, squeezing one of her stress balls as she did. Ava, Leo, and Collin were all diligently working on what they'd been assigned, including digging into Kevin Jacobs's life, tracking the identities of the two intruders, and identifying the man at the conference. Her sister, having insisted on a change of plans, was now on her way to Memphis, along with Colton's friend who'd brought her to Mystery Lake and HICC operatives Eli and Ryder.

Chad and Colton had gone to the hospital to sit in on the questioning of the man who'd been taken in the night before. Ethan was going through Gina's files and Teague was tracking the man they'd intentionally let go the night before. And she had no idea where Tucker and Killian were, although she supposed they were keeping their eyes on the HICC compound.

Which left her. Pacing the cyber lab. Back and forth and back and forth. Colton's question was driving her mad. Once Kara arrived, Ethan had asked it again. What had Jacobs been looking for? What information or item had he wanted from their mother? Neither of them had come up with anything.

Should she dig into the university network and see what

kind of archives they had? Although with eighteen years passed, she doubted any of her mother's work would still be there. Or if it was, if it had been digitized. The university had the internet when her mom was teaching, but it hadn't been nearly as pervasive as it was now. Still, it was worth a look.

Taking a seat at her desk, she brought her computer to life and started searching. An hour later, with no progress, she looked up to find Ava staring at her with an odd expression on her face.

A sense of dread spread across her chest. "What?" Sabina half asked, half demanded.

"The police file states that investigators found one of your mother's rings with the vagrant?"

Sabina nodded.

"Do you know which one?"

Sabina shook her head. "I'm sure my uncle and Gina knew, but *I* never asked. Why?" Her computer dinged with an IM from Ava, and she opened it.

"Do you recognize that?" she asked.

It had been years since Sabina had seen anything of her mother's. When they'd first gone into hiding, she and Kara had kept one picture each—one Uncle Mike had had of the three of them. Over the years, hers had become worn and tattered and several years ago, she'd put it away. After even more years passed, she'd stopped taking it out altogether.

Hesitantly, she clicked the attachment. An image filled the screen, and she frowned.

"You don't recognize it?" Ava asked, coming to stand behind her.

"No, I do," Sabina said. "It was her engagement ring from my father. But she never wore it. It had their first names engraved on the inside and the date of his proposal. That's probably how the police linked it to her."

"Hmm," Ava said, shifting behind her.

"What, 'hmm,'" Sabina said, swiveling around to look at the woman.

"It's not a smoking gun or anything, but it's odd that the only piece of jewelry to show up is a piece she never wore."

Sabina inclined her head. "I agree, but I'm not sure what it means."

Ava hesitated then pulled a chair over and took a seat. "I hope you don't mind, but I went through the crime scene photos that Gina O'Rourke sent over in her files."

Sabina drew back. She didn't mind. In fact, she'd expected it. But anticipating it happening and *knowing it happened* were two different things. Seeing the concern on Ava's face, she quickly shook her head. "Of course I don't mind," she said. "I'm not sure *I* want to see them—although I probably should have a look—but I did expect you all to review them. We'd hardly be doing our jobs if we didn't."

Ava reached out and wrapped her hand around Sabina's wrist. "That doesn't mean it's easy," Ava said.

Sabina looked into the woman's compassion-filled eyes and wondered how she could be a whiz with the computer *and* incredibly insightful with humans. Slowly, Sabina nodded. "It's not. But living this way for the past eighteen years hasn't been easy either. I've done a lot since that night—a lot with my life—and I'm proud of what I've accomplished. I love my job and know I've done good in the world. For the longest time, it was easy to tell myself that was enough. And it *was* enough."

"Until the sexy Chad Warwick walked into your life," Ava said with a grin.

Sabina's eyebrows shot up.

Ava snorted, not a sound Sabina would have expected from her. "You two are about as subtle as a new starlet at her first awards ceremony."

"I have no idea what that means," Sabina said, holding back a laugh. "Aren't up-and-coming actors and actresses usually kind of humble?"

"Oh, honey," Ava said with a shake of her head. "There is so much about life you don't know."

"I'd argue it's Hollywood and I don't need to know."

Ava dipped her head. "There is truth to that, too. But there's this passive-aggressive thing a lot of new actors do...they try to bring attention to themselves by being humble."

"Or they actually are humble?"

"Some are. But some want the media to talk about how charming and self-effacing and humble they are. Because you know...media? And for those who've been in, or around, the business for a long time, it's pretty friggin' obvious when they start to play that part."

Sabina stared at her team member then shrugged. Ava knew more about that world than she did. "Okay, what were we talking about?" she asked, wanting to get back to the original purpose of the conversation.

"You and Chad."

Sabina shot her a flat look. "We were not talking about me and Chad. We were talking about the crime scene photos of my mom." She didn't even know if there was a she-and-Chad. Sure, he'd been attentive. And he didn't appear to be holding her verbal fuckup against her. But he also hadn't spoken to her alone since they'd arrived at HICC that morning.

Ava rolled her eyes. "Right. So, do you want to see what I saw, or do you want me to tell you? Either way, I will completely support you," she said.

Sabina needed to look at the photos. She knew she did. But she also knew it would be better for her to do so—at least the first time—when she was alone. "For now, tell me."

Without skipping a beat, Ava answered. "You said your parents split when you were twelve, so when I saw the picture of the ring that had been submitted as evidence, I thought it was weird. I pulled the photos of the scene and, the thing is, your mother was *wearing* jewelry when she was killed. And not cheap jewelry, either. She had a thick chain necklace with a garnet pendant. Garnets aren't the most expensive stone, but it was huge and, well, frankly, stunning. It would have been worth *at least* as much as the ring. But not only that, she had on two other rings. One was a large ruby—"

"Her birthstone," Sabina said. "Her mother gave it to her when she finished her Ph.D. And the second ring had two sapphires, separated with a baguette diamond. Mine and Kara's birthstones."

"Birthstones?" she asked, emphasizing the plural.

Sabina inclined her head. "With our current calendar, April is diamonds. Historically, though, it was sapphires. With my mom's interests, it shouldn't be a surprise she preferred those. But the diamond in the middle is a nod to the modern take."

Ava frowned. "I didn't know birthstones had changed over time."

"And by region and by whether you go by the Gregorian calendar or zodiac calendar. Or even Western versus Eastern traditions," Sabina said.

"Look at us both learning new things today," Ava said with a chuckle. Then she sobered. "You do see the oddity, though?"

Sabina nodded. "I do. Why was a piece of jewelry that she kept in a box in her room found with the dead man when the three pieces she was wearing the night she was killed were worth so much more? I assume you have a theory?"

"It's a theory, but yeah."

"Shoot."

"I think when Jacobs realized what you and Kara had seen, his only thought was to get through the night. I think the crime scene techs came and did what they do, including taking pictures—"

"Pictures of her that included the jewelry," Sabina said,

taking up the thread. "And when he finally settled on framing the vagrant, he couldn't plant the pieces she usually wore because they were in the pictures taken after he killed her."

Ava nodded. "My guess is that he went back, found something easy but valuable to grab, and planted *that* with the vagrant. Or had whoever killed him plant it with the man."

Sabina leaned back in her chair and gave it some thought. "You're right. It's not a smoking gun, but it's certainly something to cast doubt on the theory Jacobs put forward about the vagrant. Is the ring still in custody?"

"It is. It was put into storage when neither you nor your sister came forward to claim it."

"Is the chain of custody legit?" she asked.

Ava nodded. "As legit as anything George Jacobs did was. It is cataloged correctly."

"I want all that evidence released and sent to HICC headquarters," Sabina said, sitting forward and starting an email to Stella. She'd call Kara before she sent it, but she knew her sister would be on board.

"You'll have to come forward, publicly, as her daughter," Ava pointed out.

"I know," she replied. "And I think it's about time."

CHAPTER EIGHTEEN

CHAD LOOKED at the two women curled up together on Colton's couch. It was well past midnight, and they each held a teacup. Their heads were together, and they looked to be enjoying the luxury of time. Something they hadn't been able to share for half their lives. Chad hadn't always lived near his brothers or cousins. But he'd been able to see them when he wanted. Or be there when needed. Watching the sisters, he realized it was a gift he wouldn't take for granted ever again.

"You ready for tomorrow?" Colton asked him.

Chad tore his eyes from the pair and looked at his colleague. "As we'll ever be, I suppose," he answered. He'd done a lot of interesting things in his life, and as much as he liked to plan, many of those things had required him to improvise. But how did one prepare for the consequences of Sabina and Kara stepping forward after eighteen years of being presumed missing or dead? Because that was exactly what they'd decided to do.

When he'd returned to HICC from a fruitless visit to the hospital—the man Ethan had shot wasn't talking—Sabina had laid out her plan to him. His first reaction had been a vehement "No," but he held his tongue and let his emotions simmer down before responding. Once he managed to control his own fear, he acknowledged the plan was a good one. Not only was it not practical for her to stay hidden away forever, there was no point to it. Jacobs already knew who she was and where she lived.

And Kara, too, based on the information Leo and Collin had discovered about the man from the conference. Andy Jameson was a sketchy PI from DC. *How* he'd found Kara, they didn't yet know. But Leo had dug into his financials and found a lovely little offshore account with just under a million dollars in it. An account that received regular deposits from a shell company that Collin traced to Jacobs.

Given that Jacobs knew the women were alive, Sabina was right. It was time for them to go on the offense. And not surprising, Kara had agreed with her sister. As had Stella and Hunter, who'd offered whatever resources needed to both protect Sabina and Kara and bring Jacobs down.

Chad had no doubt that the couple's decision had everything to do with their being the good people they were. But if they were successful, running for president against Stella's brother in the next election would no longer be an option for Jacobs. An added bonus.

HICC would take some heat for its role in the coming scandal. Some might even claim their involvement was politically motivated. But neither Stella nor Hunter cared. Nor did Cal, who wholeheartedly endorsed their activities.

"Did the lawyer get everything she needed?" Colton asked.

Chad nodded. At eleven o'clock tomorrow morning, the Lexington Police Department was going to get a surprise visit. On behalf of Emer Houseman's daughters, Tess Jackson, an HICC lawyer, would be requesting access to all the evidence related to the murder. She'd also be requesting the release of any personal belongings, including the ring found on the vagrant. No one thought they'd find anything in the reports or evidence. But they were counting on the request to shake things up a bit. And they were especially interested in how George Jacobs, Kevin's brother, responded. He'd been chief of police at the time, and in charge of the investigation. But there was a lot more on the line for him now as he was currently serving as the head of the Kentucky State Police.

Sabina's phone rang, and Chad's eyes went to the clock sitting above the fireplace. It was now close to one in the morning. Who would be calling at this hour?

"Collin," Sabina answered, shrugging in response to the three sets of questioning gazes that had landed on her. Everyone was bunking on HICC property for the night. But they were supposed to be doing just that by now...bunking. Meaning sleeping. They had a long day ahead of them tomorrow, including going through the truckload of Uncle Mike's belongings that Kara had brought back.

"Really? Wow, that's great...Yes, please send the info to Ryan and Chad...Thank you, really. You've done a great job. You need to get some sleep, though," she said. She listened for another few seconds then appeared to extract a promise to head to bed before hanging up.

Right as she did, Chad's phone dinged. Pulling it out, he saw a name, date of birth, and location of birth, along with a link to a document.

"Who's Jason Kline?" he asked, holding the phone up. Not that she could see the screen from where she sat, but it felt like the right thing to do.

"Our mystery patient," she answered with a grin.

"The one Ethan shot?" Colton asked, reaching for Chad's phone.

"The very same," Sabina replied.

"How did Collin find him?" Kara asked, waving off the phone Colton had offered her. It didn't surprise Chad she didn't feel the need to know more than his name; he was more or less just one of Jacobs's lackeys.

"Believe it or not, about twelve years ago, he sold a couple of video games to one of the gamer shops. As part of the process, you have to submit your fingerprints," Sabina said.

Chad blinked. "To sell a used video game?"

She nodded. "In some states, they are considered in the scope of certain secondhand goods laws that require that kind of identification."

"Then why didn't it show up in the national databases?" Kara asked.

"My guess is that it went to the local police, but then the police didn't add it to the national database," Colton suggested.

"He has quite a background, too," Chad said, having opened the document Collin had sent and scanned the contents. "Tried to enroll in the army but didn't pass the entrance exams. Then he joined a local police force in Pennsylvania where he served for eight years on the beat. After that, he moved to Markland Security. Not the best of private security firms," he said as an aside to Kara. Sabina and Colton would recognize the name. It was a decent-sized shop that farmed out personal security to clients who skirted the gray side of the law. "And from there he went to Sweet River, where he's listed as still being employed."

"Sweet River?" Kara asked.

"Think Blackwater, but even shadier," Sabina answered. "I've met a few of those guys—and they are *all* guys. They aren't people you want to spend any time with. Always wanted to jump in a shower after talking to them." She made a face that had Chad smiling despite the topic.

"I hate those guys," Colton muttered. "I'll be glad of the excuse to dig into them. Whether we find a tie to Jacobs or not, I'm guessing we won't need to dig very deep to find a pile of shit. Excuse my French."

Sabina and Kara snorted, sounding remarkably the same, even after so many years. "You do realize that I work in some of the worst hot spots in the world. Ones often surrounded by the military," Kara said.

"And I work with you lot," Sabina added, gesturing to them. "You hardly have to apologize for your language."

Colton let out a huff that was almost a laugh. "I know. You, I'm used to," he said, pointing to Sabina. "You, though. You're still new." He pointed at Kara then paused. "Only not totally new. It's really uncanny how identical you are once you get past the hair color."

Chad agreed but didn't. Now that he'd spent more time with them, he noted several subtle differences between the sisters, no doubt due to the different lives they'd led. Sabina had a small scar on her right hand and one above her left eye, just below the hairline. Kara's skin tone was a shade darker, likely from her time in places like Africa and Asia. She was also a touch leaner than Sabina. Both women were petite, but Kara had the look of someone who was used to rationing food, something he'd wager she did every time she was in the field.

"Maybe I'll let it grow back in my natural color now," Kara said, the words coming out more serious than the topic warranted. Then again, the decision had weight. Letting her hair grow back in strawberry blond was a symbol of shedding her old life—her old life of hiding.

"You're beautiful whichever you decide," Sabina said, ruffling her sister's hair. "But you don't have to decide tonight. In fact, it might be best if we all take the advice that I gave my team and get some sleep. We have a long day tomorrow."

Kara sighed as Sabina and Chad rose. They were still staying in the apartment on the top floor of the cabin, while Kara had taken Ava's spot in the second bedroom downstairs. Kara hadn't wanted to put the woman out, but Ava had insisted, saying she wanted to spend some casual time with Collin and Leo. Although after Collin's call, Chad suspected that what she really wanted was to stick close to the lab. He considered pulling up the security cams to see if any of Sabina's team had followed her orders and gone to bed. But he didn't feel like having to be the bad guy and deprive them of their fun if he found them still working.

Sabina hugged her sister, then Chad dropped a kiss on her cheek before they headed upstairs. For added security, the stairwell behind the kitchen had doors on both the ground level and the second story. As they trudged up the stairs, Colton locked the lower door and Chad did the same once they reached the upper apartment.

His gaze lingered on Sabina as he stood on the landing. She mumbled a "good night" through a yawn then headed to the room she'd slept in the night before. Once she was inside, he walked to his own, closing the door behind him. Stripping out of his clothes, he headed straight into the shower and flipped the faucet on. The cold water hit with a shock, but he welcomed it. Then slowly the temperature shifted from something close to arctic to one that steamed the glass doors.

Standing under the spray, the image of Sabina walking to her room played through his mind. The day had distracted him from everything that had happened the night before. As the heat flowed over him, though, he poked and prodded his psyche. Twenty-four hours ago, he'd been bruised and buried by his emotional scars. Did he still feel that way?

As the soap bubbles streamed off his body and circled the drain, he accepted that, yes, in some ways he did. But others? The healing had started. He understood why she'd said the things she said. More importantly, he believed her when she said they weren't meant in the way he'd taken them. She didn't gloss over the hurt she'd caused, and several times he'd caught her watching him, always with a pensive look. But throughout the day, she seemed committed to *showing* him that she hadn't meant them that way. As if she knew talking about it more wouldn't erase the pain. And in every action that she took, she gave him her trust. Explicitly and without condition.

Switching off the water, he grabbed a towel and ran it over his hair before wiping his body down. After brushing his teeth, he pulled on a pair of boxers then lay down on the bed on top of the covers. Sabina had told him she loved him, and he believed her. But there was still a small part of him that wondered how she could. Not because he didn't think he was worthy of her. But because he wondered how she could love him when he'd kept her at such a distance these past few years. Was it possible to love someone you didn't really know? Part of him thought it was—there was no way couples knew everything about each other before falling in love. Another part had to wonder, though. The space between him and Sabina wasn't about how one person loaded the dishwasher or what they thought about fiction versus nonfiction. The space between them was there because they hadn't trusted each other. Well, to be more precise, she hadn't trusted him with her secrets, and so he hadn't trusted her with his heart. He didn't think he was wrong in holding back, but with two years gone now, was there a way to even bridge that gap?

There was. There had to be. Now that he knew how she felt, he wasn't willing to let her go. He wasn't willing to let go of what he knew they could have. But how did they jump from being friends to lovers? He smiled, thinking of the romance novels he'd read while in the army. Pickings were slim while deployed, and he'd read anything he could get his hands on. His buddies had ribbed him endlessly. Until they'd started noticing how attracting female attention when he wanted it wasn't ever an issue. He'd never been a man-whore, but when he met a woman he liked, he didn't tend to have a problem earning her appreciation in return.

And he could thank romance novels for that. The stories were fantasy to be sure. But taking his cues from a genre that readers—mostly women—devoured to the tune of over a billion dollars a year seemed like a smart thing to do. Eventually, his buddies caught on and thought so, too. To his chagrin, getting his hands on a good romance became harder and harder.

And now he found himself in the classic friends-to-lovers trope. Only he didn't think it would be as easy to make the leap from one to the other as it was in the pages of the books. He didn't see himself pulling her into his arms and kissing her out of the blue. Nor did he see her making the first move—not after the way she'd hurt him. No, she'd see the ball as being in his court as to where their relationship went from here.

And it was safe to say that there'd be no drunken nights to loosen the tongue for a while. At least not until the Jacobs situation was sorted out.

A knock sounded at his door, bringing all his questions to a grinding halt. Maybe Sabina *would* make the first move...

"Come in," he called.

The door swung open, and Sabina stood there. She'd showered as well, and her wet hair swung over her shoulders. She wore a pair of sleep shorts, showcasing her runner's legs, and a hooded sweatshirt. From where he lay on his bed, with his hands behind his head on the pillow, he watched her. Waiting.

She didn't move from the doorway. A long beat passed—a beat in which her eyes drifted over his body—then she took a deep breath and spoke. "Have you ever been so terrified of something that you get tunnel vision? It's like you're so scared you can only see one way out and your body, or mind, isn't capable of processing anything else?"

Slowly, he nodded. "The first time I was in real combat was like that," he said. Twenty years had passed since that day in Afghanistan, but he remembered it as though it was yesterday. He'd just graduated from West Point, and 9/11 was still an open, weeping wound in the collective memory of Americans. He and a small team had been sent out to reconnoiter a nearby village.

Turned out the village happened to be playing temporary host to three members of Al Qaeda. He and his team had just entered when they started taking fire. Instincts and training had them scrambling for cover. But even after taking cover, the overwhelming need to just escape had nearly paralyzed him. He'd like to claim he overcame it on his own, but that hadn't been the case. As the team lead, the others had looked to him for their orders. Between their expectations, and the screams of the locals caught in the crossfire, he managed to find a way out. He managed to pull his mind from his singular focus on fleeing to the task at hand.

He and the team made it out that day. And miraculously, none of the civilian villagers had died. It had been a humbling experience, though. Before that moment, he'd believed he knew all he needed to know, that he had so much experience and training that he'd know what to do. But the truth was, there was no training that could ever prepare someone for being under active fire, and it had been a shock.

"How old were you?" she asked.

"Twenty-two. Fresh out of West Point. I thought I was ready, but the only thing that can make you ready for combat, real combat, is combat itself. I almost lost my team because the fear paralyzed me."

Her gaze softened, and he was aware that this was the first time they'd ever talked about something like this.

"My situation wasn't anything like yours. Not really. But that's how it felt," she said, shifting on her feet but still staying at the door. "I was terrified that you would become another Nate or Uncle Mike. And terrified that something might happen to Kara. The only thing I could focus on was protecting the people I loved. And the only way I knew how to do that was to keep them at a distance. I couldn't—I didn't—see any other option." She offered him a half-hearted smile. "It's like every romance novel where the heroine keeps secrets to protect someone she loves, but only ends up hurting them." She paused then shrugged. "I guess that trope is out there for a reason. Because I can tell you, my fear kept me from seeing any other options. And...I'm sorry. So very sorry," she added, her voice so quiet, he could barely hear it.

He couldn't help but smile at her reference to romance novels. It wasn't the reaction she expected, and her brow furrowed.

"What?" she asked.

He shook his head but grabbed the side of the comforter that wasn't underneath him and flipped it up. "Come here," he said.

Her gaze skittered from him to the bed then back to him. "If I get in, will you tell me why you smiled?"

"Why don't you get in and find out."

She eyed the bed again. "You'll get cold if you stay on top of the covers."

"I'll live."

She took a tentative step forward then another. When she reached the bed, rather than lie down on the blanket and sheet, she climbed under them. Once she was situated, she turned and tucked what would have been her half of the comforter around him. "You sure about this?" she asked. She'd turned on her side to face him, her hand tucked under her cheek.

He turned on his side, too, so they were face-to-face. "I'm sure."

For a long moment, they lay there staring at each other. Finally, he smiled, rolled onto his back, and held out his arm. "Come on," he said. "Snuggle up."

Everything in him relaxed when she didn't hesitate. A few seconds later, she was lying with her head on his shoulder, her body curled up next to his and her arm draped over his chest.

"Now are you going to tell me why you were smiling?" she asked, her breath fanning over his skin.

"I was trying to figure something out. You answered my question," he said.

"Are you going to tell me the question?" she asked.

He brushed a kiss across her head and gave her a gentle squeeze, tugging her body even tighter against his. "Not tonight," he said, not ready to tell her he'd been pondering how to shift their relationship from friends to lovers.

For the space of four breaths, she said nothing. Then she sighed and wiggled as close to him as she could get with the blankets between them. "What about telling me the answer?"

He smiled at that. "That's easy. The answer is: one step at a time."

CHAPTER NINETEEN

"The postcard was a limited-edition print that the distillery only made available in their sponsorship tent at the Kentucky Derby this year," Leo said, talking over his shoulder to no one and everyone.

"Any video in the tent?" Collin asked.

"Outside only. But we know Jacobs did walk in," Leo answered. "Don't know what he did when he was in there, but we know he was there and had access."

Sabina half listened as she and her sister continued to search through Uncle Mike's belongings. Kara had returned from the storage unit with everything that resembled a file, notebook, computer, or anything else that Uncle Mike might have made a note on. There were twenty-two boxes total, and so far, they'd managed to get through six. It was slow going, but Chad, Ethan, Teague, and Tucker would join them later that morning. After they'd had a second go at Jason Kline.

"Is there anything from the lab?" Sabina asked her team, not taking her eyes off the datebook she was looking through.

"They just emailed," Ava responded. "There's a partial print on the postcard that could match Jacobs's, but there's not enough to conclusively demonstrate it's his."

Kara closed the file she'd been going through and looked at her watch. "Twenty minutes until Tess has her appointment," she said. The lawyer was probably already making her way into the Lexington Police station for her eleven o'clock appointment with the current chief of police.

The three women had spoken for an hour that morning. Kara and Sabina accepted that they'd be called to give an official statement about the night their mother was killed. Tess had assured them, though, that she'd be able to push it off for several days, maybe even a week or two. As far as the police were concerned, the case was closed. Their statements would complete the file but weren't needed.

"Do you think we'll find anything in the evidence?" Kara asked, her voice reflecting the doubt Sabina shared. With George Jacobs in charge of the investigation, she had no faith any evidence that might have implicated Kevin would still be in the evidence locker. In fact, she doubted it had even made it in in the first place.

"Like everything else, maybe there will be something, but it won't be a smoking gun," she answered. Kara sighed and reached into the box beside her, pulling out a spiral-bound notebook.

"So Chad...?" Kara asked.

Sabina glanced up as she set the datebook aside and grabbed a notebook. This one looked promising. The date on the first page was only eight months before Uncle Mike died. "Yeah, Chad," she said, still not entirely sure where they stood. She'd woken up that morning, tucked up against him, her back to his front. Her fingers had been entwined with his, and she'd been hugging his arm against her chest. But he hadn't said a word before sliding from bed. He'd placed a very gentle kiss on her bare shoulder—she'd stripped out of her sweatshirt during the night, leaving her in just a tank top—but that had been it.

"I hurt him, Kara," she said. Then, keeping her voice low so her team wouldn't overhear, she told her about the incident at the diner. When she finished, she started flipping through the pages. "He knows I didn't do it on purpose, but I don't know that he's totally forgiven me. I think he's trying, though," she finished.

Kara tilted her head even as she continued perusing the notebook. "And how do you feel about it all? Suddenly having everything out in the open between you?"

Sabina flipped through a few more pages, most of which contained random scribblings about bills or appointments. "Honestly?"

Kara shot her look. "No, please. Lie to me." Sabina stuck out her tongue, making Kara smile and shake her head. "As if you could anyway," Kara pointed out.

Sabina bobbed her head. "True. But to answer your question, I'm not sure. I mean, I'm relieved it's no longer all a big secret."

"But?"

Sabina exhaled on a huff. "But I'm mad it took me so long to get to this point. I didn't just hurt him with what I said last night. Every time I pushed him away over the past two years, I hurt him. I hurt *me*. And now that it's out and we're attacking the problem the way I would normally attack any other problem—except, apparently, *my own*—it feels like I wasted a whole lot of time. I feel stupid. And maybe a little ashamed that I was so mired in my way of thinking that I never saw the gift he was offering me."

Kara studied her then asked, "Are you going to let that get in the way of moving forward?"

With zero hesitation, Sabina shook her head. "I feel stupid about how long it took me to get here. But after the diner, when it became a real possibility that he'd no longer be in my life? Well, I'd rather get over feeling stupid and give this thing between us everything I have than shy away again. I learned my lesson. If it doesn't work out, it won't be because I didn't try."

Kara smiled. "Mom would be proud of you."

Sabina couldn't help it, she laughed. Her team turned to look, but quickly went back to their tasks. "You think Mom would be happy that I'm pursuing a man? One that I've lusted after for years?"

"She'd be thrilled, and you know it," Kara said, putting the notebook she'd been reviewing to the side before pulling out a legal notepad. "She'd be happy that you found someone you wanted as a partner and that you weren't going to shy away from letting him know. At least not anymore. You know how she felt about that kind of stuff—"

"Life's too short to live with regrets," Sabina finished.

"Exactly," Kara said with a nod.

"Do you have any? Regrets?" Sabina asked, eyeing a stack of hard disks held together by a rubber band.

"I don't think anyone can get through life with no regrets," she answered. "All we can do is the best we can do."

"You sound just like your uncle," a voice came from behind Sabina. She and her sister whipped their heads around. It took less than three seconds before they leaped up and rushed over to the woman, squealing in a way that Sabina was quite sure no one in the room had heard since their teenage years.

"Gina!" they exclaimed, wrapping their arms around Gina O'Rourke. Their honorary aunt. The woman who'd come to their aid more than a few times in the past eighteen years.

"What are you doing here?" Sabina asked, stepping back. She glanced up and saw Chad, Ethan, Ryan, and Colton standing a few feet away, smiling at the reunion.

"That one offered to fly me out," she answered, gesturing to Chad. "I figured you could use a friendly face. Or maybe even a seasoned intelligence agent. I've been retired for a few years, but don't think I've lost my edge."

"Never," Kara said, grabbing Gina's hand and tugging her toward the boxes. Not wasting any time in putting the woman to work, she handed Gina a notebook from one of the open boxes.

Sabina watched as the two dived into the contents without missing a beat. She walked toward Chad as the others drifted off to pick up other tasks. "You called Gina?" she asked.

He smiled, and his dimple appeared. "I thought you and Kara might appreciate having her around."

There was still a distance between them, but she could feel it dissolving by the hour. It would take some time to disappear completely. The important thing was, though, they were trying.

"Thank you," she said, going up on her toes and kissing his cheek. His hand came out and curled around her waist as she moved. It remained there when she was back on her feet.

"How are you? Really?" he asked, his dark eyes holding hers. Filled with concern.

She lifted a hand and rested it on his arm. "I'm equal parts terrified and relieved. I didn't think those two feelings could exist together, but they do. I have no idea what's going to happen, but it feels good to be doing something. To be coming out of the shadows." She paused. "Even if it took me a long time to get here."

His fingers twitched against her waist as he held her gaze. Then he leaned down and whispered, "The important thing is, we're here. Together. All of us."

Involuntarily, her hand gripped his arm. He drew away slowly, his cheek brushing against hers. When he'd pulled back enough that she could see his eyes again, her stomach jumped at the heat she saw there. It had been a long time since she'd seen that in his eyes. So long that she'd wondered if she'd extinguished it altogether. If she had, she had every intention of trying to reignite it. But with the way he watched her now, she knew it wouldn't take much to fan the spark into a flame. Even more thrilling, though, was the fact that he was letting her see it. That he wasn't hiding it from her.

The memory of him curled up behind her that morning washed over her. She stepped away rather than give in to the urge to move her hand from his arm to his neck and pull him down into a long and deep kiss.

"Did Jason Kline say anything?" she asked as they approached Ethan, Gina, and the others who'd joined Kara at the boxes.

"Only as much as he felt needed to be said," Colton answered. Sabina and Chad sank onto a couple of chairs, and she picked up the notebook she'd been going through earlier as he grabbed one of the hard disks. He popped it into an external drive Collin had found and started perusing the files.

"Kline claims they were hired to investigate a threat," Colton said. "To whom the threat was made, he couldn't say. Only that they'd been ordered to do the job and it was a legal hire."

"What exactly was the job, though?" Sabina asked. Chad cast Colton a look before shifting his gaze to her.

"He claims they were there to reconnoiter," Chad answered.

"But?" Sabina pressed.

"Their weapons say otherwise," he said. "The one who was killed was carrying a very expensive, high-powered sniper rifle. A rifle that, incidentally, matched the one used during the ambush on your car. As for Kline himself, he had three weapons, all handguns, all with silencers. No one carries a silencer unless they plan on killing something, or someone, quietly."

"Any ID on the one who died?" Gina asked.

Colton nodded, brought up a file on his phone, and handed the device to the woman. As her eyes scanned the information, Chad watched. He hadn't bothered to look up Gina O'Rourke's file before arranging to bring her to Mystery Lake. With a name like O'Rourke, he'd expected someone of Irish descent, like Sabina. He had not expected a five-foot-ten, whipcord lean Black woman, with a shock of gray hair that hugged her scalp in a cap of curls. She also didn't appear to prescribe to the belief that women of a certain age needed to dress a certain way. Unless that *certain way* was however the fuck she wanted to dress. Wearing ripped, skintight black jeans, a gray Ramones T-shirt, motorcycle boots, and a leather jacket, she looked as though she could have been out partying at CBGB during the height of its punk rock popularity.

"I don't believe that the sins of the parents should be visited on the child, but that man's father is the worst kind of prick," Gina said, handing the phone back. "If he's anything like his dad, it doesn't surprise me that he's the one who's dead. The whole family is filled with arrogant pricks who think they are smarter than everyone. My guess is he tried to do something he thought was badass, but actually had about as much finesse as an actor playing a part?"

Ethan shrugged and nodded in confirmation. "Pretty much."

"I've lost track of his dad, but I'd think about looking into him. Unless something's changed in the past few years, his son would not have had the skill to handle the kind of rifle you talked about," Gina said. "My guess is that his dad is involved in Sweet River and somehow managed to get his son a job. I don't recall him having any ties to Jacobs, but they swim in the same cesspool, so it's possible."

"On it already," Leo called out, making Sabina smile at her eager team. They might be working magic on their computers, but they were still listening.

An hour and four boxes later, Tess Jackson called with an update on her meeting with the Lexington Police. Predictably, George Jacobs had tried to stop the release of the evidence, arguing that the women formerly known as Bela and Nala

Houseman needed to be interviewed and their identities confirmed before any evidence was released. Tess had anticipated that objection, though, and had presented notarized documents confirming their identities through fingerprints. When a technician matched those to ones on file from when the girls had worked as lifeguards in high school, there'd been no question that Sabina and Kara were who they said they were. And no question that they had rights to the evidence, especially their mother's belongings. It hadn't helped George's argument that it was his name on the file that had closed the case all those years ago.

While Tess had overseen the packaging up of the evidence, George Jacobs had peppered her with questions about Sabina and Kara that revealed more than the fact that he was nosy. Since Kevin Jacobs already knew about the two women, George either wasn't conspiring with his brother anymore or, if he was, he wasn't being told everything.

After the update, Teague and Tucker popped into town and brought lunch back. The break was a welcome one, though short, and soon, they were all back to work.

It was close to dinner when Ryan returned, having left after lunch to check on things at the station. "Jason Kline was released this afternoon, and his bail hearing was just a bit ago. The Sweet River lawyer paid it, but he's not allowed to leave the county, so we'll be keeping an eye on him."

"What'd you book him for?" Gina asked, not looking up from the laptop she was working on. A few hours earlier, she'd swapped with Chad and was now looking through the remaining hard disks.

"Trespassing, intent to commit murder, and a few other things," he answered, picking up a notebook from one of the last few boxes. Uncle Mike hadn't left any obvious notes, at least none they'd found so far. Which meant that whatever information he found was either in code or very subtle, and they'd missed it. Or, the option Sabina didn't care to think about, that he hadn't written anything down at all.

Suddenly, Ava's chair flew back as she jumped up with a great big whoop. So startled at the movement and cheer, Sabina nearly dropped her notebook. She wasn't the only one caught off guard, nor was she the only one who smiled when Ava started doing a little celebratory dance, chanting, "I got it. I got it. I got it."

"Care to tell us what you got?" Ethan asked.

She held up a finger then walked to the printer that was spitting out paper. Taking the documents, she rearranged them into a particular order then joined them at the table. As she passed out the stacks of papers, she started to explain. "Kevin Jacobs was looking for something when your mother was killed," she said. Sabina and Kara nodded. "Which made me start to wonder what was going on in his life *at that time*. Leo and Collin are looking into his current situation, including finances and all that, but something triggered him eighteen years ago, and I wanted to find out what it was."

A trill of excitement vibrated through Sabina. Leaning closer to Chad to better see the stack they shared, she started to scan the first page. Without question, he handed the papers over and into her control.

"And?" Ethan prompted.

"Long version or short version?" Ava asked, practically bouncing on her toes.

"Short," everyone replied at once. They could dig into the long version later.

"Short version is that Jacobs was involved in all sorts of illegal activities from gambling to high-end prostitution to bootleg liquor," she said.

"You make him sound like Al Capone," Ethan muttered.

"Not far off," Ava said. "Although Kevin was just a player in the organization, not the head."

"What does that have to do with our mom's murder?" Kara asked.

"I believe that whoever was laundering the money for the organization stole it from Jacobs, which then put Jacobs in a panic. And I think, for whatever reason, he thought your mom might have information on who that person was or where to find them."

"But what would my mother know..."

Sabina felt Kara's eyes on her as her sister's voice trailed off. But she kept her attention on the information in her hand.

"Sabina?" Chad asked. "Didn't you say your father was an accountant?"

"He was. Or is," she said, looking at the group and holding one of the pages up. "And this is what Uncle Mike found. Hidalgo Jose." She pointed to a name on the list of shell companies Ava had found that had been used to launder the money. The same name she'd seen scribbled in one of Mike's notebooks. She'd thought it was the name of a person, and one so common that she hadn't bothered to run a basic internet search on it. Of course, even if she had, she wouldn't have found what Ava had.

"So Uncle Mike found evidence of Kevin Jacobs's illegal activities and Jacobs killed him," Kara posited.

"It would make sense," Chad said, his voice heavy. "Is it also possible that your dad was the accountant and *that's* what Kevin Jacobs was looking for from your mother? A way to find him?"

Gina made a small sound of disgruntlement. "Mike finding a link between Hidalgo Jose and Kevin would be enough to warrant Jacobs killing him. But if he also managed to find a link between Hidalgo Jose and Richard Houseman, then it would have been imperative that Jacobs kill him because the authorities would have been able to connect Kevin to not just the illegal activities, but also the murder of your mother," Gina said.

"But is it possible your father was involved?" Ethan asked.

Sabina looked at her sister and slowly, Kara nodded. "I can't say for certain," Kara answered. "But it's possible."

"Tell us about him. Your father," Ava urged. She, Leo, and Collin had all swiveled in their chairs and rolled them closer to the rest of the group.

Again, Sabina looked at her sister, but this time, she answered. "He left when we were twelve. I don't remember any big fights or anything. He wasn't always the best of dads. He wasn't terrible to us, but Kara and I were always..."

"Kind of an afterthought," Kara finished her sentence.

Sabina nodded before continuing. "When our mom told us they were getting a divorce, she simply said that sometimes people aren't always who you think they are and that they'd grown apart."

"Do you think she knew he was involved in illegal dealings?" Colton asked. "Assuming he was, of course, which we don't know for certain," he added when Chad sent him a quelling look. Sabina appreciated his attempt at tact, but it wasn't needed.

"She never said anything to us, but after he left, she definitely erased him from our lives," Sabina responded.

"Not that it was hard," Kara interjected.

Again, Sabina nodded. "He wasn't a part of our everyday life much anyway, so it wasn't hard to move on as usual after he was gone. I know that sounds weird, but that's the way it was. After she told us they were getting a divorce, she never mentioned him again."

"If he was involved and she didn't *actually* know, she probably suspected," Kara said.

"I agree," Sabina confirmed.

"Which would be another reason for her to cut him out of your lives completely," Chad said.

Kara inclined her head. "The three of us were close. She

would have done anything to protect us if she thought there was a threat."

"Even if that threat was our own father," Sabina added.

"So where is he now?" Ethan asked.

At Ethan's question, everyone looked at her and Kara. But like her, Kara raised her shoulders. "I—we—have no idea where he is," Sabina said. "Like I said, we never saw or heard from him again after he left. Then of course, after the murder, we were in hiding. If he tried to reach out to us after that, he wouldn't have been able to find us."

"Is it possible he's dead?" Kara asked, her question sounding more curious than concerned.

"If our theory holds true, he was alive at least long enough to steal from Kevin Jacobs," Chad replied.

"But that was eighteen years ago," Sabina pointed out, looking at her team in silent question.

"I'll look for him," Collin said. "Ava, you stay on Jacobs and see if he's still involved in those activities. Or any other illegal activity, for that matter."

"And I'll stay on the Sweet River angle," Leo said. Without a word, her team swiveled and scooted their chairs across the room until they were once again in front of their weapons of choice.

"We need to call Tess," Chad said. "We have bits and pieces of evidence, but nothing solid. I don't know what she'll be able to do with it, but she's best positioned to have the answer since none of us are attorneys."

"I agree," Sabina said. "Why don't we do that then break for dinner? I know you wanted everyone to stay on HICC grounds, but any chance we can head out to the Dirty Boom? I could really use a cheeseburger—"

"And a beer," Kara interjected with a mutter.

"And a beer," Sabina agreed.

Chad glanced at Colton, and some sort of communication

passed between the two. Finally, Chad nodded. "I also think it might be better for you three to stay at my place tonight," he said, pointing to Sabina, Kara, and Gina. "I know Leo, Collin, and Ava bunked down in the dorms last night, but I think we should move them to the cabin. The operatives can split watch duties between here and my property."

"Why split up? It seems like we should be sticking together?" Kara asked.

"It sounds dramatic, but the world now knows you're both alive," Ethan answered. "When it was just Kevin Jacobs, he could send his henchmen to do whatever he ordered with no one as witness. Now that it's on record that you are alive, who you are, and what you do, it will be much harder for him to come after you."

"Don't get complacent, though," Chad warned. "He'll still want you out of the picture. But he'll have to regroup and think of a new strategy since his current one leaves him too exposed."

Ethan nodded. "And with the danger levels lower, everyone may as well be comfortable. I suspect Leo, Ava, and Collin will like the beds in the cabin better than those in the dorms. I *know* you, Gina, and Kara will prefer the ones at Chad's."

"And the grounds and house are safe," Ryan said, stepping into the conversation for the first time since he arrived. "It's not so much a strategic decision as one of comfort," he reiterated. "We're going to have a couple of long days ahead of us. We shouldn't underestimate the importance of a decent night's sleep."

Sabina couldn't argue with that. She was an eight-hours-a-night kind of gal. Still, she wasn't the only one impacted. She looked to Kara and Gina.

"Fine by me," Kara said. "Especially if that means I can have a burger and a beer."

"A bed is a bed," Gina said. "If that's what you girls want, I have no objections."

"Then it's settled," Chad said.

"I'll go over to the cabin to tidy up a bit," Sabina said.

Kara stayed her with her hand then rose. "You stay and talk to Tess. I'll go to the cabin. I'll pack our things, change the sheets, that sort of stuff."

"I'll go with you," Ethan said, rising. "I can pack Chad's things and help with the beds."

Before either she or Chad could say anything, the two were out the door.

Sabina glanced at Colton and Ryan, both of whom wore similar looks of amusement. Maybe she wasn't the only one who'd picked up on a spark of interest between Kara and Ethan. Or at least on Ethan's part. Unusually, she couldn't get a read on her sister. Pushing aside that interesting observation, she turned to Chad.

"Are you ready to call Tess?" he asked.

She smiled. Like a shark. "You have no idea."

CHAPTER TWENTY

The conversation with Tess, and subsequent follow-up, took longer than expected. They spent an hour walking through every piece of evidence and information they had. Then she'd asked them to package it all up into a coherent form and send it to her. Which meant they'd had to coordinate with the lab in DC before sorting all the information into discrete, logical categories with cross-references.

To Chad's surprise, Collin's skills weren't limited to what he could do with a computer. He had an uncanny ability to lay out complex data in a way that made it easy to reference and cross-reference. He'd been a godsend in getting everything they'd collected in order and sent to Tess.

They finally arrived at the Dirty Boom close to nine. It was a Friday night, though, and the place was still packed. Angelica, the owner's daughter, saw them walk in and gestured to Chad to head to the back room. He nodded his thanks and led the way to the room located to the left of the bar and accessed through a large sliding door. It was normally reserved for private parties, but it was the only place they'd all be able to sit together.

"Menus, everyone?" Angelica asked as she waltzed into the

room, effortlessly carrying a tray with twelve water glasses on it.

"Please," Sabina responded as she started passing waters down the table. Once the tray was empty, Angelica handed him and Sabina each a stack of menus, which they also dutifully passed down the table.

"And drink orders?" Angelica asked, taking out a notepad. A few minutes later, she exited the room, promising to be back shortly with the first pitchers of beer. The few folks who'd ordered cocktails would have to wait a little longer.

Within minutes, conversation flowed around the table. He smiled as Kara, Sabina, and Sabina's team tried to get Ethan to tell them why the town was named Mystery Lake. Gina, Ryan, and the others were talking baseball. When it seemed appropriate, he tossed a comment or two into both discussions. But his mind was occupied with Kevin Jacobs. And more specifically with how this would all end.

What *did* the end state look like? Jacobs in jail? Dead? Admitting his guilt?

Jacobs meeting his maker was the easy answer. With the crimes he committed, Chad wouldn't be sad to see him leave this earthly plane. It had the added bonus of being the surest way to guarantee Sabina and Kara's safety.

Despite the extreme temptation, though, that wasn't Chad's plan A. Maybe it would be his plan B, or even plan A, version 2. But it wasn't what he'd lead with. It was too easy a way out for the man.

Over decades, Jacobs had used his power not just for his own gain but to hurt others. And the idea of watching him lose everything—of seeing him stripped of his power and revealed for the man he really was—was perversely enticing.

Also, if Jacobs was dead, their chance of getting a confession died with him. Not that Chad was convinced they'd *get* a confession. The man had lived with his sins for a very long time and didn't seem bothered by them. But if possible, Chad wanted Sabina to have that closure.

Yes, humiliation and a confession seemed like the right plan A. They needed to bring about the man's complete and utter downfall without giving him the luxury of death.

His mind jerked back to the room when Sabina's foot brushed along his calf in a deliberate slide. She smiled at him from her spot across the table. Between that tempting tilt of her lips and her foot still rubbing his leg, a wave of *need* crashed over him. His hands twitched with the urge to grab her and take her somewhere. Anywhere dark—or not. Anywhere where it was just the two of them.

She must have sensed the leashed desire coursing through his body, because she stilled. Everything about her froze. Except for the vein in her neck that pulsed with the same craving flowing through him. Unwilling and uninterested in pulling his gaze from her, he stared. Tension arced over the table until he was certain their heartbeats matched. She was the first to move, though not by much. She licked her lips and her eyes darted toward the door, as if she was contemplating the same thing he was.

His breath caught in his lungs. He was seconds away from asking her if she wanted to go for a walk, or anywhere. Then Kara, who sat at her side, lurched into her sister in what looked like an attempt to get away from something.

Chad's adrenaline spiked at Kara's familiar movement. His body tensed to defend the women, and his attention shifted from Sabina to assessing the situation. Leo was standing up, tossing napkins onto the table. Ethan was doing the same. Ava was laughing at something.

Water. Leo had knocked his water glass over, startling Kara and breaking the moment between him and Sabina. His body grumbled and complained about the abrupt end to the odd, and not entirely unwelcome, intimate moment. Given that they were in a bar with ten other people, it was probably a good thing, though.

He offered up his napkin as well, but Kara waved him off. Leo had the situation under control.

"Are you okay?" Sabina asked. He wasn't. His body was still primed and wanting her, but he didn't think that's what she meant.

"You seemed a little lost in thought there," she added, clearing up any confusion as to how to interpret her question.

He didn't want to talk about the direction his thoughts had taken. There were confidentiality reasons, of course. More importantly, though, he didn't want to shift the convivial atmosphere of the group. It wasn't as if they'd been in the trenches for weeks or months. It had only been two days since all hell had broken loose. But he had enough combat experience to know that it was important to take breaks when they could. As the SEALs were famous for saying, the only easy day was yesterday. No one could predict what tomorrow would bring.

He shook his head and smiled at her. "I find it funny that you all are so obsessed with the name."

She eyed him. "Okay, we'll go with that, even though that was so obviously *not* what you were thinking. The name has to come from somewhere, we just want to know where."

He shook his head and laughed as Angelica walked in with three pitchers of beer on a tray. Reaching to take one from her, he answered. "Are you this obsessed with other town names? Like Truth or Consequences?" he asked, naming the town in New Mexico.

"Named after a game show," Sabina answered, pouring herself a beer from the second pitcher.

"Coward, South Carolina?" he asked, sliding his pitcher down after pouring his own drink.

She made a face. "Is that a real place?"

"It is. So is Superior, Wyoming," Angelica commented before double-checking the table then leaving.

"And Kill Devil Hills, North Carolina," he added.

"That I don't believe," she said before taking a sip of her drink.

He lifted a shoulder. "You don't have to, but it is a place. Google it."

She started to pull out her phone then dropped it back into her bag. "Why do I get the feeling that you're trying to distract me because *you* know the origin of the Mystery Lake name."

He barked out a laugh. He actually did know. Not the reason per se, but the inspiration. It had been passed down through the generations of the founding families. It wasn't something he was allowed to share, though. Sure, it wasn't against the law to tell people, but it was most definitely against Mystery Lake tradition. His grandfather—and about seventy-four other people in the know—would have his hide if he talked.

Sabina opened her mouth to say something but stopped when Angelica waltzed into the room with a tray full of cocktails and announced that everyone better be ready to order. He knew Sabina would order a cheeseburger, because she'd been craving one earlier. But he also knew she'd still examine every item on the menu before making her final choice. She was not a woman who made decisions without all the data.

"Start with him, please," she said, almost in a panic when Angelica looked at her expectantly. Angelica raised an eyebrow but complied and turned to Chad. He ordered his favorite tri-tip sandwich with fries and a side salad. No need to look at the menu for him.

By the time Angelica had made it down his side of the table and back up Sabina's, Sabina was smiling. "I'll have the cheeseburger, no lettuce or tomato, please. And fries," she said, handing her menu over.

"Salad?" Angelica asked.

Sabina darted a look at him.

"You're not stealing my salad," he said.

She huffed then turned to Angelica. "Yes, a salad please, with blue cheese dressing."

Angelica scribbled the note on her pad then scanned the table once more before heading back to the bar and kitchen. Before Sabina could turn the conversation back to the origins of the town name, he asked her what it was like growing up in Lexington, Kentucky. At first, habit had her answering slowly. But by the time their food arrived, she and Kara were sharing stories from high school—stories about the sports they played, their group of friends, and the underage party scene. There'd been a moment when he'd worried that talking about the friends they'd left behind would turn the conversation somber. That hadn't been the case, though, and rather than focusing on the years they'd lost, the sisters talked excitedly about getting back in touch with some of them.

Two and a half hours later, they all stumbled out of the Dirty Boom. None of them were drunk, but fatigue and a full belly had made a few of them a little giddy. With his own SUV still parked in his garage at home, Chad, Sabina, Kara, and Gina all piled into Ethan's car and headed to Chad's house. Ethan wasn't on duty that night, but he planned to check in with Killian and Ryder, who were. The two men would patrol the property throughout the night while Chad stayed on duty inside. In the early morning, Tucker would take over for him and remotely monitor his security system from the HICC offices so that Chad could get some sleep.

When they arrived, Ethan helped carry in the bags and get each of the women situated in the three guest bedrooms. As Chad watched them disappear into their temporary lodgings, he was glad Ethan's mom, who was an interior decorator, had insisted he furnish the entire house as soon as he moved in. It also did not escape his notice that Ethan had directed Sabina to the room beside his own.

Pushing aside the thought of Sabina sleeping so close, he called Killian and Ryder and asked them to come to the house. A few minutes later, he and Ethan met them outside in the shadows of the garage. Calling Tucker, the five men then walked through the plan for the night. If Chad managed to fall asleep when Tucker relieved him at four in the morning, he'd be able to fit a full five hours in before needing to be back at the office.

Ethan offered to take a shift, but he'd had a couple of long nights already, and Chad wanted his cousin to get some sleep. Ethan's reluctance to leave probably had a little—or a lot—to do with Kara. But after a few minutes of negotiation, he finally agreed.

Heading back into the house, Chad checked to see that his guests were well settled, making sure to tell them they were free to help themselves to anything they needed. Like Ethan, Sabina offered to stay up with him. He politely declined. The last thing he needed was to be in his command station—a small, secluded space—alone with her.

Once he heard the women shuffling around and getting ready for bed, he made his way to his office then down to the safe room. Flipping on the monitors, he identified Ryder's and Killian's locations then sat back and watched. And watched.

Four hours passed like molasses in January, and he was glad when four o'clock rolled around. Handing the duties off to Tucker, he dragged himself upstairs.

Entering his bedroom, he shut the door then eyed his bathroom. Should he shower now or in the morning? His bed called to him, but he'd also just stared at a computer for four hours. He always had a hard time falling asleep after long periods in front of a screen.

Decision made, he stripped out of his clothes as he crossed

the room. Tossing them into the hamper in the corner of the bathroom, he then flipped the shower on. This time, he waited for the water to heat up before stepping under it. When he did, it hit him with a sting, cascading over his head and down his body.

Having been born and raised in California, a state with a history of crippling droughts, long showers weren't the norm. But tonight, he indulged in the feel of the pounding spray hitting his shoulders, relaxing his muscles, and sliding down his body. Turning his face into the water, it ran over his scalp and through his hair, easing the hint of a headache he'd been fighting for the past few hours.

Finally, when his body felt heated and subdued, he flipped the water off, grabbed for his towel, and froze.

"Sabina?" he managed to say. Although why it came out a question, he didn't know. She was most definitely standing in his bathroom. Wearing nothing more than a pair of sleep shorts and a short-sleeved shirt.

He pulled his towel from the rod and started drying off, his eyes never leaving her. She said nothing as her gaze followed his movements. He dried his hair, then his chest and back, and finally his legs. When he was done, he considered wrapping the towel around his waist. With the way his body had reacted to her proximity, though, there was no way it would stay in place. So instead, he held it in front of himself.

"Is everything okay?" he asked, then winced at the stupid question. She was clearly fine. She was also very clearly in his room for one obvious reason. He wished he were a little smoother, that he knew what to say to her. But logic, and words, seemed to be outside his grasp.

He opened his mouth to say something else, though what it might have been, he didn't know. Thankfully, Sabina finally spoke.

"I heard you come in," she said.

He nodded. What else was he supposed to say?

"I..." Her gaze drifted to the small scratch on his arm then dropped to the one on his thigh.

The flash of vulnerability in her eyes woke all his senses. And it wasn't a subtle awakening, either. Every part of him—body, mind, heart—roared to life, and desire poured through him.

Without further thought, he dropped his towel and walked to her. Grasping her face between his palms, he dipped his head and slanted his mouth over hers.

Tasting her for the first time.

Their lips and tongues danced and mated. As the seconds ticked by, every ounce of restraint he'd shown over the past two years slid away, leaving him starving for her. For her touch, for her body, for the sounds she'd make when he finally buried himself inside her. For her surrender. Not to him, but to *them*.

She was on the same page, and her legs wrapped around his waist as he picked her up. Without breaking their kiss, he carried her into his room, the heat between them chasing away any chill. Not wanting to deprive himself of her touch for even a moment, he lowered them both to the bed, keeping her tight against him, then shifted to the side as he came down over her.

Coasting his hand over her rib cage to the dip in her waist, he snagged the hem of her shorts and managed to remove them without his lips leaving hers. Wanting to imprint the feel of her skin against his, his fingertips caressed her body. From the curve of her hip down to the indent of her knee, then back up again along the softness of her inner thigh. She sighed at his touch, and her own hands traced lines down his spine and over his backside.

Shifting from her side to over her, he slipped a hand under her shirt then cupped her breast. Pulling his lips from hers, he trailed kisses down her neck as he reveled in the feel of her in his hand.

A gentle bite at the sensitive spot where her neck met her shoulder, timed with a firm pinch of his fingers, had her legs wrapping him as she arched up.

"Get this shirt off me," she managed to say.

He raised his head and grinned down at her, but as commanded, he shifted away. Her heels dug into his thighs as she yanked her top off. And then they were both naked. Physically, mentally, and emotionally.

Taking his time, he skimmed his fingers from her collarbone, down between her breasts, over her belly, then to her waist. Her skin was fair, much fairer than his, but at the moment, it was also flushed.

He was lost. As he'd known he would be if they ever managed to get to where they were. There was not a single doubt in his mind that he wanted everything from the woman who now lay under him. He wanted her trust, her wit, her humor, her intelligence, her body. Her heart. He even wanted all her quirks. The road might not always be smooth for them—it never was for any couple—but he could still see it stretching far ahead.

She lifted a hand, and her fingers traced his jaw. His eyes met hers, and they stared at each other for a long moment, their chests rising and falling with each breath.

She raised her other hand and cupped his cheeks, much as he had in the bathroom. "Come to me," she said. "Please."

She tried to pull him down into another kiss, but he resisted. "Are you sure?" he asked. She was. He knew she was. But he needed to hear the words.

She knew why he'd asked and why he needed a clear answer. And as that memory slipped into the moment, a look of pain flashed in her eyes.

"I'm sor—"

"Don't," he said, cutting off her apology by placing a finger across her lips. This bed, this time between them, didn't need to be marred by his past. Regardless of what had happened to him all those years ago, consent was important. But what was even more important to him was not just her consent, but her willingness, her desire, and her need.

"Are you sure you want this?" he asked again. And to be sure she understood the full import of his question, he added, "And I don't mean this, tonight. I mean everything. I need to know you are sure about me. About us."

Her hands were still cupping his cheeks, and her thumb brushed along his cheekbone. Her eyes never left his as she spoke. "Before you, I never let myself dream about this *everything* you're talking about. It was always out of reach, something I could never have, so why bother thinking about it? But then you walked into my life."

Her thumb traced another gentle path along his jaw. "I remember every detail about the first time I saw you. It was your first day at HICC. You were in a conference room with Hunter, and he handed his son to you. He doesn't do that with just anyone, and it caught my attention. You probably never even noticed I was there, but I stopped to watch. You took Mateo without batting an eye, like you were used to handling precious things. Precious people. I didn't know who you were, but I envied Mateo that day, to be held by hands so sure and so gentle.

"Something came to life in me in that moment. I both craved and hated the thoughts and dreams I wove around you. Around the possibility of us. I told myself I couldn't have those dreams, but I couldn't give them up, either. It hurt to fall in love with you and it hurt to push you away. I hated myself for it. I hated myself for hurting you as much as I hated myself for not being able to move on and let you go."

She paused and let out a soft sigh, her breath brushing against his cheek as her fingers slid into his hair. "But by some miracle, we're here. Together. I'm *not* going to let it slip away, and I will fight for it. So, to answer your question, Chad Warwick: yes, I'm sure. About you, about me, about this. About *everything*."

He held her gaze as her words settled deep inside him. Then slowly, like a seed taking root and unfurling, a smile emerged from within him. "I intend to fight for it, too. I want you to know that."

She smiled back at him. "I know. You've been fighting for it for two years. I'm not going to let you stop now. Not when I'm finally alongside you."

He leaned down and brushed his lips against hers. "Good."

"Yes, good," she said, arching up into the kiss. A kiss that turned into an inferno. "There is one thing, though," she said, her voice shaky as she fought for breath.

He'd just started to slide his hand down toward her thigh, and his lips were a hair's breadth from nipping her earlobe. He froze and looked up. "What's that?"

Running her hand down his chest, then around his waist to his back, she gave him a soft, teasing smile. "Promise me that fighting for *us* means there will be lots of *this*," she said, pressing her palm against his lower back and pulling him closer. "Because I plan to get *very* used to the feel of your body moving with mine."

Her nails scraped down his backside, and his hips jerked forward. He dipped his head and kissed her as he rocked his body against hers, feeling her legs tighten around him. "You are brilliant," he said between kisses. "Your plan is brilliant." Another kiss. "And now," he said, moving back enough to be where he wanted. "If you don't mind, I'd like to get started on it," he said before sliding deep inside her.

CHAPTER TWENTY-ONE

"THIS ISN'T GOING to be an awkward morning after, is it?" Sabina asked. It wasn't. She'd never been more comfortable in her whole life. But she did like to tease Chad.

"Every morning without you was awkward. This? This is the way it should be," he murmured from behind her. He was wrapped around her body, still half asleep. She didn't know how he managed such sweet words in his half state, but they made her smile, and she snuggled closer against him.

His body responded to her movements, the way she knew it would. Especially since it was morning. Unfortunately, they had to leave in twenty minutes if they wanted to make it to HICC as planned. And she needed a shower. Not to mention she could already hear Kara and Gina moving around downstairs.

Straightening her body into a long stretch, she shifted away. He remained on his side, but the hand that had been wrapped around her waist started a leisurely trip down her thigh then up toward her breast.

"Shower," she said.

"Hmm," he replied, spanning his hand across her stomach and pulling her against him again.

"And not together," she said. "We have to leave in twenty minutes if we're going to get to HICC in time."

"Shit!" Chad exclaimed, jerking upright.

Startled, Sabina rolled to her back and looked up at him. "What?"

He raised a knee and rested his elbow on it as he ran his hand through his hair. Then he looked away.

"Chad?" Her voice was quiet, unsure of what was on his mind.

"We didn't use a condom. Not that first time," he answered, then he turned and met her gaze. "I'm so sorry. I'm clean, I can promise you that. But, well, that wouldn't help with the...other thing."

"You mean pregnancy?" she said, unable to stop a smile at his seeming inability to say the word.

He nodded.

"Do you want kids?" she asked.

His eyes widened, and he went still. Then he inhaled and answered on the exhale. "Yes, eventually. If the stars align and all that and you want them, too. But call me selfish. I've been wanting you for two years, and now that we're here, I don't want to rush anything. I want to enjoy this a little. In a lot of ways, we know each other well, but in others? We have a long way to go."

His assumption that if he had kids, they'd be with her, gave her the warm fuzzies, but she agreed with him. And she was selfish, too. She wanted time for just the two of them.

"Well, I could draw this out and torment you a little more, but I won't because I'm everything that is good and right in your world." He snorted at that, as she knew he would, then she continued. "I have an IUD. It's good for another two years. And I'm clean, too."

"Two years?" he asked. She nodded. "So no need for

condoms for at least two years?" Again, she nodded, not at all unsure where his mind was now.

"But while we don't need to think about condoms, we do need to think about Kevin Jacobs." She rolled her head and looked at his bedside clock. "And the fact that we now have fifteen minutes before we need to leave."

He stared at her, clearly weighing whether he could convince her of a better way to spend those fifteen minutes than showering and getting ready. It wouldn't take much, but just then, both their phones dinged with incoming texts.

Kara: *Ethan texted and has some news. Believe me, I didn't want to interrupt, but thought you should know he's waiting for us*

Chad groaned as Sabina threw the blankets off. "Sometimes decisions get made for us," she muttered as she started hunting for her clothing.

"Take my robe. It's hanging in the bathroom," Chad said, swinging his feet to the floor.

She poked her head in, found the flannel robe, and wrapped it around herself. It was huge, but cozy and smelled like him. "Fifteen minutes downstairs?"

He nodded. "Oh, and Sabina?" She turned before opening the door. "When this is all over, maybe we could take a vacation? After my grandad's Halloween party or something. A long weekend in Cabo or Belize? Maybe even a week?"

She'd never been to Cabo before and now that she was in California, it was only a short hop away. Lazy days at the beach and long nights with Chad sounded like a dream come true. She'd never allowed herself to think of such things before. That she could do so now, and with a man she loved, was almost overwhelming. She smiled and nodded. "I'd like that. A lot."

He met her smile with one of his own. "Good, I'll make the plans then once we're free." She stared at him for another long minute as he sat there on the side of his bed, the blankets draped over his lap but with his chest and feet bare. She doubted their relationship would always be smooth sailing, but she made a promise to herself to not ever take it for granted that she had the opportunity to have one.

Forty-five minutes later, the four of them pulled onto the HICC grounds with Ryder and Killian trailing behind in one of the company SUVs. Chad had tried to convince them to get some sleep, but she suspected they'd grab a few hours in the dorm and stick around. Bringing Kevin Jacobs down wasn't an official operation, but Sabina appreciated the fact that everyone was treating it as one. In fact, Colton had even suggested it was a good training exercise for the team before taking on official business.

Ethan waved them into a large conference room as soon as they walked in. Ava, Leo, and Collin were already seated, as were Colton, Ryan, Teague, and Tucker. Tess's voice was projecting through the speaker sitting in the middle of the table.

"The rest of the gang is here now," Ethan said, interrupting what sounded like an explanation of some statute of limitations.

"Good, now I can get to the meat of the matter," the lawyer said, not missing a beat. "I had a fascinating conversation with a former colleague who now works at the SEC. They've had their eye on Kevin Jacobs and some of his businesses for several months. Needless to say, they found your information informative. They aren't the only ones interested, though. The Federal Election Commission is also investigating him. Neither investigation may end up being related to your situation, but they do help us. He's done something, or several things, to land on their radars, and that won't be a comfortable place for him to be."

"What is the SEC looking at?" Ava asked.

"He's the majority shareholder of three companies that have had some infusions of cash in the past few years that the forensic accountants can't account for," Tess answered. "My contact wouldn't say which companies—"

"No need," Ava said, then flashed Sabina a look letting her

know that she'd research it. Sabina's plan A was to bring Jacobs to justice for the murder of her mother. But if there wasn't enough evidence to support that charge, then her plan B was to throw him to the wolves in every way possible. Well, plan B might also be a component of plan A. She was nothing if not thorough.

"Right...so, moving on," Tess continued. "I have my people preparing a new file on the murder of Emer Houseman. I'll be including all the evidence we've found to date, along with your statements, Sabina and Kara. It would be helpful if there were video evidence of Jacobs near Sabina's apartment the morning the postcard was dropped off..."

"We'll look into it," Sabina answered, glancing at Leo, who nodded in return.

"What was in the evidence turned over to you?" Kara asked.

"To be clear, I had it turned over to the lab at HICC," Tess responded. "They are licensed and authorized to process crime scene evidence. I didn't want there to be a chain of custody issue if they discover something. But to answer your question, very little. Photos and the reports, of course, but you already had those from Gina. Your mother's clothing and jewelry, the ring found with the dead man, and the scarf used to kill her."

She and Kara flinched at the image as well as the memories. Under the table, Chad's hand wrapped around hers. His touch didn't chase the demons away altogether, but it did steady her.

"The scarf will have his DNA on it, won't it?" Sabina asked.

"Yes, but the statement he gave eighteen years ago addressed that. He said it was a scarf she wore often, and he'd handled it on more than one occasion. Usually while helping her into or out of her coat," Tess said.

Sabina looked over at Chad, who was frowning. "What?" she asked.

He tipped his head. "There have been a lot of advances in DNA technology in the past few decades. I can see his DNA being on the scarf if he handled it. But handling it to help someone is one thing. Using it to strangle someone—which takes a lot of strength—is another."

"Hmm, you have a point," Tess said. "I'll ask them to test for quantity and, if possible, the pattern of the DNA."

"It could amount to nothing. I don't know how much DNA degrades over time," Chad said.

"But it's worth looking into," Tess said, and Sabina and Kara nodded.

"Anything else?" Sabina asked. Tess spent another few minutes walking them through everything that had been delivered to HICC. She'd call the lab later, but it was good to hear from the lawyer what she should be asking about.

When Tess wrapped up the summary, Kara asked, "What's next? I feel like I should be doing something."

"You've done a lot already," Ethan said. "Yesterday was a long day."

Kara made a face. "It was a long day of sitting on my ass and going through Uncle Mike's things. Surely there's something I can do?" Kara looked at Sabina. Now that they'd gone through all the boxes, Sabina planned to join her team and follow up on the cyber leads. But Kara didn't have those skills—or that outlet.

"Your father," Ethan said, drawing the women's attention. "Ava is looking for him, but maybe you know more about him than you think you do. You could spend some time thinking about where he might have gone after he and your mom divorced."

Kara frowned but didn't dismiss the suggestion as Sabina might have.

"What might I know?" Kara asked.

Ethan lifted a shoulder "I don't know. *We* don't know. Not until you give yourself the space to think about it. Maybe it will be nothing, but maybe you'll think of something."

Kara shot him a doubtful look. "I'm supposed to sit around and think about our dad?"

Ethan shook his head. "We'll go for a walk, and we can talk along the way. You can let the memories flow. You were just complaining about sitting around. This will get you out of the house—so to speak—and out of your head a little."

Sabina recognized the look on Kara's face. She was debating whether to be offended by Ethan's comment about getting out of her head. In truth, Sabina was the one who usually needed that reminder. Kara was more of a go-with-the-flow kind of person.

To Sabina's surprise, Kara nodded. "As you said, it might not come to anything. But at the very least, I'll get a walk out of it."

"Let me know if you think of anything," Tess said.

"Of course," Kara replied. A few minutes later, everyone filed out of the room. Kara and Ethan turned toward the stairwell that would take them to the closest exit. Chad and Sabina trailed behind her team as they walked to the cyber lab. The operatives peeled off to go do whatever it was they were going to do. Probably planning how to assassinate Kevin Jacobs. Not that she thought they would, but as Colton was so fond of saying, it was a good training exercise.

They were ten feet from the lab when Chad's phone rang. Sabina paused as he pulled the device from his pocket and looked at the screen. "Stella," he said. She nodded, knowing he'd need to take the call in the privacy of his office. Lifting the device to his ear, he answered as he walked to his domain.

Joining the others in the cyber lab, Sabina went straight to her computer and powered it on. This was her first time leading a team, and it was a little disconcerting how many tasks they'd taken on, leaving her with little to do. She trusted them to do their jobs, and didn't want to duplicate efforts, but what was left for her?

Leaning back in her chair, she idly watched her screen as it went through the safety protocols and scans that she'd installed. What was something she could bring to the table that was uniquely hers?

She drummed her fingers on her desk and considered the situation. The only thing really left to dig into that she—and her sister—might have special insight into was the whereabouts of her father. Kara was taking her walk, giving her mind the space and serenity to think about it. That was one approach, but it wasn't one Sabina thought would work for her. She liked nature as much as the next person, but it wasn't what got her thinking.

But something else did.

With the beginnings of a plan, she smiled and logged in. After navigating through a few systems, she found herself in the records department of the courts for Fayette County, the county in which Lexington was located. Only it wasn't the files on her mother's murder she sought. No, she was looking for records from twenty-four years ago. The year her parents divorced.

It took her thirty minutes to find the file she was looking for. And after that, she disappeared down the cyber rabbit hole. At some point, Chad texted her to let her know he was taking care of a few things in his office. So lost in the trail she'd picked up, she'd only responded with a "K."

She picked and poked her way through database after database. With each new lead, adrenaline pulsed and coursed under her skin. Not a burst, but a slow flow that gained strength with each fork in the trail she took. From court records, to planes, to hotels, to banks, to real estate sales, she was closing in on her father.

And then she found him.

Leaning back in her chair with a grin, she just about jumped out of her skin when Chad's hand came down on her shoulder.

"Everything okay? I've stopped by a few times, but you were so focused, I didn't want to interrupt."

She glanced at the clock on her computer. She felt as if she'd traveled the world, but only four hours had passed.

She smiled up at him then tugged him down and pressed a kiss to his lips.

"Whatever you found must be exciting," he murmured, lingering a little longer.

She considered jumping into his arms and celebrating a little more, but she pushed the urge down. Instead, she gestured to her computer. "I found him."

"Who?"

"I know where he is!" Kara exclaimed, bursting into the room with Ethan on her heels.

"São Paulo!" the twins said at the same time.

Kara drew to a halt beside Sabina. "You figured it out, too?"

Sabina nodded then gestured to her computer. "How'd you figure it out?" she asked.

"I didn't know for certain," Kara said, leaning forward to read the information on the screen. "But I remembered him talking about Brazil a lot. About how it was a good place to hide. It was always in the context of *other* people hiding away—mainly the nazis. But as I started to remember those conversations, I also started to remember little things. Like how his voice would change when he talked about the country and how one day, I saw him looking at travel brochures for São Paulo. Like I said, I wasn't certain, but it seemed like somewhere he'd go."

"And he did," Sabina said, motioning for everyone to gather chairs and take a seat. Once they were circled around her, she brought up the image of a stark white modern villa. Set in a lush landscape in a high-end neighborhood, the house was large, bordering on a mansion, with a pool and a tennis court.

"Is that where he's living?" Chad asked.

Sabina nodded. "I was able to trace his movements from Lexington to here." She pointed to the house. "I started with the day he and my mom signed the divorce papers. It was done in person, so I knew he was still stateside that day. From there, I searched flight records, then hotels, banks, etcetera, until I found this. He purchased the house five years ago, and as far as I can tell, still lives there."

"I know it wasn't easy, but you make it sound easy," Ethan said, his voice pitched with a hint of awe. Sabina didn't miss Chad's quirk of a smile. He'd always been vocal about how talented she was and for right or wrong, she knew he was pleased his cousin saw it, too.

"It got a little touch-and-go about a year and a half after he arrived. He changed his name, and that threw off my search. But while he may have changed his name, he did not change his habits. I was eventually able to track him through his movements and pin down his new name."

"Which is?" Chad asked.

"Benicio Silva," Sabina answered, bringing up a picture of the man neither she nor her sister had seen for twenty-four years.

Kara let out a wry chuckle. "Think he's had a little work done?"

Sabina laughed. Benicio Silva looked remarkably like the man she remembered except for the slightly plasticky look to his skin.

"What do we do about this now?" Ethan asked.

Sabina looked to Chad, and she wasn't disappointed. He knew what she wanted and looked ready to go along with it.

He grinned. "Now we take a little trip."

CHAPTER TWENTY-TWO

CHAD CLOSED the email he'd been reading and relaxed back in his seat. They'd flown from Mystery Lake to Miami, where one of the larger, more luxurious HICC planes had picked them up for the nine-hour flight to São Paulo. Now they were somewhere over the Caribbean with eight hours left in the flight.

"Transport and hotel are booked," he announced to everyone who could hear. Kara and Sabina were napping in one of the bedrooms, but Ethan sat across the table from him. Teague and Killian were also nearby. They'd be overseeing overall security during their time in São Paulo while Ethan and Chad focused on the sisters.

"What do we need to know?" Teague asked, looking up from the crossword he'd been working on. Chad wasn't sure if crosswords and sudoku were just how he passed the time while flying, or if they were something he did regularly. Either way, he'd had one or the other in front of him since they'd taken off from California.

"All the details are in your emails," he answered.

Without a word, Teague set his crossword book down and pulled his computer out. Killian had appeared to be dozing on one of the couches, but he, too, reached for the bag at his side and pulled out his computer, only opening his eyes once the device was sitting on his chest.

"Is travel always like this?" Ethan asked, nodding to their surroundings.

Chad chuckled. "Sometimes. Depends on the op. Stella and Hunter have a lot of resources and treat their employees well. They also know that arriving at a location exhausted isn't optimal. If it were just us," he said, gesturing to the four men, all of whom were ex-military, "we'd probably be on something a little less luxurious."

"They did it for Sabina and Kara?"

Chad wagged his head. "Probably. But it's more than that. Stella and Hunter do a lot of work that most people don't know about. They get involved in everything from preventing human trafficking to ensuring affordable childcare. Having someone like Kevin Jacobs in a position of power—a man who made his money through illegal gambling, prostitution, and organized crime—isn't something they'll sit back and let happen. Not now that they know about it."

"After all these years, do you think Benicio will still have evidence of Jacobs's crimes?" Ethan asked.

"Who knows?" Chad answered. "Assuming he is the one who stole Jacobs's money, it's unlikely they've done any business together in the past eighteen years. Given that it was so long ago, if he does have something, though, he might be willing to turn it over."

Ethan turned his head and looked out the window. Chad remained silent, giving him the space to think. As with his cousin, the military had taught Chad all about how to run ops, tactical assaults, and similar engagements. But it hadn't been until he'd joined the FBI that he'd learned about the cat-and-mouse game that was the mainstay of investigatory and intelligence work. HICC's business blended those aspects of security

—they had the ability to strike, with guns and weapons, but also with knowledge. Ethan didn't yet have the training that Chad had on what he often considered the more sinister side of things. He'd get there, though.

"You don't think this is a fool's errand?" Ethan asked, curiosity ringing true in his voice.

Chad shook his head. "Kevin wasn't the head of the organization, we know that. So who was? And is he or she still in power? If so, who are they in bed with? These are the kinds of things Benicio might know. He might not be willing to share with us if he's worried about coming back onto their radar after stealing that money. But if *we* found him, chances are he'll realize others can, too. And if he's worried about his *life*, he might be willing to sing like a canary if he thinks it will keep him safe."

Ethan considered the words. "And even if he's not willing to talk about the organization he worked for, he might know something about other organizations. I doubt a man like Jacobs will change his spots, so to speak. If he stopped working with one conglomerate, I'd bet he took his business to another."

"Exactly," Chad said, then paused. "Stella and Hunter have another reason, though." Ethan rolled his head against the back of the seat and looked at him. "The contact at the SEC that Tess spoke to yesterday?" Ethan nodded. "Well, *she* has contacts with the CIA and FBI. Those agencies are also interested in Jacobs's dealings. Not so much in him as an individual, but who he's working with, how the business is working, and the flow of money. In the past few years, there's been an increasing concern of foreign money making it into our election system enough so that the FEC isn't the only agency interested. They've asked Stella and Hunter to help where they can."

Ethan's gaze never left his as the gears turned. "And it never hurts to have a marker to call in with the alphabet agencies. Not that they wouldn't agree otherwise, but it helps."

Chad inclined his head. "It does help, yes. Especially in our business."

"How do you want to handle check-in?" Teague asked, ending their conversation.

"You and Killian in the lead," Chad answered. "Check-in, get a feel for the lobby, then we'll bring Sabina and Kara in. I'm not anticipating any problems since no one knows we're coming, but I'd rather play it safe."

They spent two hours running through what would happen in the next day and a half. Tonight, they'd lie low at the hotel and rest up. In the morning, they'd make their way to Benicio's home. Ava and the team back in Mystery Lake now had eyes on the place and would be their guides. They planned to be back in the air by late tomorrow night and home the day after. It was a solid plan, but Chad was never happy with just one plan. In that, he and Sabina were remarkably alike.

Teague eventually claimed the other bedroom for a nap, and Killian crashed out on the couch again. They'd have all night to study the roads and potential routes to their destinations. Chad, on the other hand, had other plans for his nocturnal activities. If he'd been traveling alone or on an op, he never would have considered taking a break. But Sabina was going to be nervous about confronting her biological father. He both wanted and needed to focus on her. Which was, admittedly, no hardship.

The remainder of the flight and hotel check-in went without a hitch. HICC had reserved a suite with two bedrooms for them. Chad presumed it was a family suite, as one room had a king bed—which he and Sabina claimed—and the second, two full-size beds. Ethan eyed the two beds then shifted his gaze to the couch. Chad empathized with his cousin. There was no way he would have wanted to be in the same bedroom with Sabina if he couldn't also, at the very least, hold her. In the end, Ethan said he had some work to do before going to bed, then said good night to Kara before she disappeared into the bedroom. The look Sabina shot Chad told him she'd seen his evasion technique, too, but neither spoke of it. In fact, once they closed the door to their room, neither spoke very much at all, preferring to let their bodies say what needed to be said.

After the languorous night, they rose, showered, then joined Ethan and Kara in the main room where a large breakfast was already laid out. He gestured for Sabina to get started while he checked in with Teague and Killian. As predicted, all was quiet on the home front.

At fifteen minutes to nine, Teague swung a large SUV under the portico in front of the hotel. Everyone tossed their bags in the back, then the four of them climbed in, and he pulled away. Killian followed behind in a smaller, more nondescript, SUV.

An hour later, they pulled to a stop in front of a small shop a quarter of a mile from Benicio Silva's house. If they needed to make a quick exit, it was easier for four people to slip away than to get a car through the closed gate of his property, so they'd agreed to walk the short distance.

Killian took the lead at a respectable distance ahead of them. Then Chad, Sabina, Ethan, and Kara followed. Teague brought up the rear.

Eight blocks later, Chad pressed the button on the panel outside the gate to Benicio's house and waited. A few seconds later, a voice crackled over the intercom. Chad wasn't fluent in Portuguese, but he knew enough to translate the dismissal. Ignoring it, he pressed the button again, this time holding it down until a man appeared at the door set into the fence to the left of the gate.

He was armed, not a surprise, but so were Ethan and Chad. Although Chad intended to do everything in his power to keep the situation from devolving to a point where those weapons were needed.

The man stared at them through a pair of beady eyes and shifted his coat to reveal more fully the gun at his hip. Chad nearly rolled his eyes. They were standing less than eight feet apart, nowhere near enough time to unholster it if he and Ethan decided to rush him.

Despite the lack of any real risk, he and his cousin took subtle steps to put themselves between the man and Sabina and Kara. Although, to be fair, neither woman seemed particularly fazed by the weapon. As an employee of HICC, Sabina was no stranger to guns. And given the kinds of places Kara traveled, he suspected she had her fair share of experience, too.

"Americans?" the man asked in English, his voice heavily accented.

Chad nodded sharply. "You can tell Benicio Silva that Lalibela and Nalanda Houseman are here to see him."

The man eyed them, then withdrew a phone from his pocket. Hitting a button, he brought it to his ear. What followed was a conversation too rapid for Chad to understand, although he did hear the sister's names. Less than four minutes later, they were being escorted into the very modern house.

They followed Beady Eyes through a pair of tall glass doors and into a foyer. Then continuing up a wide set of gleaming metal stairs, they traipsed down a hallway, around a corner, and finally, into an office with panoramic views toward the city.

And there stood Benicio Silva. The man formerly known as Richard Houseman.

Despite the hour, he held a glass of whiskey. He didn't move from his position behind the desk, not even after his guardian left, closing the door behind him. With one hand in his pocket and the other holding the tumbler, he studied them.

"You both look like your mother," he finally said.

Neither Kara nor Sabina moved. No one had expected a joyous family reunion, but his cool appraisal surprised Chad. The man had spoken as if observing a piece of art that he didn't quite care for. He showed no shame for what he'd done. No curiosity about how they were or what they'd been doing the past twenty-four years. No familial affection whatsoever.

"Tell us about Kevin Jacobs," Sabina said.

Benicio stilled for one brief second then he smiled. Or at least Chad thought that's what he'd intended. It was hard to tell with the amount of work he'd had done on his face.

"You were always bright children. I'm going to assume you've turned into bright women and that you know I stole a fair bit of cash from the man." He gestured for them to take seats, but when neither Sabina nor Kara moved, Chad and Ethan stayed standing as well. Benicio sighed, as if put out.

"I was running the accounting business for a man I'd worked with for a few years. *He* was the one who did business with Jacobs. To make a long story short, he decided Jacobs needed to be taken down a peg or two. He authorized me to take the money. He didn't need it, so he told me to keep it. He was more interested in making a point."

"And what was the point?" Kara asked.

Benicio's gaze shifted between the sisters before landing on Chad. "It wasn't about the money. That was the point," he responded. "He wanted Kevin Jacobs to know who was calling the shots. And that it wasn't Kevvy."

"And that everything could be taken from him at the drop of a hat if he stepped out of line," Sabina said. Benicio switched his gaze to her then nodded and took a sip of his drink.

"Why are you telling us this?" Kara asked. It was a good question and one Chad had been wondering.

"Because neither I, nor the man I worked for, are in the business anymore. We both retired five years ago."

"It doesn't work that way in the kind of organization you worked for, Silva," Chad said. "You don't get to start talking. Not even when you retire."

There was an odd tug on the corner of Silva's mouth. Again, maybe a smile? "You're right," he said. "When we retired, my boss's son took over the organization. I got out because the kid could barely piss into a toilet on his own. Turns out, I wasn't the only one who thought so. Two years after his takeover, there was another power grab. This one by a different organization. Killed pretty much everyone I knew. So you see, it doesn't matter if I talk about them. They're all dead."

"Except you," Sabina pointed out.

He raised his glass to her. "I'm nothing but a lowly accountant. I know nothing about the new organization in control, so I'm not worth bothering. I find that it's a rather nice spot to be."

Chad suspected it was. He appeared to have all the money he'd ever need and was left alive to enjoy it. If only Chad bought into that story.

"Is Jacobs still involved in those kinds of activities?" Sabina asked.

Benicio studied her then lifted a shoulder. "As of five years ago, yes. The specific activities have changed over time, of course. But if you're asking whether the senator is engaged in activities unbecoming of a public servant, then I'd say you have it right."

"With whom?" Kara asked.

"*That* I'm not at liberty to say," he answered. Regardless of what he'd told them about his ability to speak freely, Chad thought there was a lot he'd already said that he wasn't at liberty to say. It could be he felt some guilt for Emer Houseman's murder, and giving them information about Jacobs's past dealings assuaged some of that. Or there could be another reason.

"I assume you know why we're here," Sabina said. "I'm not naive enough to believe that you have any feelings toward Kara or me that would induce you to help us bring Jacobs to justice for the murder of our mother. But as you say, what's in the past is in the past. If everyone is dead, there's no one to make you pay the price for talking to us. If you have any records that might help, we'd be happy to take them off your hands."

His eyes flickered between his daughters, and Chad would have liked to say he saw something in his gaze—maybe compassion or some sign he realized what he'd missed out on when he walked out of their lives—but he didn't. Benicio could have been talking to two women off the street for all he appeared to care.

"I have nothing," he finally said. "When I retired, I destroyed everything. But even the files I had would not have brought you the justice you seek. I had plenty of records of his finances, but nothing that tied him to Emer's murder."

That was a statement Chad did believe. There would have been no reason for him to have any evidence related to the murder. It was a possibility Chad had considered. Expected even. But that didn't make it any easier to accept. At least they had confirmation that Benicio had, in fact, laundered money for Jacobs. Even if they had no evidence to support that fact. Nor, for that matter, did they learn any of the information that Stella and Hunter had hoped for.

"Well," Benicio said on an exhale. "Since you came without warning, I haven't cleared my schedule. I have a meeting in town, so if there's nothing more?"

Chad had to work very hard not to react to the man's dismissal of his daughters. Despite what Sabina and Kara had said about him earlier, it *had* to hurt to be so casually brushed aside by a man who was supposed to care for them. A man who should have loved them, but who had, in fact, been little more than a sperm donor who then ruined their lives. Not that the sisters led terrible lives. But what they'd built, who they'd become, was in spite of him, not because of him.

Sabina didn't need his outrage, though, so he held his reaction in check.

Instead of responding to the man now walking them to the door, he took Sabina's hand and held tight. Ethan didn't reach for Kara's, but he did keep his hand on her lower back, letting her know he was there.

Benicio led them back downstairs, calling for a man named Vitor who Chad assumed was the beady-eyed henchman who'd let them in. When the man hadn't appeared by the time they reached the front door, the little hairs on Chad's neck started to twitch.

"Does your manservant often go missing?" he asked, pausing at the door.

Benicio half bobbed, half shook his head. "I'm sure he's in the garage pulling the car out."

Chad looked at Ethan and barely tipped his head. Reading the message correctly, Ethan subtly moved Kara a step behind him. Sabina's arm stiffened, and she squeezed his hand. She might not have the same intuition that he did in situations like these, but she knew him well enough to sense that *he* sensed something off. With no debate, she stepped behind him when he tugged her back.

"Do you have a driver?" Benicio asked, swinging the door open.

"We do—"

Chad never got to finish his answer as a hail of bullets tore through the entry.

CHAPTER TWENTY-THREE

CHAD SPUN and yanked Sabina farther into the house, pressing her back against a concrete pillar and shielding her body with his. He spared a look across the hall and saw Ethan had Kara in much the same position.

Peeking his head around the column, Chad quickly ducked back when a second volley of bullets hit. He'd had enough time, though, to see Benicio's body bleeding and sprawled across the steps. What he had not seen was the shooter. Although he'd wager it was Vitor and that Vitor was positioned in the greenery near the gate.

"We should have worn earpieces," Chad muttered, cursing the fact that they hadn't. Now he needed to hold both his phone and his weapon. Juggling the two wasn't going to be easy.

"I'll call Teague," Sabina said. "You manage your gun." Her bag with her phone was pressed between her back and the pillar, so rather than try to reach around, she dug into the front pocket of his jeans for his.

Trusting Sabina to do what needed to be done, he took another quick look outside. He had his Glock out, as did Ethan, but he didn't want to take a shot unless he knew what he was shooting at. His magazine held fifteen bullets. As did Ethan's. But up against the Heckler UMP submachine gun that Chad was nearly sure Vitor had, he wasn't going to test their odds—not with Sabina and Kara in the picture.

Scanning the room for an alternative, Chad cursed the open layout of the house. He was aware of Sabina and Teague making a plan, but his mind was too focused on how to get them out to participate.

"Back door?" Ethan suggested.

"If there's more than one person, they'll be waiting there. The garage is our best bet," he countered. "I'm going to kick the door closed. When I do, can you make it over here?"

Ethan glanced around the corner of his pillar then back at Chad. Chad could tell from the look on his face that he'd seen Benicio's body. Something neither Kara nor Sabina needed to witness. Seeing one dead parent was already more than enough.

Ethan nodded. "On zero?"

Chad gave a sharp nod in response then started counting down from three with his fingers. When his hand clenched in a fist, he stepped away from Sabina and placed a well-aimed boot at the thick glass. It wouldn't hide them from Vitor's view, but it might distract him enough not to get a good series of shots off.

Ethan spun Kara around, keeping himself between her and Vitor, as they bolted from their spot. A hail of bullets streamed across the middle of the door. The force pushed it back open, but the glass held long enough for his cousin and Kara to make it to the same side of the threshold as him and Sabina.

Silence fell after the last barrage of bullets, and Sabina shoved his phone back into his pocket. "They want us to make our way to the garage. Killian is already on his way with an ETA of less than five minutes. He's going to come over the fence through the back in case there's anyone there that…that needs to be managed," she said. "Once he clears the back, he'll circle around the front to distract whoever is out there."

"It is Vitor," Ethan confirmed. "I saw him."

Sabina inclined her head. "Once Killian starts engaging with Vitor, we need to head out and over the back fence. Teague will pick us up at the bottom of the road. When we're clear, Killian will disengage and make his way back to his own SUV."

For the first time since they walked onto Benicio's property, Chad smiled. "Nice plan," he said.

She grinned back. "I even know the best path to get from the fence to where we'll meet Teague." He didn't doubt it. And he'd wager she'd lead them on the same path he'd identified when he'd studied the maps and satellite images.

Another round of bullets pelted the glass of the dining room to the side of where they stood. Kara and Sabina ducked on instinct and Chad and Ethan pulled their respective charges closer to their bodies.

"I guess there's some good news in that the glass appears mostly bulletproof," Ethan said, leaning over to look at the damage. It wouldn't hold indefinitely, not against the kind of weapon Vitor had, but it was better than nothing.

Chad poked his head around the pillar to assess their options. While the house was open plan, the modern architecture was a mix of materials. Including a three-foot-high section of concrete that was the bottom part of the front wall. It was intended to hold the heavy glass that made up the rest of the wall, but for their purposes, it would make excellent cover.

He leaned back and looked at Sabina.

"Crawl?" she suggested.

"Definitely crawl," he confirmed. "You all ready?" When Ethan and Kara nodded, he dropped to his hands and knees. Taking the lead, Sabina and Kara stayed behind him with Ethan bringing the rear. They were halfway across the dining room when Chad heard something he didn't like at all. The sound of footsteps crunching on the shattered glass right outside the front door.

"E?"

"Got it," Ethan said.

"Sabina and Kara, go!" he ordered. The two women scrambled by him as the first bullets tore across the room. His heart stopped when Sabina's hand slid out from under her. She almost went down, losing precious seconds, but she quickly righted herself and kept going. At the same time, Ethan got off a couple of shots, forcing Vitor to take cover.

"Follow the women, C. I'll keep you covered. Once you're in the kitchen you can return the favor."

Chad almost chuckled at that. He'd never had the chance to work with anyone from his family before. And although he'd wanted Ethan on the team, and known he'd be a good asset, he hadn't realized how much he'd enjoy it.

"Always wanting something in return," Chad muttered, making Ethan snort.

"Yeah, I'm not a giver like that. Now go make sure the women are okay."

Sabina and Kara had made it to the relative safety of the kitchen. To Ethan's point, though, that didn't necessarily mean they were okay. Keeping to the wall, he crawled as fast as he could toward them. A scuffle sounded behind him, then a shot from Ethan's gun.

Chad was only a few feet away from the kitchen when the sound of Vitor's gun echoed through the house again. Ethan's follow-up shots were nearly instantaneous. But they weren't fast enough to stop a bullet searing its way across Chad's calf.

He hissed in pain and jerked his leg closer to his body. Fighting the urge to stop and check the damage, he kept his eyes locked on Sabina and dragged himself the rest of the way. The second he was within arm's reach, she reached out and grabbed him, hauling him close.

"Kara," she snapped.

"On it," Kara said, kneeling beside Chad's calf.

"Can't. Not right now," Chad said, flipping around so his belly was on the ground. From his position, he had a line of sight to Ethan as well as the muzzle of Vitor's gun. Despite the pain radiating up his leg and the blood dripping down his calf, he knew he'd be able to cover his cousin.

Ethan looked back at him, and Chad gave him the "go" sign. In a flash, he was on his feet, bolting toward the three of them. The muzzle of Vitor's weapon shifted. Chad fired off a warning shot. It hit the wall an inch below where the gun rested. With a weapon like Vitor's, he wouldn't need eyes on his target to lay down deadly fire. But he would need to expose his arm and Chad wanted him to know that if he did, Chad's aim would be true.

Two seconds later, his cousin was with them, but Chad held his position until Ethan moved in to take his place. Then scooting farther into the room, he flipped over and got his first look at the damage to his leg. The bullet had ripped a long hole in his jeans, and the denim was dark and wet with his blood. He knew enough about gunshot wounds to know this one wasn't serious, nothing more than a deep graze, but it hurt like hell.

"You need stitches," Kara said. Chad looked at her. She made a face. "Okay, maybe not *right now,* but you do need stitches."

"What can we do *now*?" Sabina asked. Chad switched his focus to her. Her fair skin had gone even more pale, and he thought she was muttering something about three bullet wounds.

"I'll be fine, Sabina," he said, almost smiling. The first two bullets from the ambush really had just grazed him and he'd all but forgotten about them.

She didn't bother responding. "Kara?"

"Sabina," he said, then waited until she looked at him. When she finally did, he reached for one of her hands and curled his around hers. "I'll be fine. It hurts and it's bloody, but it's not deep and didn't hit anything major. Believe me, I'd know."

Her blue-green eyes studied him, and she bit her lip. She must have come to some conclusion in her mind, because she nodded. "Okay, fine," she said, sounding not that fine. "Let's get something tied around it. Can you walk?"

"Yes."

"Good, then we stick with the plan. Ethan, you good with that?"

"Yep," he responded, not leaving his lookout spot.

"Killian should be here any minute," she said, as she and Kara started digging through the drawers. Kara withdrew a clean dishtowel from one, looked at it, then grabbed a second.

"I'll tie these together and then it should be long enough," Kara said. Sabina nodded but kept looking. When she pulled out a pair of scissors from another drawer, he knew what she intended. Quickly, she cut away his pant leg, then Kara moved in and wrapped the dishrags tightly around his calf. Electric pain shot through his body as she tied off the makeshift tourniquet. Not wanting to further worry Sabina, though, he bit back his reaction.

"Ready?" Ethan asked.

Sabina and Kara helped Chad stand, and he tested his leg before putting all his weight on it. He wasn't worried about it buckling, but he didn't want the pain to catch him by surprise. When he was firmly on both feet, he motioned the women toward the hall that would lead them to the garage.

"We're on the move," Chad replied.

As planned, Chad stopped at the edge of the hall and called to Ethan. His cousin glanced back as a round of bullets came flying through the doorway to the kitchen. From where Vitor was positioned, his range was limited, and Ethan had good cover. Chad wasn't worried. Well, not too much.

But then once again, he heard something that gave him

pause. Ethan must have heard it, too, because his head snapped up, even as he continued toward Chad's side.

"That wasn't the UMP," Ethan said when he reached Chad. It wasn't. There'd been several shots fired, but not from Vitor's weapon. "Killian?" he asked.

Chad hoped so. Only the shots hadn't come from the front of the house, and the plan had been for him to circle around to that part of the property. Then again, Vitor had moved from his original position; it was possible Killian had needed to adapt his approach.

Another blast from Vitor's weapon echoed through the house, followed by a deafening silence. Chad was pretty sure he'd heard the second weapon fire but couldn't be certain in the cacophony of noise.

Ethan looked to Chad for orders. It was possible the second gun was Killian. Likely even. But he wasn't going to take any chances. Motioning Ethan toward Sabina and Kara, who were huddled in one of the three doorways that lined the hall, he spoke. "We stick with the plan."

With a nod, Ethan took off. Rushed footsteps echoed down the hallway, letting Chad know that the three of them were on the move. In the distance, he also heard sirens. Violence wasn't uncommon in São Paulo. But even so, the volume of gunshots in the neighborhood they were in wasn't something neighbors would ignore.

Despite knowing they should stick around for the authorities, Chad wanted to be far away from the house by the time the police arrived. Evidence of their presence was all over, so it wasn't as though he thought they wouldn't be tied to the events of the past fifteen minutes. But he'd prefer for it to come out when they were in the relative safety of the United States.

Walking backward down the hall, he joined the trio as he motioned Ethan to clear the garage. Sabina and Kara stepped into the final alcove along the hall, while Chad moved in front of them. His cousin slowly opened the door and when no sound came from within the space, he opened it more fully before stepping through.

"We're as clear as we're going to get," he said. The open-air garage was protected on two sides, but left them exposed on two.

"Slight change of plans," Sabina said. He glanced back at her to see her holding her phone before returning his attention to the mouth of the hallway. "Ava texted and the neighbors aren't home. We can go over the side fence into their yard, rather than drop down into the waterway that runs behind the houses. Once we're there, they have a gate out the back that we can use, which will make it easier to keep our feet dry."

And it would. The original plan had them going up and over the fence at the back of the property. It wasn't a difficult maneuver, but it put them smack in the middle of the runoff waterway that ran behind the houses lining this side of the street. With the rain the city had had over the past week, it would have been soggy going. But the waterway didn't bump right up against the neighbor's property in the same way it did Benicio's. They'd be able to pick a trail alongside it and down to Teague.

"Ready, E?" he asked.

"Ready," he called back. Less than five seconds later, Sabina and Kara had followed Ethan out the door and into the garage.

Chad didn't know what awaited them outside, and he hoped Killian had done his job. The house was beginning to feel as if it was closing in on him, and fresh air sounded heavenly. With that thought firmly in mind, he started to move toward the door to the garage.

He wasn't even halfway there, though, when footsteps behind him had his heart clawing its way into his throat. Turning to face whoever it was, he stood exposed, in the middle of the hallway. Time slowed, and his thoughts turned to Sabina and everything they had ahead of them.

He'd promised to fight for her. For them.

Raising his gun, he stood his ground. And watched the form of a man—and a gun—appear at the end of the hall.

CHAPTER TWENTY-FOUR

SABINA'S HEART stopped when she caught a glimpse of a man at the end of the hall through the garage door. The light from the kitchen at his back made it impossible to see his features, but the outline of his gun was more than clear.

Ethan moved between her and the door, as if sensing her urge to rush to Chad. Before she'd given it a moment's thought, she cried out his name. Then just as quickly, she snapped her mouth shut. She didn't need to distract him.

Blood rushed through her system, drowning out any other sounds. He was a sitting duck in the hallway; the alcove was too far away and he had nowhere to go. An armed sitting duck, but still, there was no cover for him.

Both men raised their weapons, and an unholy panic flooded through her. She lunged forward, desperate to get to Chad. She made it two feet before Ethan's arms caught her around the waist and held her back. Even knowing she was no match for him, she fought to get away. She was not going to stand there and watch Chad die. She might have been afraid before, but it had been nothing like what she felt now. And she intended to use every bit of that energy to get to Chad.

"It's okay, Sabina." She heard the words but was too busy fighting Ethan to let them sink in.

Then she heard a chuckle and found herself unceremoniously dumped into Chad's arms. "Chad!" she cried, wrapping her legs around him and hugging him tight as she burrowed her face against his neck.

"It was Killian," he assured her. "He's cleared the house and grounds." She heard him. She even sort of understood what he was saying. But she was too busy appreciating his warm, alive, body against hers to care. She didn't even mind the butt of his gun digging into her back as he held her.

Then she remembered his leg and immediately jerked away from him. He wasn't so keen to let her go, though, and her body slid slowly down his.

"In case there was any doubt she'd fight for you, I think we put that one to bed," Ethan said from behind her. She was no longer wrapped around Chad, but she didn't want to let him go and still had her arms looped about his waist. As his encircled hers. For one more moment, her gaze stayed glued to his face. Then she loosened her grip and turned toward the others. They were all watching her and Chad, but her attention snagged on Ethan. He was sporting a bright red mark on his cheek.

"You headbutted me, if you were wondering," Ethan said with a grin.

"Oh my god, I am so sorry," she exclaimed, slipping her hand into Chad's and taking a step closer to his cousin to examine her handiwork.

"No, you're not. You'd do it again in a heartbeat," Ethan countered. There wasn't much she could say to that, because it was true.

"Not to cut in on this little moment of joy," Killian said. "But Teague texted, and the police are five blocks away. Unless we want to be the welcome crew, I suggest we head on out."

As one, they walked toward the side fence, Kara reaching up

and checking Ethan's cheekbone as they went. When they reached the solid wall, Ethan boosted Chad up and over it in one smooth motion. Chad let out a soft curse when he landed on the other side. Sabina didn't have time to think about that, though, because in her next breath, Killian was lifting her up and over. She wasn't nearly as graceful as Chad, but she managed to shimmy over and, with him guiding her down, land on her feet. Next came Kara, whom he helped as well. Ethan and Killian came in quick succession after that.

In silence, they picked their way across a lush lawn and to the gate Ava had said they'd find in the far corner. Fifteen minutes later, she, Chad, Kara, and Ethan were climbing into the large SUV with Teague behind the wheel as Killian made his way to his own car. Without a word, Teague pulled out into traffic and headed toward the airport.

"I called the pilot, and she has everything ready," Teague said. "We'll be able to leave as soon as we arrive at the airport."

The original plan had them leaving later that evening, but Sabina was glad for the change. As the miles clicked by, the adrenaline ebbed from her system, and she was itching to get home.

"Was he after us?" Kara asked the question Sabina's mind hadn't gotten to yet. Hers was still filled with concern about Chad and his wound. She'd seen enough operatives come back to HICC from the field to know that once his adrenaline dropped, he'd be feeling a whole lot worse than he did now.

Chad shook his head. "I don't think so. There was no way Vitor could have known we were going to be there—"

"There's always a way," Sabina interjected. She didn't disagree with Chad, but she also didn't want to discount the possibility that they were being watched.

He sighed. "You're right. But he would have had to know that we located your father and that we knew Benicio was involved with Kevin Jacobs eighteen years ago. Then he would have had to track our private flight. If someone on the team talked and leaked the info to him, it's possible he knew we were coming, but I don't think that's the case. Besides, if it was about us, he could have taken us out at the hotel or anytime along the way. No, I think he was a plant."

"I agree," Ethan said. "It's more likely that he was a stooge for one of the other crime families and he was placed with Benicio to keep an eye on him."

"And he had orders to leave Benicio alone so long as he didn't start talking," Kara spoke, picking up the thread. "But when he did, even though he didn't tell us much, Vitor's orders were to eliminate him." She paused, then added, "That does make more sense."

Sabina had to agree. What was possible wasn't always what was likely, and the scenario laid out made far more sense. Inasmuch as anything that day made sense.

"Is he dead?" she asked.

Teague nodded. "Killian took him out."

"Anyone else?" Chad asked.

Teague shook his head. "It was just Vitor."

Ten minutes of silence passed when Sabina's phone vibrated with a text. She pulled the device out and read the message from Ava. Her team was tracking their phones so knew they'd all gotten out, but she'd still wanted to check in. Not wanting to get into the details of Chad's wound via text, Sabina sent a confirmation that all was well. Then, on a whim, she asked her to look into Vitor no-last-name. Ava would be able to pull a picture from somewhere and start the process. If he was employed by one of the other families, maybe it was the family who had current dealings with Jacobs. It was a long shot, but long shots sometimes paid off.

An hour later, they were taxiing down the runway and lifting off for Miami. As soon as the pilot gave the all-clear, Sabina insisted that Chad take one of the beds so that Kara could tend to him. The first thing Kara did was give him some pain meds from the well-stocked medic kit on board. Then once he was stripped out of his jeans, he lay on his stomach and submitted to her ministrations.

Sabina, not usually a big fan of blood, hovered over her sister. Thankfully, Kara didn't seem to mind. She even put her to work getting cleaning supplies together, gathering up used ones, and generally acting as her unskilled nurse.

The "graze," as Chad had called it, was more than a graze. The bullet had cut across the wide part of his calf, from left to right, leaving a gash an inch and a half at its deepest. By the time Kara was done cleaning and suturing it—with eleven stitches—Chad had succumbed to the pain medication and fallen asleep.

Sabina covered him with a blanket then rose and stood beside her sister. "He's dead," she said, knowing Kara would know to whom she referred.

"No big loss," Kara replied. "I hate to say it, but our mother did not pick the right man to share her life with."

Sabina chuckled at that. "At least she got us out of it."

"Only for eighteen years," Kara replied, her voice tinged with sadness.

"I think if you love someone, you're grateful for whatever time you're given with them," Sabina said.

Kara was silent as they watched the rise and fall of Chad's back as he breathed deeply in his peaceful slumber.

"I think you're probably right," she finally said, and Sabina knew her sister was thinking of the soldier she'd loved and lost. "Maybe when this is all over, we can finally visit Mom's grave." Uncle Mike had attended the funeral but for obvious reasons, neither of her daughters had. He'd also overridden his stepsister's wish to be cremated and her ashes spread at various archaeological sites. Sabina and Kara had been mad at the time, but now she understood why he'd made the decision he had. He'd known that someday, they'd be free, that they'd be able to reclaim their lives. And when that happened, he wanted them to have a place they could go and say goodbye to their mother in a way they hadn't been able to when she died.

"I would like that," Sabina replied, then stifled a yawn.

Kara turned and smiled at her. "We have eight more hours until we reach Miami. Why don't you get into bed with him and take a nap?"

It was only early afternoon, but the lure of curling up next to Chad was strong. She probably *would* sleep, but even if she didn't, she'd be happy tucked up beside him.

"I think I will," she said, starting to undress. She'd leave her shirt and panties on, but she didn't want to wear her jeans, socks, and bra to bed. She paused before climbing under the covers and turned to her sister again. "Thank you," she said. "I know Ethan and Killian have medic training but thank you. Seeing him stitched up wasn't something I'd like to repeat, but knowing it was you doing it helped me…to, well, not freak out entirely." She offered Kara a wry smile, and an answering one tugged on her sister's lips.

"I'd say any time, but I hope it's never again. For both your sakes." Kara leaned forward and wrapped her arms around her. Holding her sister felt as though a piece of her had come home, and it settled something deep inside.

Kara gave her one more squeeze then stepped away. With a last look at Chad's calf, she slipped from the room, shutting the door quietly behind her. Sabina didn't waste another second. Crawling over Chad to the other side of the bed, she pulled the blanket over them and tucked herself against his warm body.

When Sabina and Chad emerged from the bedroom seven hours later, she was wired. Except for about a thirty-minute stretch, when Chad had woken her in the most delicious of ways, she'd napped the entire time. She was rested, probably too much, and knew that meant she'd be awake long into the night.

"How's the leg?" Ethan asked as Chad took a seat at the table and reached for his computer.

"Leg is fine, but those pain meds put me out," he answered.

"They always have," Ethan commented, and Chad nodded. A little something Sabina hadn't known about him.

"I don't think we should go back to Mystery Lake yet," Chad said, drawing everyone's attention. "I've been thinking about it, and I think it would be best for us to go to DC for a few days. Jacobs has to be feeling the heat by now. Sabina and Kara have stepped into the spotlight, and HICC has all the evidence from the case," he said, looking at her and Kara, who were sitting beside each other on the couch. "And now, with the attack on your father, I'm guessing it's going to start getting around that Benicio might have said something that warranted his death."

"But he didn't," Sabina pointed out.

"Jacobs doesn't know that," Ethan said. "All he'll hear is that we met with him and right after, he was assassinated. He'll believe that we were intended targets as well, but that we got away. Any updates from Tess or the Zatoros?" he asked, directing the question to Chad, who'd opened his computer.

"Give me a minute," he responded.

"So we head to DC and what?" Kara asked. "Stalk him? Make him feel the pressure?"

Ethan grinned. "Not a bad idea, but no. Like C said, he'll be feeling the pressure. Knowing you're in town and under HICC protection will make him even more nervous."

"So nervous he might make a mistake?" Sabina asked, doubtfully.

It appeared Ethan agreed, because he shook his head. "He's been in this game a long time. He'll be feeling the heat, but I don't think he'll make any dumb moves like trying to flee the country or anything."

"He might, however, be quietly divesting some of his interests," Chad said, his attention on his screen.

Sabina rose from the couch and took the seat next to Chad, angling his computer so she could read over his shoulder. Sure enough, her team had documented seventeen transfers of funds and three transfers of shell companies out of Jacobs's name.

"Damn, I picked a good team, didn't I?" she said with a grin.

"And in case you're wondering, they did email this to you. They only cc'd me," Chad said, pointing to the address line. She didn't really care who received the information first, but it was a good decision to send it to more than one person.

"Won't that make him look more guilty?" Kara asked. "I know your team is good, Sabina, but if they can track it, can't the SEC as well?"

"Actually..." she started to reply, then paused to read the rest of the email. "The SEC is working on it in collaboration with my team. It appears they had a warrant but aren't as fast as we are, so they contacted Stella and Hunter and worked it out."

"What about the election commission?" Ethan asked.

"Whatever the SEC finds that's related to election funds, they'll hand over," Chad said. "Then the election commission's investigation will follow."

"It looks like this is really happening?" Kara said.

Sabina didn't want to extinguish the hope she heard in her sister's voice, but she wanted to be sure she recognized the scope of what was happening. "It looks like he will be held accountable for his financial, and potentially his election finance, misdeeds. But that doesn't mean he'll be held accountable for what he did to Mom."

Chad reached over and took her hand. As much as they didn't wish it were the case, it was. All the evidence they had tying him to the murder was still circumstantial. And while it might be enough to hold him accountable in a civil trial, the burden of proof was much higher in a criminal case and what they had wouldn't amount to a showing beyond a reasonable doubt.

"What about the DNA on the scarf?" Kara asked.

Sabina looked at Chad, who clicked back into his in-box to check for any messages from the HICC lab. "Nothing yet," he said. "That doesn't mean they won't find something, but DNA takes time."

"But even if we find DNA on the scarf that supports what Sabina and I saw all those years ago, will it be enough to convict?" Kara asked.

Chad paused then lifted a shoulder. Sabina could feel his reluctance. He didn't want to be the messenger of this particular message, but he wouldn't gloss over the truth. "It's possible, but it won't be a slam-dunk case," he answered.

"What would make it one?" Kara asked. "A slam dunk, as you say?"

"A confession," Ethan said with a rueful twist of his lips. "If you got one of those, you might not even need to go to trial."

"Then we'll get one," Kara said, startling Sabina with her vehemence.

"Um, it's not that easy," Sabina replied. "Don't get me wrong, you know that I'd like one as much as you would. But getting someone to confess to murder isn't like getting someone to confess to cheating on an exam."

Kara sent her a withering look. Tinged with love, of course, but still withering. "Don't patronize me, Sabina. I know it's not easy. If we were going to get him to confess, though, how could we do it?"

"What do you mean by 'we'?" Chad asked. His question was tentative, as if he didn't want to hear her answer.

"Well, it's safe to say that someone like Jacobs would never confess to the likes of you two," Kara said, gesturing to Chad and Ethan. "That means it would be up to me and Sabina."

Sabina glanced at Chad. His expression had gone stony, and

it wasn't because Kara had cast aspersions on his interrogation skills. No, he very much did not like the idea of her and Kara questioning Jacobs. Honestly, Sabina couldn't blame him. She wasn't too crazy about it, either. But Kara was right. *If* they were going to try to get a confession, no way would Jacobs talk to anyone other than Kara and Sabina. And he definitely wouldn't talk to a former FBI agent or naval officer.

Sabina took a minute to revisit her train of thought then she groaned.

"See, you know I'm right!" Kara exclaimed. Not only was she right, she had Sabina contemplating the possibility.

"It's not a good idea, Sabina," Chad said, his voice tight.

"I agree," Sabina said. He let out a slow breath at her statement. "But that doesn't mean we can't or shouldn't at least consider it," she added. His hand jerked in hers, but to his credit, he didn't immediately shut the possibility down.

The tense silence was interrupted by the pilot's voice filling the cabin to let them know they were starting their descent into Miami.

"Let's play this out just for fuck's sake," Ethan said. "How would you do it?"

"*We*," Chad corrected. "How would *we* do it? Kara is right in that if Jacobs agreed to talk to anybody, it would only be them. But that doesn't mean they are on their own."

Ethan nodded. "I stand corrected. How would we do it?"

"Trick him?" Kara suggested.

"He's going to be looking for something like that," Sabina said. "I think we'd need to catch him off guard, but not try to trick him."

"You mean like show up at his favorite coffee shop and ask him if he murdered our mother?" Kara asked, only somewhat sarcastically.

Beside her, Chad narrowed his eyes at Kara's tone. Sabina couldn't say for certain, but she thought Ethan might have nudged him under the table. When Chad turned to look at his cousin, Ethan gave a small shake of his head. Chad's jaw tightened, but he nodded in return and held his tongue.

"His staff would never let us near him. If he even has a favorite coffee shop," Sabina said, ignoring her sister's snark.

"Then what?" she prompted.

"I was thinking more along the lines of making an appointment to see him."

"And how is making an appointment to see him catching him off guard?" Kara asked.

This time, Chad didn't stay silent. "Because it will give him time to develop a false sense of confidence."

Kara's gaze bounced from Sabina to Chad then back again. "I don't get it."

"If you call and ask for an appointment, what do you think he's going to think?" Chad asked.

"That we're stupid?" Kara answered without hesitation. Then she stilled with the implication.

"Exactly," Chad said.

"He'll think that we're stupid and that we're trying some last-ditch effort to get him to talk because we have nothing else on him," Kara continued.

"And he'll get more confident that he has the situation under control," Sabina said.

"But won't he?" Kara asked.

"We'll go double wired," Sabina said.

"What?" Ethan and Kara asked at the same time.

"They'll wear an obvious wire and a secondary wire," Chad jumped in. "They'll ask him straight up if he killed Emer. When he doesn't answer, they'll cry and wring their hands, then finally pull off one of the wires."

"And when he thinks we're not wired at all—that we only want to hear the truth for ourselves—he *might* be willing to talk," Sabina said.

"I'm sure it will do his ego good to see you both crying and appearing to crumble at his power," Ethan commented, bobbing his head as he appeared to mull over the tentative plan.

"Uh, how is that different from my suggestion to trick him?" Kara pointed out.

Sabina rolled her eyes. "Fine, it's a trick. But when we pull the first wire off and appear to give up the chance to prosecute him, it will also catch him off guard."

Kara narrowed her gaze at Sabina but opted not to argue the point. It was only relevant insomuch as it was a sibling quarrel that she wanted to win. Sabina could have been annoyed at getting sidetracked. The truth was, though, she and her sister hadn't been able to have a sibling quarrel in a long time, and it felt kind of good. Petty, sure. But good.

"I still don't like it," Chad said.

Ethan chuckled, and Kara rolled her eyes in much the same way Sabina had moments earlier. "Color me surprised," Kara said.

"I'm shocked as well," Ethan chimed in.

"Fuck off. Both of you," Chad said, glaring at them. Which only made them laugh. Sabina bit back her own laugh and leaned over and kissed his cheek.

"I know you want to protect me, so thank you for that. But aside from my role in the plan, what do you think of it?" she asked.

"Potential plan," he muttered. "Stella and Hunter would have to sign off on it. They aren't going to like putting their best cyber lead in front of a man like Jacobs any more than they are going to want to throw a civilian into the mix," he said with a nod to Kara. Sabina refrained from pointing out that HICC wasn't a military organization so technically, they were all civilians.

"What do you think of the *potential* plan?" Kara asked.

The wheels of the plane touched down smoothly on the

Miami runway, and the cabin filled with the sounds of the engines reversing as they slowed to a taxi. Finally, when it quieted enough to speak again, Chad sighed. "Jacobs might not take the meeting. And even if he takes the meeting, he might not talk. Not even when he believes you're not wired."

"But?" Sabina pressed.

His shoulders dropped as he met her gaze. "I don't like it, but I don't have anything better to offer."

CHAPTER TWENTY-FIVE

THEY LANDED in DC six hours after touching down in Miami, and Chad was still feeling uneasy. They'd called Stella and Hunter from the plane, laid out the rough workings of the plan, and gotten sign-off. If they could get Jacobs to agree to meet in a public place, Chad didn't think he'd do anything too dangerous. But that didn't mean he might not try something either before or after the meeting. He'd already shown himself as a man who didn't shy away from violence. And the way Jacobs had taunted Sabina with the postcard made Chad's skin crawl. As if he enjoyed tormenting her.

And yet here he sat, awake in the early hours of the morning, staring out at the DC skyline contemplating the plan. HICC had booked a hotel for them not far from the Capitol building, and they'd only stumbled in an hour ago. Sabina was sound asleep in bed, and he assumed Kara, Ethan, and the others were as well. But not him.

Kevin Jacobs was a guilty man. Guilty of murder. Guilty of funding and benefiting from criminal activity. And probably guilty of everything the SEC and the election commission were investigating him for. Chad understood Sabina and Kara's desire to bring him to justice. What he couldn't wrap his head around, though, was their willingness to put themselves in his crosshairs to try to get a confession that Chad had some serious doubts they'd get. Jacobs might be an arrogant prick, but he wasn't stupid.

A man darted down the street below the hotel, and it sparked an errant idea. Was it worth sneaking out now, catching Jacobs off guard, and doing *his* best to get a confession out of him? Jacobs might be smart, and he might be a little twisted, but Chad had learned a thing or two in the army and FBI that he was quite certain the pampered senator wouldn't be able to withstand.

"Come to bed."

Chad turned to see Sabina walking toward him, her silhouette lit by the ambient light coming in through the window. She'd been a part of his life—a part of him—for so long, and yet everything between them was new. And not.

She wrapped her arms around him from behind and rested her cheek against his back. He'd always hoped they'd end up here. Not quite in this scenario, but here, like this, together. It felt more right than anything had in a long time. They were *good* together. She made him laugh, made him think, and made him a better person. He hoped he did the same for her.

"Are you out here planning how you might torture Jacobs into confessing?" she asked. He could feel her smile against his back.

He grunted. "Maybe."

"You know confessions gained through torture aren't generally admissible." Now she was laughing at him. Not outright, but he heard it in her voice.

"I'm not sure why you think I'd care," he countered, fighting his own smile. It was kind of a ridiculous conversation. He wasn't *actually* going to torture Jacobs. But he did like the idea of it.

"You care, because I care," she said. "I know he might never get convicted of the murder, but I do want him to admit to it. It's not all that logical. What good is a confession if it doesn't lead to him paying for his crime? But it's how I feel. He's manipulated so much over the past decades, and I guess this is Kara's and my way of saying *enough*."

He turned and wrapped his arms around her, resting his cheek on the top of her head. "I know. I get it."

"But you don't like it."

He shifted, a little uncomfortable. He wanted to support her—he did support her—but he couldn't lie. "It doesn't matter if I like it or not. I love you, and this is what you want. You deserve this opportunity."

She drew back and looked up at him, her eyes sparkling in the dim light. "You love me?"

He studied her face, not understanding the confusion he heard in her voice. Not confusion, exactly. But maybe uncertainty?

"Of course I love you. I have for a long time," he said. "Even when I wasn't sure I wanted to, I couldn't stop myself. That's why I kept my distance from you. It hurt to only get bits and pieces of you. It was like a constant reminder that I wasn't good enough. Keeping my distance was the only way I could feel like I wasn't torturing myself. But once I fell in love, there was no way I was falling out. Not even on those rare occasions when I wished I would."

She blinked, and his heart stuttered. He'd made her cry. "Please don't cry," he said, tipping her head up and brushing kisses along her damp cheeks.

"That's the first time you've said it," she said, squeezing her arms around him and burrowing her face against his chest.

He ran his hands through her hair as he stared into the dark room. "Is it?"

She nodded against him. "I've said it. But you haven't. Not until just now."

A wave of emotion crashed through him, leaving him almost unable to stand. She *had* told him she loved him. More than once. And he'd not said anything in return. Once she'd put herself out there, she'd held nothing back. Her courage humbled him, and he pulled her tight against his body.

"I'm sorry," he said.

She shook her head. "Don't be. I wouldn't want you to say that until you meant it."

He touched his lips to the crown of her head. "I mean it, every word. And I will always mean it." Of that he was certain. All relationships had ups and downs—he'd seen it with his aunts and uncles and even with his grandparents. But he'd also seen enough of love to know that what he felt was true and lasting.

"Say it again, please?" she asked, her voice muffled against his chest.

He smiled. "I love you."

She sniffed. "Good, now can you take me to bed, make me lose my mind for a little while? Then in the morning, we can plan exactly how we're going to bring Kevin Jacobs to his knees?"

Her train of thought had him chuckling. But despite his misgivings about confronting Jacobs, her plan for the next few hours sounded pretty good.

"Happily," he said. Then he swept her up and carried her to bed, where he proceeded to make her lose her mind for more than just a little while.

"Tomorrow at nine a.m.," Tess Jackson said. Chad, Sabina, Ethan, Kara, Stella, and Hunter were at the conference table with her. Ava, Leo, and Collin were on speakerphone. Teague and Killian had gone off with some of the DC-based operatives to hit the gym and, presumably, learn more about the company.

"That easily?" Ava asked, raising a question Chad had been pondering.

"Not easily," Tess responded. "But I convinced his lawyer it would be good for Jacobs's optics. If he didn't have anything to do with Emer Houseman's death, how would it look to have him refuse a meeting with her daughters? Especially when they've been in hiding, fearing for their lives, for the past eighteen years. After all, he was a man who cared for their mother, right?"

Chad smiled at that. Tess might have laid it on a little thick, but apparently, it worked. Although Chad suspected it only worked with the lawyer because the lawyer didn't know his client was guilty.

"Have we scheduled a press conference announcing that you'll be pushing to reopen the case of Emer's murder?" Hunter asked.

Tess inclined her head. "At three today."

That gave them three hours to grab lunch and prepare. As if reading his mind, Stella spoke. "Lunch is being delivered in thirty minutes. We'll eat here while we plan."

"What kind of wires are you going to wear?" Leo asked.

"The basic run-of-the-mill wire for the obvious one," Sabina answered. "But the secondary one is a small prototype we've been developing."

"Prototype?" Collin and Ava asked at the same time. Only the excitement in their voices was the exact opposite of what was going through Chad's mind.

"You're going to test a prototype on something so important?" he asked.

Sabina started to respond, but Hunter cut her off. "We've tested it. Rigorously. It will be fine tomorrow."

Chad fixed his gaze on his boss. To his annoyance, Hunter grinned. "Relax, Warwick, it's fine. It's only still considered a prototype because we haven't been able to produce enough of them to use in the field. That's in the works, and the operatives will start using the devices in about four months."

"Everyone will be able to listen in as well," Sabina said. That gave Chad some assurance. He, Ethan, and Tess would be nearby in case the shit hit the fan. Something he didn't want to think about too much, but knew he'd obsess over until they walked safely away from the meeting. But it would be good to have his HICC colleagues on both coasts listening in as well.

"And where is the meeting?" Leo asked.

"His office in the Capitol building," Tess answered. "Neither the House nor the Senate is in session tomorrow, so there will be fewer people around. It was a compromise I made with his attorney, but one that also works in our favor. With less activity, there won't be as many distractions for Jacobs."

"Sabina, we should start testing the wires," Ava suggested.

Sabina looked at him, and he nodded his agreement.

"Kara and I will head down to the equipment lab in a few minutes, and we'll call you from there," she replied.

"Sounds good, boss. Talk soon," Ava said, then hung up.

"With Sabina and Kara testing the equipment, what's your plan?" Hunter asked him.

"Ava got a picture of Vitor from some camera feed. I'm going to see if I can chase down who he worked for," Chad answered. He was better at tracking people physically than electronically, but he wasn't a slouch, either.

"And you, Ethan?" Stella asked.

"We studied some of the big crime families in the police academy. I'm sure the information we had wasn't as in-depth as what HICC has access to. I thought I'd start looking into a few of those," he answered.

"That's a big pond to wade into," Hunter pointed out.

Ethan nodded. "But Sabina found her father by tracing his movements. I thought I'd trace Jacobs's movements in the past few years and see if there are any crossovers with the key players of the families. It's possible that everything was done over the phone or computer. A lot of those people are old-school, though, and I'd bet at some point, they met in person. It *is* a big pond, but if I don't drop a line in, I definitely won't catch anything." He paused and looked at his new bosses. "Unless there's something else you think I should be doing? If so, I'm happy to do that," he said, looking at Stella and Hunter before glancing at Chad.

"No," Stella said. "That sounds like a good plan. As you say, it might net us nothing or it might net us something, and we won't know unless we try. If we can tie Jacobs to a specific family, it will make it easier to track his illicit activities."

Beside him, Ethan let out a quiet breath, and Chad fought back a smile. His cousin might appear the epitome of calm and confident, but it was nice to know he was human.

"That's it then, folks. Sabina, Kara, let us know if you need anything," Stella said, rising from her seat. "Lunch should be in the kitchen in a few minutes if you want to grab something before you head down to the equipment lab. Chad, you can show Ethan around."

"I'm going back to my office to prepare a few more talking points," Tess said. "I'll expect you all there around half-past two," she said, sweeping her gaze over the sisters as well as him and Ethan.

A few minutes later, the room was empty except for him and his cousin. It was hard to believe that this thing was almost over. In some ways, this hunt had only started a few days ago—a quick op as ops went. But to Chad's way of thinking, it had been going on for years. Years that Kara and Sabina had to hide who they really were. Years that they lived with questions that had no answers. Years that they kept their distance from everyone they cared about, including each other.

All of that was almost over.

"Let's get ready for the final curtain," Ethan said.

Chad grinned. "You took the words right out of my mouth."

CHAPTER TWENTY-SIX

IT WAS five o'clock by the time they walked out of Tess's law firm. The press conference had run for forty-five minutes, but they'd spent some time going over the plan for the next day. Tess, Ethan, and Chad would accompany the women to Jacobs's office, although knowing it would stifle Jacobs, none would participate in the meeting. Chad hated the idea of not being in the room with Sabina, but he wanted her to have this moment. He wanted her to have this chance to confront the man who had changed the course of her life.

He held Sabina's hand tight in his as they made their way to the parking garage where the HICC vehicle they'd borrowed was parked. The K Street Corridor was starting to let out, and men and women in suits were beginning to fill the streets.

Ethan and Kara had opted to walk back to the hotel and planned to stop somewhere along the way for a drink. Chad suspected a drink would turn into dinner, and it was up in the air whether they'd invite him and Sabina to join.

"Will you miss this?" he asked, watching several people in suits bustle down the street. Sabina had lived in DC for longer than he had. She didn't live near K Street, but it was still her city. Once they eliminated the threat from Jacobs, she'd be able to come back. He didn't think she'd want to. Not anymore. But a small part of him still couldn't quite believe that everything he'd wanted was within his grasp. Nor was he certain that what he wanted was what she wanted. She wanted him, he didn't doubt that. But staying in Mystery Lake, maybe marriage, maybe kids? They hadn't really talked about that and, despite their two-year buildup to getting to where they were, it felt too soon to be discussing such things.

Beside him, Sabina shook her head, her strawberry blond hair swinging with the movement. "I loved my time in DC because I loved my work, and being in a city let me hide. But growing up, well, Lexington isn't as big as you'd think. I was part of the community there. I knew families and businesses and which Little League team won the championship. I miss that."

His hand squeezed hers. "And you think Mystery Lake will be enough for you?"

She paused then drew him to the edge of the sidewalk close to a building. Surprising him, she then dropped his hand and wrapped her arms around him, pulling him close. He didn't hesitate to respond, and his arms came around her and he hugged her tight.

After a beat, she pulled back enough to look him in the eye, but their bodies were still touching. "Mystery Lake is everything I ever wanted and never thought I'd have. Provided that you're part of it. I get to have work I love, a man I love, a community I can be a part of, and a large extended family. Assuming the Warwicks take me in like I think they will. On top of all that, my sister is only five hours away and I will get to see her whenever, and as often as, I want."

He stared down into her blue-green eyes and though it was too soon—or perhaps not soon enough—images of them together at his house danced through his head. Quiet nights with the two of them, family nights with the extended Warwick clan, barbecues, birthday parties, and, maybe someday, kids running in the yard. There might even be a dog or two.

"It's everything I ever wanted and didn't think I'd ever have, too," he said. "Don't think for a second that I ever plan to not be a part of that with you."

"Good," she said, then smiled and tipped her head up. Obligingly, he lowered his and kissed her.

He was starting to think it would be a good thing if Ethan and Kara didn't call when a throat cleared to his left. With an annoyed huff, Chad drew back. Really, it wasn't as if they were playing tonsil hockey on the street, and so what if they were? He made a face at Sabina, making her smile, then turned to the source of the disruption.

Instinct had him reacting and in a flash, he was standing between Sabina and the person who'd interrupted them. In front of him was not a man annoyed at two adults sharing a kiss on the street. No, this man had come looking for them. For *her*.

Chad scraped his gaze over the intruder, taking in every detail and wishing he had enough time to reach for his weapon.

"Yes?" Chad snapped. Though dressed in a suit, the man was not someone he'd underestimate. He was skilled enough in hand-to-hand and, if needed, he could at least hold him off long enough for Sabina to get away. But judging by the cold steel in his eyes and the dark energy radiating from his lean six-foot-five body, Chad wasn't sure it was a fight he'd ultimately win. The only good news Chad could see was that he didn't seem to have a weapon either.

"Sabina O'Malley," he replied, his voice heavily accented. Much as Vitor's had been.

Sabina was smart enough to recognize the uncertainty of the situation and remained silent.

"You are?" Chad asked. The man's attention shifted from

where he'd been trying to get a glimpse of Sabina tucked behind him, to Chad.

Chad held his gaze with a steely one of his own. The longer they stayed in this weird sort of standoff, the more populated the streets would get. Not that the adage "safety in numbers" was always true, but it was definitely safer than if they met alone in an alley.

"I mean you no harm," the man finally said, holding his hands up in a placating gesture.

"You are?" Chad repeated.

"My name is Larry Salinsky. I'm a lawyer for certain aspects of Benicio Silva's estate." Neither statement was one Chad had expected. The name didn't fit with the man. Nor had it occurred to Chad that Benicio would have estate matters that involved the daughters whom, until the day before, he hadn't seen for more than twenty years.

However, there was a more pressing question. "How did you find her?" He did *not* like the idea of Sabina and Kara coming onto the radar of *anyone* in Benicio's life.

Larry inclined his head in Chad's direction, but when he spoke, he looked at Sabina. "Five years ago, Benicio hired our firm to locate you and your sister. It took a year, but we eventually tracked you to DC and your sister to Los Angeles, to the extent she remained in the United States. After Benicio's untimely death, it was little more than to track private flights out of São Paulo. It was not a surprise to see you come home to the headquarters of HICC."

Sabina had loosened her grip on the back of his jacket, and reluctantly, he shifted to the side so she could step out from behind him.

"My father tracked us?" she asked. Larry nodded. "Why would he do that?"

"He wished for you to have this." Larry started to reach for something in the inside pocket of his jacket. Chad's body went on high alert, and he rocked onto the balls of his feet. He held an arm out, ready to push Sabina out of the way if needed.

Noting the shift in Chad, Larry nodded then raised his hands in front of him. "You are right to be cautious," he said. "There is an envelope in my coat pocket. May I retrieve it?"

"Slowly," Chad said. To his credit, the lawyer didn't seem to mind being treated with such suspicion. With one hand, he plucked the side of his jacket back far enough that Chad could see he was unarmed. When Chad nodded, Larry reached inside and pulled a standard business-size envelope from the pocket of the silk lining.

Then dropping the jacket back into place, he handed the envelope over. "For you and your sister," he said.

"What is it?" Sabina asked, taking it and turning it over in her hand. It had the name of what Chad assumed was Larry's law firm in the upper left corner but was otherwise blank.

Larry shook his head. "I do not know. He paid us to hold on to it with the proviso that it be delivered to either you or your sister within forty-eight hours of his death if, and only if, he did not die of natural causes."

"A deathbed confession?" Sabina mulled out loud.

Chad thought it likely, but of what? The reason he'd left them all those years ago? His activities with the crime family? Something else?

"Is there anything else?" Chad asked, still not entirely trusting Larry.

Again, the lawyer shook his head. "There are other matters of the estate, of course. But those are not so timely and will take some months to sort out. You and your sister are his sole heirs, of course," he said. Until those words, Sabina's attention had remained focused on the letter.

Her gaze lifted. "His estate?"

"A substantial one," Larry answered.

"All built on ill-gotten gains. No, thank you," Sabina said.

"And I know my sister would feel the same. We don't want anything to do with it."

"Unfortunately, that is not the way it works. You could try to disclaim the inheritance, but that would take years."

"And if they don't?" Chad asked.

"As I said, it will be settled in months."

Sabina started to say something, but Chad took her hand and squeezed. "I know why you want to disclaim it," he said. "But you should talk to Kara first. It might be worth taking it then turning around and giving it away. If your goal is to have as little to do with him as possible, that might be a faster way to get him out of your life for good."

Her eyes held steady on his then she nodded. "Yes, I'll talk to Kara tonight. Do you have a card?" she asked, turning to Larry. The lawyer glanced at Chad, who nodded, then he reached into his pocket and pulled one out.

"Please contact us at your convenience and let us know how you wish to proceed. It goes without saying that certain aspects of the distribution will need your involvement. If you wish to close the proceedings quickly, I'd contact us as soon as possible."

Sabina took the card and nodded. Larry's gaze flickered between the two of them one more time then he nodded and strode off. Chad and Sabina remained where they were. Larry ducked down into the Metro station, but Chad continued to wait. Before they resumed their walk to the car, he wanted to be sure the lawyer wasn't going to come back up and follow them. Finally, when he was comfortable that Larry wasn't going to reappear, he urged Sabina back into the flow of pedestrian traffic.

"What do you think it is?" she asked, one hand still firmly in his, but the other holding the envelope. She inspected it as they walked, although what she thought the blank envelope would tell her that she hadn't already deduced, he didn't know.

"Could be any number of things," he said, leading her to the stairwell of the parking garage. "Want to call your sister and we can pick them up on our way to the hotel? I know they wanted to stop for a drink, but I'm going to guess that"—he gestured to the envelope—"changes things."

Without another word, she tucked the envelope in her bag and dug out her phone. Fifteen minutes later, they pulled over and Ethan and Kara climbed in. A few minutes after that, they dropped the car with the valet and headed up to his and Sabina's room.

Sabina held the envelope out to Kara. "Open it."

Kara gave a quick shake of her head and stepped back. "No, *you* open it."

Chad glanced at Ethan and they both grinned. It wasn't a laughing matter, but he liked these glimpses of what they must have been like as kids.

Sabina rolled her eyes then carefully unsealed the envelope. Inside was a single sheet of paper folded into three. Holding it between two fingers, she took a seat at the desk. Kara sank into a chair next to her, then he and Ethan moved behind them.

Cautiously, as though it might bite her, Sabina unfolded it. And they all stared.

"What the hell is that?" Ethan asked. Kara glanced up then returned her attention to the paper. In the middle of the sheet, perfectly centered, was a series of numbers, twelve in total.

"Phone number with a country code?" Kara suggested.

"Serial number for something?" Chad offered.

"Could be an IP address," Sabina said.

"It could be any of a thousand things," Ethan countered. Chad shot his cousin a look. If he wasn't going to be helpful, he needed to keep his mouth shut. To his credit, Ethan mumbled an apology.

"Why don't you enter it into your favorite search engine and see what pops up," Chad suggested.

Sabina set the paper down and reached for her bag. A few

minutes later, the search engine on her laptop brought up three possibilities. One was a phone number, one was a tracking number for a package, and the last was a unique identifier from India.

Sabina entered the tracking number only to discover that the associated package had been delivered to a residential location in Ontario four months earlier. To be thorough, she searched the ownership records of the home. The house had been in the same family for over a hundred years. The current occupants were a young couple and their three kids. Not likely to be people Benicio would have known.

The phone number was an elderly woman in Romania. The unique identifier was a college student in Mumbai.

"That's—" Ethan cut off whatever he was going to say and shifted gears. "Why don't I place an order for room service while you dig in a little more," he offered. Everyone nodded and provided their orders. When he stepped away to make the call, Chad turned back to Sabina.

"Would an IP address show up in the search? If not, why don't you try that," he said. She was ahead of him and was already typing it in. It wasn't as straightforward as a URL, but this was second nature to Sabina, and her fingers flew over the keyboard.

He sucked in a breath when a page popped up. Had it not been for the text above the password box he would have thought it was another bust. But the words "Nala and Bela" told him otherwise.

Kara exhaled in surprise, but Sabina went utterly still. "Well, now we know what the numbers are. It would have been nice if he'd given us a hint about the password," she said, not hiding her irritation.

"Is it possible he set up a virus or something to infect your computer if you manage to get in?" Chad asked. He didn't think Benicio would go to the trouble of getting information to his estranged daughters only to cause damage, but he had to ask.

"It's possible, but I don't think so. And even if he did, he'd never get through my security. There are only a handful of people who could, and I assure you, they are all friends. They would have told me had they been approached to do something like that."

As usual, her logic was sound. And practical. "What do you think you'll find when you get through?" he asked.

Sabina hadn't taken her eyes off the screen, but she shook her head. "I don't know. Kara?"

"Don't look at me," she replied. "By giving us the IP address, he meant this for you. If he'd meant it for me, it would have been something medical."

Chad wasn't so sure about that. "If he needed a safe place to store files, electronically is the most obvious and that *does* fall into Sabina's wheelhouse. But my guess is the password will be something you'll know, Kara. Or something you'll both know."

Ethan rejoined them but remained silent as the women stared at the screen. "How many tries do you think we'll get?" Kara asked.

"You think it will disappear if you have too many wrong entries?" Ethan asked.

Sabina nodded. "If he went to the trouble to protect the information, he wouldn't then make it vulnerable by allowing endless password attempts."

"I know you don't know the answer, but what would be your guess as to how many tries you get?" Chad asked.

Sabina bobbed her head from side to side. "Five to seven would make sense. But given that he provided this to us without any clues whatsoever, I'd guess it's more like ten to twelve. Although I wouldn't stake my life on that."

Chad held his tongue, as did Ethan. This was something the sisters would need to figure out. It was probably something from their past, or perhaps something they shared. It wouldn't be anything Chad or Ethan could help with.

"Try Gomer," Kara said.

"Good one," Sabina replied. "Our dog growing up," she added, no doubt for his and Ethan's benefit. After typing the words in, she hit the Enter button. *Incorrect Password* popped up in tiny red letters.

"What about Kentucky Lake?" Sabina said.

"Can't hurt to try. It's really the only spot we vacationed at more than once," Kara said.

Sabina typed it in, but the results were the same. The sisters let out identical breaths.

"We don't know how many tries you have left," Ethan said. "Is it worth coming up with a list using a pen and paper and then evaluating them before trying again?"

Sabina looked at her sister, and they seemed to communicate something without speaking. After a beat, Sabina shut the computer down and pushed it to the center of the round table. Chad turned and grabbed a pad of paper and pen and handed them to her. Once Sabina and Kara had their heads together, Chad gestured to Ethan, and they stepped away.

"That was a good suggestion," he said. "I don't think they have too much of a shared history with their dad. Making the list will take some of the pressure off. They'll be able to brainstorm without constraints. Once they're done, I think they should sleep on it, though."

Ethan studied him. "You mean not make any more attempts tonight?" Chad nodded. "And you want my help in distracting—or convincing—Kara."

Chad inclined his head. "I know you two got thrown together because of Sabina and me. But I don't think I'm out of line in thinking that there's more to spending time with her than being the HICC operative assigned to the role."

Ethan crossed his arms and his gaze drifted to the two

women, heads still together at the table. Sabina had torn a piece of paper off and pulled another pen out from somewhere, presumably her bag, and they were each making lists.

Ethan inclined his head but didn't outright confirm Chad's presumption. "We could get them drunk."

Chad barked out a laugh. The two women turned and stared at them. "It's nothing," he assured them. Sabina's gaze lingered, but after a beat, she went back to her list.

"Actually, that's not a bad idea," Chad said. "I don't want them so drunk they won't want to get out of bed in the morning. But enough that they're distracted tonight and then feel enough under the weather tomorrow that they forget to be nervous? Not a bad idea."

Ethan's eyebrow went up. "Seriously?"

Chad shrugged. "We can't force them to drink, but if we make it available, it might not be a bad thing."

Ethan's steady green gaze held his then he shook his head. "That's kind of fucked up, but I can see where you're coming from. I ordered a bottle of wine with dinner, but there's a liquor store around the corner. What's their drink of choice?"

"I don't know about Kara, but Sabina's is tequila," Chad answered without missing a beat. He may not have spent many nights drinking with her, but he'd heard her talking with colleagues often enough to know what liquor she favored.

"High or low end?"

"High," Chad answered. "We don't want them feeling like a cat crawled into their mouths overnight and died."

"Memories?" Ethan said with a smirk.

"Ones I'm not revisiting. Not even for Sabina."

Ethan laughed. "Liar. You'd totally revisit those for Sabina."

Chad shrugged then grinned. "Probably."

Ethan smiled then sobered. "I know you don't need anyone's approvals. But I like her. I like you with her. She doesn't *need* you, but she likes you. She wants you, too. Which is always good."

Chad's gaze drifted to the woman in question. Ethan was right. There was something heady in knowing that she didn't need him, but that she wanted him. And in more ways than one, it *was* good to be wanted rather than needed.

"It is good," he agreed. "It's new. Ish. And in a lot of ways, it feels that way. In so many, though, it doesn't."

Ethan nodded, understanding what Chad said and what he hadn't. What was between him and Sabina wasn't something that he could easily describe. But it was more real than anything he'd ever experienced.

"Well, I'll pop around the corner. Dinner should be here by the time I'm back," Ethan said before slipping out of the room.

His timing was spot-on, and twenty minutes later, they all sat around the table eating and drinking. As the night went on, neither he nor Ethan imbibed much. They were, however, conscientious about keeping Sabina's and Kara's glasses filled. The drinks were strong enough to keep them on the tipsy side, but not so strong as to push them over the line to being drunk.

As Chad had hoped, the sisters relaxed and, for a little while, shed the weight of the situation. Another benefit of the tequila, one he hadn't predicted, was that it loosened both women's tongues, and memories. Over the course of the night, they added several more options to their growing list of potential passwords. But the side effect Chad enjoyed the most was when the sisters started telling stories and the hours filled with "remember whens."

It could have been bittersweet, but neither woman seemed interested in letting it become that. There were tears of laughter rather than sorrow as they recalled their friends, the pranks they'd played on each other, and one particularly cringe-worthy trip with their mother to Lalibela, the archaeological site for which Sabina was named. Apparently, naming your US-born daughter after a town in Ethiopia was endlessly entertaining to those who lived there.

At the end of the night, Ethan walked Kara to her room while Chad made sure Sabina drank a big glass of water before they sank into bed. He expected her to curl up beside him and fall fast asleep—it was late, it had been a long few days, and she'd had a fair bit to drink.

He wasn't at all disappointed when he learned that verbal inhibitions weren't the only things that fell to the wayside when tequila was involved.

CHAPTER TWENTY-SEVEN

"YOU DID THAT ON PURPOSE, didn't you?" Sabina said, the dull ache in her head mildly subdued by Chad's fingers brushing through her hair, massaging her scalp.

She was draped over him, a leg thrown over his, an arm across his stomach, and her head on his chest. His chuckle rumbled under her cheek. "Maybe," he replied.

She raised her head and glared at him, though in truth, she wasn't all that upset. The minor hangover was a small price to pay for the laughs she'd shared with Kara last night. And the list of potential passwords they'd come up with once their minds loosened up.

Chad's phone rang, and she closed her eyes against the sound as he reached for it.

"Yeah...We'll be ready...Yeah...See you then," he said, then hung up. "Ethan and Kara are going for a walk and grabbing some breakfast. They'll be back in an hour, and we can walk to the Capitol together," he relayed.

She groaned then forced herself to roll out of bed. When her feet hit the ground, she paused, sitting on the edge. The dull ache ratcheted up to a deep throb then subsided into something distracting but not unbearable.

"There's Advil in the bathroom. Why don't I make some coffee while you shower?" Chad suggested. "Or would you prefer tea?"

"Coffee, please," she managed to mutter before pushing to her feet and dragging herself to the shower. When she emerged, wrapped in a towel, he handed her a cup. Taking a sip, it was sweetened exactly how she liked it—just enough to take the bitter edge off. It was an odd thing to notice—especially given everything else on her mind. But the fact that he'd given her the drink just as she liked it struck her. They'd been circling around each other for two years and keeping the other at arm's length, but he'd always shown her how much he paid attention.

She paused, halfway to her suitcase. Chad was already going through his, picking out clothes for the day. "You are a remarkable man, Chad Warwick," she said.

He paused and looked up. "Uh, thank you?"

The mixture of pleasure and confusion on his face was adorable, though she doubted he'd like it if she mentioned it.

She smiled. "I just wanted you to know. And I love you," she added, because it was true. It had always been true. And now that she *could* say it, she planned to say it a lot.

He grabbed a stack of clothes in one hand and walked to her. Slipping a hand into her wet hair, he tipped her head up and kissed her. When he pulled back, he rested his forehead against hers. "I love you, too. Now let's go get this thing with Jacobs over with so we can hit that beach vacation."

"Sounds good." She went up on tiptoe and kissed him again, a quick brush of her lips against his. "And why is it always a beach vacation?" she asked, as he stepped away.

"What do you mean?" he called over his shoulder as he walked to the bathroom.

"In romance novels, the couples always talk about beach vacations. Why not the Alps or Banff, or the Amazon?"

"Easy," he said, toothbrush in hand. "Beach vacations imply someplace warm. Someplace warm implies bathing suits and not a lot of clothing. But if you want to go somewhere cold, I can arrange that, too."

She considered that answer as she started to dress. Oddly, in all her years of reading romances, she'd not thought of that. She'd always assumed that beach vacations meant relaxation. And, after going through whatever the couple went through, relaxation was usually well-earned.

She pulled a sweater on and when her head emerged, she saw Chad watching her. "Do you want to go somewhere else? Somewhere we can hike or ski?" he asked.

Her eyes swept over his body. Dressed only in boxers, he was a sight to see. She grinned. "No, a beach vacation will work out just fine."

Sabina glanced at Kara as they sat in the lobby of Senator Kevin Jacobs's office. She was sure the look on Kara's face was mirrored on her own—a mix of determination, anticipation, and unease. Most people didn't meet their loved one's killer, let alone have a conversation with them. What they were doing was the right thing. But as the seconds ticked by on the clock, and memories of that night pressed to the forefront of her mind, it occurred to her that perhaps they hadn't thought it through as much as they should have.

"It will be okay," Kara said, reaching over and taking her hand. Sabina wasn't sure which of them the words were meant to reassure.

As if sensing her growing discomfort, Chad settled his hand

at the base of her neck and started to massage the muscles there. On his other side, Tess looked at her watch.

A young man stepped out of an office, drawing their attention. He couldn't have been more than a year or two out of college, but he had the arrogant look of someone who thought that working with a powerful man made him special. He was the type of person who casually slipped into every conversation the fact that he worked for Senator Jacobs.

"The senator will see you now," he intoned.

She flickered her gaze to Chad, who pulled her toward him and dropped a kiss on her temple before releasing her. Gripping her sister's hand, they rose together. Shoulder to shoulder, she and Kara would face the man who killed their mother.

They followed the young man, who hadn't bothered to introduce himself, through two rooms before he paused at a door and knocked. "Come in," a voice called. A voice Sabina hadn't heard in years. One she recognized well from her nightmares.

In a flash, anger replaced her unease. Confronting the man wasn't going to be easy, she didn't kid herself about that. But anger—at what he'd done, at what he'd gotten away with—flooded her body. And as the door swung open, she dropped her sister's hand. They were still side by side, but she wanted Kevin Jacobs's first glimpse of them to be two women standing on their own. Not two sisters clinging to each other.

Kevin Jacobs's head was down, and he was writing something in a notebook when they stepped in. Without a word, the young man moved out of the room and shut the door.

Sabina recognized a power play when she saw one. Kara did, too, if the slight tip of her lips meant what Sabina thought it did. He would make them wait until he was good and ready.

They had two options, either wait or draw his attention. Sabina considered the second; it was likely what he was expecting—it would give him a chance to further ignore them.

But then she decided that turning the tables would be much more fun. Gesturing with her head to a pair of chairs in front of Jacobs's desk, she and Kara each took a seat. Then they sat back, pulled out their phones, and, for her part, started scrolling through the news. He might be trying to assert his dominance by making them wait, but that game only worked if they submitted. Which they had no intention of doing.

A full four minutes passed before he finally looked up. Four minutes in which Sabina checked her horoscope, scanned the headlines, and scoped out flights from San Francisco to Cabo.

"Bela, Nala, it's good to see you. I'm sorry about your mother," he said.

Sabina shared a look with her sister. Kara slipped her phone back into her purse, but Sabina kept hold of hers.

"Thank you," Sabina said. "We're sorry you killed her, too."

He blinked at her open salvo but didn't otherwise react. At least not for a few seconds. When he did, his response was what they expected.

"I don't know what you're talking about. I'm sure by now you've read the police reports your lawyer picked up a few days ago. I wasn't there. A vagrant killed her."

"You mean the reports on the investigation led by your brother?" Kara asked. Then she frowned. "Tess is going to have those overturned or overruled or whatever it is they call it in the justice system. You know, it being a conflict of interest and everything."

Again, Jacobs blinked, and Sabina wondered how he'd survived in politics so long with such an obvious tell. She'd been in his presence for six minutes and she could anticipate a lie by his facial expression.

"She's welcome to try, but you'll find the evidence supports my story," Jacobs said. Which was a stupid thing to say. Of course the evidence supported his story. His brother had made sure of that. But Sabina let it pass.

Out of the corner of her eye, Sabina saw Kara glance over. They were off script now. Way off script. But the idea of crying and pleading to Jacobs, as planned, was one she could no longer stomach. She didn't know how the conversation would unfold, but she was going to go with her gut. She and Kara had lived a lifetime in the shadows. They'd learned a thing or two about human nature. And Jacobs was not as strong as he thought.

"We had a little chat with our father a few days ago," Sabina said. That comment resulted in a double blink.

"What does that have to do with anything?" he asked, glancing at his watch.

"You're not curious about the twelve million dollars he stole from you all those years ago?" Kara asked. "I mean, I know it was a while ago and you've more than made up for the loss. Still, if I were you, the loose end would bug me."

Jacobs swallowed then shook his head. "I don't know what you're talking about."

"Oh, but you do know, Kevvy," Sabina said, employing the nickname Benicio had used once. Kara stifled a laugh with a cough. "It's why you killed our mother. You wanted her to tell you where he was, and she wouldn't. Do the words 'I'm sorry I had to do that, but if you'd given me what I asked for, I wouldn't have had to,' ring a bell?"

The blinking was back. But then he seemed to regroup. Taking a deep breath, he leaned back in his chair. "This is harassment, ladies," he said. "If you want to talk about what happened all those years ago, if you want to *accuse* me of something, then talk to my lawyer. Or the police."

Kara bobbed her head. "I assure you, it's on the agenda."

Jacobs's gaze lingered on Kara. "You'd like me to believe that, wouldn't you? But you have nothing. There *is* nothing," he insisted. Then he sighed and tossed the pen he'd been holding onto the desktop. "Look, I'm sure you came in here thinking you could get some sort of confession out of me.

That maybe you'd get some answers about what happened that night. And I understand you wanting those. Like pieces of a puzzle coming together, you want to fit everything into place and have a nice complete picture. Something to make sense of what happened. It's what every family member of a victim of violence wants. But I'm not the person to get that from. All I can tell you is the same thing you read in the reports. I'm sorry you don't believe the vagrant killed her, but I have nothing else to say."

Sabina had to give him credit. He *did* sound sincere. She was weighing her next move when his words started to niggle at something in her brain—in her memory. Sifting through them, she searched for what had subconsciously caught her attention.

She jerked and her spine hit the back of the chair when it clicked into place. She looked to Kara, who seemed to have made the same connection.

"Mad Libs," they said at the same time.

"What?" Kevin said, but neither sister paid him any attention.

"Try it," Kara urged, pointing to the phone Sabina still held in her hand. Unlocking the device, she pulled up the browser and keyed in the IP address from the note Benicio had left. When the password box popped out, she typed in "MadLibs." The name of the game was actually two words, and it was possible they needed to be separated with a dash or an underscore, but she tried the one-word version first.

And two seconds later, they were in.

"All one word, and it worked," she said. Kara could see that it had, but she wanted her colleagues at HICC who were listening in to know, too.

Kara leaned over. "What is it?"

"What the hell is going on?" Jacobs asked.

Sabina and Kara ignored him as they scanned the list of files that filled the small screen. "Open the video," Kara said, pointing to one. Sabina complied, and when the image of Jacobs filled the screen, she knew they'd hit pay dirt.

The video was taken from behind a man sitting at a desk. They could see little of him except his receding hair and the shiny top of his head. But pacing the room in front of him was Kevin Jacobs.

"I never should have let my people let you in," the man at the desk muttered. He had a slight accent that Sabina would place as either from New York or northern New Jersey.

"I want to know where my money is," Jacobs said, pacing back and forth. "You know where it is. I want it back."

The man chuckled. "Why would I do that, Kevvy?"

"Because your fucking accountant stole twelve million dollars from me, Lou," Kevin all but spat. "I want my fucking money back."

"We don't always get what we want in life," Lou said. To Sabina, he sounded like he was enjoying the conversation. She couldn't be certain, but she'd guess he was the head of the crime family who'd allowed her father to steal the money to teach Jacobs a lesson.

"Just tell me where your accountant is," Jacobs said, stopping in front of the desk.

Lou tipped his head to the side. "I'm not going to do that. If you want him, you find him."

"I tried. His bitch of an ex-wife wouldn't tell me."

"She can't tell you something she doesn't know," Lou said. Sabina would parse that statement later, but assumed it meant that Lou knew her father had cut all ties to Emer and his daughters.

Kevin laughed. "She can't tell me anything anymore. I killed her."

The air in Sabina's lungs froze. For the first time since opening the video, she remembered Jacobs was in the room with them.

She lifted her gaze to him even as the video continued to play.

"Killing ain't good, Kevvy. It's harder to hide your tracks than you think." Her eyes remained locked on Jacobs as Lou's voice broadcast from the device. The senator had risen from his seat and was now leaning over his desk in much the same way he had in the video. Cold calculation simmered in his eyes. He looked so menacing that she found herself trying to remember if members of Congress were allowed to have guns in the Capitol building.

"It's a lot easier than you think when your brother is the chief of police," Kevin responded in the video. With evidence of George Jacobs's corruption, Sabina considered how busy the Kentucky justice system was going to be cleaning up his mess. But that thought was short-lived when Jacobs shouted.

"Give me that!" He lunged across the desk. It was too wide for him to make it, but even so, Sabina and Kara leaped up and away. The files were stored in the cloud, and it wouldn't matter if he managed to get hold of her phone, but she still pulled it protectively against her chest.

"Take this as a friendly warning, Kevvy." With the device pressed against her sweater, Lou's voice was muffled. "You try to play me again, it will be more than just your money missing."

In front of her, Jacobs reached for a drawer. Instinctively Sabina knew what he was planning. "I wouldn't," she said.

"Why not?" Jacobs responded, retrieving a small revolver.

Sabina glanced at Kara, who was frowning but didn't look particularly worried.

"Well, because it's a cliché, to start with," Sabina said. Jacobs frowned. "And we have two ex-military men sitting in your lobby waiting for a reason to come in here."

"We already have that reason," Chad said as he threw the door open. It hit the wall hard enough that the floor rumbled under Sabina's feet.

"I told them they couldn't come in..." The young man who'd ushered them in earlier faltered at the door then stopped. His gaze swung wildly around the room before fixating on the gun in his boss's hand. He'd followed Chad, Ethan, and Tess in and now inched behind them even farther.

But it wasn't only Chad, Ethan, and Tess who'd arrived.

"Gina?" Sabina and Kara said at the same time.

Gina grinned but stayed to the side and a little behind Chad and Ethan. "You didn't think I'd miss this moment after all these years, did you?"

Sabina wasn't sure how to respond to that and instead looked to Chad.

"You going to put that down, Senator?" Chad asked, his attention focused on the man.

Jacobs's gaze darted among the people now crowded into his office. When it landed on her, and the phone she still held clutched to her chest, his hand twitched.

"I wouldn't do that if I were you, Jacobs," Chad said. His voice was calm but had a steel to it she hadn't heard before. It was enough to give Jacobs pause.

"I wouldn't do that, either," Ethan said when Jacobs's hand made a slight turn, shifting the muzzle toward his own torso, though not directly at it.

"Sabina, Kara, come over here, please," Chad said when Jacobs stilled. She and her sister scuttled across the room. Kara went to Gina's side, but Sabina stopped next to Chad.

"What now?" Jacobs asked. His voice didn't carry a tone of surrender, but more one of curiosity.

"Now we let the lawyers sort it out," Chad said. A small, bloodthirsty part of her wanted to tell Jacobs to rot in hell. She wanted to tell him that she'd be releasing the video to the public so everyone could see what a murdering, corrupt jackass he was. Okay, fine, it was a not-so-small part of her. But before she could open her mouth, Chad reached over and held his hand out for her. Taking his in hers, she stepped closer. Close enough to feel the heat of his body against hers, like a warm, comforting blanket.

Sanity returned, and she bit her tongue. She was still bloodthirsty, but she needed to put her trust in Tess and the other ongoing investigations. She didn't want to say or do anything that might give away any of the leverage they now had or compromise any evidence.

"Or I could shoot at least one of you," Jacobs said. Behind Sabina, his assistant gasped.

Chad inclined his head. "You could. But in front of all these witnesses, it would be hard to defend that course of action."

"We both know I don't have much of a defense on any of it," Jacobs said. "What's one more thing?"

"Maybe you do, maybe you don't. But since you don't know what any of the charges might be, is that a chance you want to take?" Chad asked, appealing to the man's desire for power. If Jacobs willingly walked out the door and turned himself in, he'd have a fighting chance at holding on to some of it. Even if that power was only an illusion.

A noise from behind her drew Sabina's attention. Not wanting to be surprised by anyone sneaking up on them, she jerked around. Then she let out a long, slow breath. She had no idea how the Capitol police had arrived so quickly, but she was glad to see them.

Sensing their arrival, Chad stepped to the side as four uniformed officers walked in followed by two plainclothes ones. The taller of the two not in uniform, a woman who looked to be in her forties with short hair and the build of a basketball player, continued straight to Kevin Jacobs.

"Kevin Jacobs, we're arresting you for the murder of Emer Houseman..."

Sabina leaned into Chad as the detective finished Mirandizing the senator.

It was over.

After eighteen years, her mother's killer was going to be brought to justice. After eighteen years, she and her sister could come out and into the light. After eighteen years, she could once again have the things in life she'd taken for granted as a young woman. Things she'd given up on entirely after that night—real friends, community, a family. A life without the fear of loving someone.

Chad turned and wrapped his arms around her. Vaguely, she was aware of the police leading the senator out, but she didn't bother to watch. She'd done what she wanted to do, and the rest was in someone else's hands. Well, not entirely. HICC would always be willing to assist if the ongoing investigations asked it of them. And she *was* curious about the rest of the files her father had sent.

But that could wait. For a while.

Because now she wanted to go home. Home to Mystery Lake, which was only hours away from her sister. Home with Chad.

"Can we go home now?" she asked, her face still buried in Chad's chest.

"Please?" Kara added. Sabina turned her head and opened one eye. Gina and Ethan each had an arm around her sister. Their eyes met and, in that moment, a shared memory floated to the surface. Slowly, Sabina grinned.

"We sound like we did that time Mom took us to Sudan. Do you remember that?" she asked.

Kara smiled back. It was a little watery, but genuine. "Remember? Of course I remember. It was the worst trip she took us on. Eating MREs, living in the desert, dust *everywhere*."

"Really *everywhere*," Sabina added, remembering how uncomfortable it had been when she and her sister had realized all the places the fine dirt managed to lodge itself.

Kara snorted. "You remember the mac and cheese MRE?"

"Oh my god, don't make me gag. I'm still a little hungover," she said, nudging Chad in the ribs. He chuckled and released her enough that she could move.

"Or the bike?" Kara asked, leading them out of the office.

"The one without the seat?!" Sabina said, laughing. "And that time we found the snake sleeping in its frame?"

"Don't even talk to me about that snake. It nearly killed me," Kara said.

"It wasn't venomous. I told you that!" Sabina said, as they walked through the halls of the Capitol and toward the future.

"Bullshit. It so was. You've never been able to identify snakes," Kara said. "Chad, if you ever go camping with her, you need to know that. She's *terrible* at wildlife identification."

Chad, Ethan, and Gina all laughed, happy to let her and her sister reminisce. With each step they took away from their past and toward their new lives, the weight on her shoulders lifted more and more.

And by the time they touched down in Mystery Lake, she'd never felt lighter, stronger, or more hopeful in her life. The road she'd taken to get there might not have been the most efficient or easiest. But none of that mattered. Not anymore. She was finally on a journey she'd chosen. One that filled her with awe and wonder. No one knew what tomorrow, or even the next second, might bring. Whatever it was, though, she wasn't ever going to face it alone again.

EPILOGUE

"Let's go!" Chad said, yanking the comforter from Sabina's body. He paused to admire the sight. She'd more or less been living with him since they'd returned from DC before Halloween, but she'd only officially moved in with him six weeks ago on New Year's Day. Gina was now living in her old apartment and settling into life in Mystery Lake. The wily intelligence agent had even struck up a friendship with his grandad. One that included whiskey nights and brutal games of Battleship.

"Ugh. It's freezing out there," she muttered. "Where are you dragging me?" She tried to grab the comforter, but he lifted it out of her reach. She rolled onto her back, giving him a particularly spectacular view, and glared at him.

He grinned. "You won't want to miss it. I promise."

She studied him and by the softening of her expression, he knew he wasn't hiding his excitement very well.

"But you're not going to tell me?"

He shook his head.

"Not even a clue?"

He started to shake his head again then paused. "When we

get there, I want you to remember that I never lied to you," he said.

"But you misled me?"

"More like omitted to mention something," he clarified. Her gaze was steady, and he loved that she didn't assume the worst, as many would. Their relationship was solid. Better than he'd ever imagined or hoped. That she felt the same was written in her every expression.

"Well, I guess with that vague but intriguing statement, I best get my tush out of bed," she said, swinging her legs over the side.

"And dress in warm clothes. I'll get us some coffee to go," he said over his shoulder as he left.

Fifteen minutes later, she joined him in the kitchen, dressed in layers as he'd suggested. Another five minutes after that, they were in his car on the way to the large expanse of land on the northeast side of the lake owned by the Warwicks. The resort his cousin Brad ran occupied most of it, but the family had left a couple hundred acres untouched.

Parking along a dirt road, he grabbed his hat, gloves, scarf, and jacket and made sure Sabina did the same. When they were bundled up, he slid from the car and slung the backpack he'd packed early that morning when she'd still been asleep over his shoulder. Then he grabbed the snowshoes.

"Ready to go?" he asked, his feet crunching in the snow as he joined her.

Her eyes flickered to the snowshoes, and the spark of curiosity in them brightened. Always game for a new experience, she said nothing as she reached for her pair. Within minutes, they were traversing through the woods across virgin powder, accompanied only by the occasional sound of a winter bird or snow falling from branches.

"It's beautiful here," Sabina said from a few feet behind him.

"It is. We used to come here as kids all the time. It was our favorite place to play in the winter."

"You'd come here to this forest or 'here' to wherever you're taking me?"

"Both," he said, looking over his shoulder as he answered.

There were questions in her eyes, but she fell silent as they hiked their way through the evergreens. Every now and then, they'd catch a glimpse of the lake, the edges coated in ice and untouched.

After thirty minutes, they reached their destination. Or at least the entrance to it. He paused and smiled as he snapped his snowshoes off and gestured for her to do the same.

"We're here. Well, mostly here," he said.

She looked at the pile of rocks he was leaning against. Then she turned to see if there was a view or anything that would make this spot special.

"You're not looking in the right place," he said. Her arched eyebrow told him he better get to the point. "Come here," he said, holding out a hand. She reached for him, and he guided her to his side then pointed. She leaned forward and squinted.

"Is that a cave?" she asked.

"A special cave," he said, turning sideways and starting to inch his way through the gap in the boulders.

"*Special* like it's filled with crystals or *special* like it's a den for serial killers?"

He shot her a look. As if he'd bring her to a place like that.

She held up her hands in supplication. "Fine, not a serial killer den. It's just that the word *special* can have so many meanings. It's kind of special that way."

He huffed. "Are you going to follow me or not?"

"Of course I'm going to follow you. I have to bug you about it, though, since you're being so mysterious..."

He'd inched forward a few more feet, but he turned to look at her when her voice trailed off.

Her eyes were wide and shimmered with excitement. "Oh my god, it's the lake, isn't it? I don't mean the lake lake," she said waving in the direction of the big lake. "But *the* lake. The *mystery* lake." She didn't wait for him to respond before shimmying into the gap behind him. "Go, you slowpoke," she said, poking him in the side and drawing a laugh from him.

He did his best to maneuver quickly through the last eight feet before finally arriving at the opening of the cave. Pulling a flashlight from the backpack, he flicked it on and shone it down the long corridor.

"What is this?" she asked, taking his free hand in hers and moving up close behind him.

"Originally, it was a mine shaft. Now it's an entrance to a place that very few people know about." She held her tongue as they walked a little over a hundred yards into the earth. When they reached the gate that his family had installed twenty years ago, he pulled out a key.

"Is there a reason this is locked?" she asked. Mystery Lake was a safe town and while it had its fair share of petty crimes, violent crime was almost unheard of, and it wasn't unusual for people to leave their doors unlocked.

"Just precautionary. We didn't want anyone wandering down here by accident." He gestured for her to precede him then locked the gate behind them. Continuing on, they followed through a slight bend of the shaft.

"It's getting warmer in here," Sabina said. "Is that because we're underground?"

Instead of answering with words, he pulled her around the final turn and flicked on the battery-operated lights Brad had installed several years ago. Then he stopped to watch her reaction. And he was glad he did.

Her mouth dropped open, and she gaped at the sight in front of her. The shaft opened up to form a circular cavern about twenty feet tall and fifty feet in diameter. Large rocks lined the lower edges, and ferns and mosses grew along the walls, draping down the sides and dripping with moisture.

And right in the middle of it all was an almost perfectly round lake.

"It's a natural hot spring," Chad said, keeping his voice gentle so as not to echo and disrupt the moment.

She whipped her head around. "Can we swim?"

He grinned and set the backpack down. "I have bathing suits —which are optional—and towels. I also packed us a lunch so we can stay for a while."

He hadn't even finished his sentence before she started undressing. He watched in appreciation as she removed each layer of clothing. When she was naked, she turned to him with a huge grin and launched herself at him. He caught her with a kiss, but she was gone from his arms before it could go any further. Then, with a hum of appreciation, she lowered herself into the heated water.

"Oh, this is amazing," she said, moving away from the edge until it was deep enough to swim. Then pushing herself off the last rock, she started stroking across the small lake. In reality, it was more of a pond, but "Mystery Pond" didn't sound as good as "Mystery Lake."

He watched her frolic in the water, her lithe body gliding through it. It was hard to believe that four months ago, he'd been forcing himself to accept that she'd never be a part of his life in the way he wanted. But all that was well and truly behind them now.

The day before, Jacobs had signed a plea agreement. He'd pled guilty to the murder of Emer Houseman and to several financial and elections crimes. In exchange for a reduced sentence for those misdeeds, he'd given up a lot of names. Names of the police officers who'd helped hide his crime and names of the crime syndicate he'd been working with for the past several years. He'd even blabbed about the connection between the syndicate and Sweet River, the security firm he'd sent to kill Sabina.

Chad and Sabina were pleased with the outcome. Even with his reduced sentence, Jacobs would still be behind bars for at least forty years. That is, if he lived that long. The men he'd ratted out might have something to say about that, and that possibility didn't upset Chad—or Sabina—at all.

In fact, they'd had a little celebration that night. First with the family, then just the two of them. Now he hoped they'd have even more to celebrate.

Shucking his own clothes, he went to his favorite rock and dived in, rising out of the water beside a laughing Sabina.

"I'm guessing you know the spots that are okay to dive from and that I don't need to worry about you breaking your neck?" she asked, wrapping her arms around his shoulders and her legs around his waist as he treaded water.

"You do not," he said. "I've been coming here since before I could walk. There isn't a rock or ledge I don't know well."

She raised her head and looked around. She seemed happy to stay attached to him, and he was happy to have her there. "Is this really Mystery Lake?" she asked.

He nodded.

"You knew about it all along?"

"This is where I'm skating a thin line, and I know it," he said. She dropped her gaze to him, and the look in her eye suggested he explain. "You always either asked if I knew where the name came from or why the town was named Mystery Lake. I don't actually know why they picked the name or where it originally came from. Honestly, it always seemed a little crazy that the founders picked it, since they also went to all this trouble to keep it a secret."

"You don't know where it came from or why it was picked, but you did know there was an actual lake?"

He made a face and nodded. Then hoping to distract her, he kicked his feet up and backstroked to a rock. Sliding to a sitting position on the slick surface, he gripped her waist in a gentle hold, her skin soft and silky under his palms. Water swirled around their chests and bodies, but his weight kept them anchored.

"Who knows about this place?" she asked, her eyes once again drawn to the grotto-like beauty of it.

"That's a bit of a weird story," he started. She glanced down at him, but her gaze drifted away again. "I'm sure you know from your research that there are four founding families of Mystery Lake. The Warwicks are one. Oscar and Angelica's family is another," he said, naming the owner of the Dirty Boom and his daughter. "You met a few members of the other two families at Gramps's Halloween party, but you might not remember them."

She dropped her eyes to his, and his heart started to thud. He had her complete attention. It was what he wanted. But even so, his heart rate kicked up.

"At some point after they discovered this lake, all four families agreed that it would be something they'd keep among themselves," he said. "I don't know why they made that decision, but it's been that way since the mid-eighteen hundreds."

"Only members of the four founding families know about it?" she asked.

He nodded. "There are about seventy-five of us alive," he continued. "But there are only four keys to the gate. One for each family."

She made a face. "That's kind of elitist, isn't it?"

"In a way, yes. But the lake is on Warwick land. Land that's been in the family since before the gold rush days. We wouldn't have to let *anyone* use it if we didn't want to."

She seemed to consider this then nodded. "I have to believe that over the years, someone has leaked the secret. Unless you take a blood oath or something?" she teased.

"If anyone has leaked the secret, we haven't discovered it. And now there's no way anyone other than one of the family members can get in. They might try, but they wouldn't succeed."

"But to keep it a secret..."

"It's tradition among the families. Once you know about it and are old enough to talk about it, it's stressed that it isn't something you *should* talk about. Every one of us knows that only members of the four families are allowed to use it."

Her blue-green eyes held his. "I'm not family, though, Chad," she said, her voice tinged with curiosity and confusion.

This was it. The moment he'd been planning for three weeks. He took a deep breath. "But will you be? Will you be my family, Sabina? Will you let me be yours?"

She blinked and damned if he didn't see moisture gathering in the corners of her eyes.

"Are you asking me to marry you, Chad Warwick?"

He swallowed and nodded. "I am," he said. "I love you. I want you to be my family, and I want to be yours. I want my family to be yours, and I want Kara to think of me as her brother. And maybe, if we decide to, and we're lucky, we can start a family of our own."

A single tear tracked down her already damp cheek. "Truly?"

He brushed the tear aside and frowned, a little confused by her question. "You don't doubt me, do you? I mean, I know I'm not always the most demonstrative of people and I know—"

"Yes, please," she said, cutting him off.

He hesitated. "Yes?"

She nodded. "Yes. Please be my family, Chad Warwick. And please let me be yours."

The air whooshed out of his lungs, and he slid his fingers into her wet hair, pulling her in for a long, deep kiss. When he drew back, the happiness flowing through his body made him almost giddy. "We're getting married," he said, grinning.

She grinned back. "Yes, we are. But I have to say, there's no ring."

He chuckled. "You don't wear jewelry, but I'll get you one if you want. I did, however, get you something to mark the occasion. Something I hope you'll like." Arching his back, he reached behind him and pulled out a piece of paper from the backpack. Careful to keep it away from the water, he held it out to her.

"You didn't have to get me anything, you know. I was teasing about the ring. Having you, being with you, is enough. It's more than I ever thought I'd have and all I want."

He smiled. "That's nice, and I'm glad, but I still got you something. Want to see?"

She eyed the paper, then releasing his neck, she snatched it out of his hands with a laugh. "Of course I do."

He held her as she leaned far enough away from him that she could unfold the document and read it. Her eyes tracked the print and when she reached the bottom, they jerked up to meet his. Then they dropped down again before resettling on him.

"You endowed a scholarship for me?"

He nodded, hoping he'd done good but unable to tell from the tone of her voice or the expression on her face. "The Emer Houseman Scholarship for Computer Science. I was thinking it could be something available to the kids in town. But it's up to you if you want to structure it differently."

Her eyes went to the paper again. "Chad, this is…it's a huge sum of money."

Now she sounded perplexed, but pleased. He hoped he was reading her right and that she was, in fact, pleased.

"Warwick coffers are pretty deep," he cut her off. "Not *billionaire* deep, but deep. We also have a few connections that come in handy on occasion. And to put your mind at ease, the family took a vote on this, and everyone supports it. The twins even want to help when it comes time to select the student or students."

She dropped her gaze to the paper again, and this time two

tears escaped. Reaching for the document, he gently removed it from her hands, folded it up, and returned it to the backpack.

"Did I do okay?" he asked. "Or do you want a ring, too?"

She stared at him for a beat then threw her arms around his neck and squeezed him. Tight. Almost to the point he couldn't breathe.

"I love you," she said, her voice muffled against his neck. "So, so much. Not because you gave me that scholarship program—which is perfect and better than any ring that I'd never wear. Although, once we're married, I would like us both to wear bands." He agreed but didn't have a chance to say so because she rushed on. "I love you because you *thought* of this. I love you because you noticed that I don't wear jewelry and that I love working with the Hedy Experience students. And because you remembered that I'd been looking for a way to honor my mother and everything she taught me—including to love learning. I love you because you see me. And you hear me, even when I'm not talking. I only hope that I'm half as good at it as you."

She was. She was more than half as good. She was better. But he held back from saying so because when he said it, he wanted her to know it was from the heart, and not something simply reciprocated. Instead, he kissed her, then made love to her, then fed her. They spent the day laughing and talking and laughing some more, marveling at what they'd found. At what they'd pulled from their dark pasts.

And with each laugh, each smile, each quiet conversation, they promised each other that while their future might hold many things, they would never hide in the shadows again.

THE END

Thank you for reading *Defenseless*!

. . .

With a missing person, a fatal accident that might not have been an accident, and a stalker that's seemingly come back from the dead, architect Josh Warwick and movie mogul Sofia Parisi find themselves delving into far more than just their new relationship.

Book 2 in the Mystery Lake Series, *Exposed*, will be coming soon.

In the meantime, did you know that we first meet Chad and Sabina in book 2 of my **Doctors Club Series**?

Meet Cyn, Six, Devil, and Nora—four women with brains, bank accounts, and a huge, shared secret. They don't need anyone to save them. In fact, they've been trained since the age of twelve to handle any trouble that comes their way. But when their handler suddenly decides they each require a backup, the women discover that wanting help, and the men who provide it, is an entirely different question. Especially when danger comes knocking on their doors.

Read on for a sneak peek of book 1, CYN!

EXTRACT OF

CYN

#1 Doctors Club Series

A dead body, a dubious admirer, and an explosive conclusion is just another day at the office for Cyn Steele.

A body in the driveway of her seaside mansion is the last thing Dr. Cyn Steele expected to find when she returned home from a trip abroad. It's not the first time she's seen a dead man, it's not even the fiftieth. But it is the first time one has been left as a calling card. Is it a warning or a message? She doesn't know, but the sexy new chief of police is more than interested in helping her figure it out.

When Joe Harris accepted the position as chief of police for the small town of Cos Cob, he was expecting jaywalking tickets and the occasional fender bender. He was not expecting body dumps, Somali pirates, or the whirlwind that is Cyn Steele. And while he'd rather forgo the first two, spending time with Cyn is definitely no hardship.

Unraveling the message of the body takes a dark twist when Cyn and Joe discover the young man's ties to some rather unsavory people—people intent on wreaking havoc on the city of Boston just as it celebrates a beloved national holiday. It's a race against time that takes them from Massachusetts to East Africa and back again. Failure is not an option, even if it costs them their lives.

EXCERPT

Early December
Massachusetts

Cyn Steele swung her feet up onto her desk and leaned back in her chair. Juggling two Rubik's Cubes in her hands, she eyed her target on the other side of the room as the speakerphone beside her droned on—and on and on. Well, to be precise, the *phone* didn't drone, but her uncle did.

"And that's why it's impossible for you to resign, Hyacinth," he said, using her dreaded—and no longer legal—first name as he brought his argument to a close. "You were well aware of the obligations you'd be held to when you agreed to your extension. It wouldn't do to renege."

Uncle Franklin wasn't just her uncle, he also happened to be her handler for the work she did with MI6. And because she was his favorite niece, most of the time he was putty in her hands. Most of the time.

"I told you, Uncle, my heart isn't in it anymore," she said, her attention on the small trampoline hanging on the wall twenty feet away. If she threw the Rubik's Cube with the right amount of force, and hit it at the right angle, it would bounce off the target and come back to her.

"Be that as it may, my dear, you made a commitment," her uncle replied.

She threw one of the Cubes and hit dead center, but then it bounced far off to her right. She grimaced. It must have rotated in flight and hit the trampoline on a corner.

"*Commitment,* Uncle? We're usually much further into a conversation before that word comes out."

"Hyacinth."

"Cyn," she corrected.

"Hyacinth."

She let out a dramatic sigh and eyed the second Cube in her hand. Three years ago, her friend Violetta Salvitto—better known as Six—had given her the pair for Christmas. Cyn had yet to solve the puzzle, but she was certain that whenever she got close, her friends—Six, Devil, and Nora—rearranged the stickers. When solving it became a Sisyphean task, she'd changed the game and hung the trampoline. It was much more fun to throw things anyway.

"You would have me do the work even though my heart isn't in it?" she asked. The question was ridiculous. They were British. The heart had nothing to do with it. The *Great Families of England* always did their part to protect queen (or king) and country. The Steele family had counted themselves among that blessed lot since the days of Henry VIII.

Franklin let out his own sigh. "Just don't make any reckless decisions," he said. "We both know that's a bit of a challenge for you, but it's all I ask. Go home for the holidays. Spend Christmas and Boxing Day at Greyswood with your family," he said, referring to the ancestral estate. "If you still have the same opinion when you return, we will revisit this conversation."

"Aren't you joining the family this year?" she asked. Franklin was her father's youngest brother. He had no partner or children of his own and was, more often than not, taken into the fold of his eldest brother's family.

"I am not. I have some concerns I need to attend to down here."

Franklin lived in Florida of all places. Although why that always struck Cyn as odd, she didn't know. Maybe because it was hard to see her uncle in a pair of shorts and a T-shirt. Not that she ever *had* seen him in that attire, but she assumed he must don it every now and then.

"I've already booked my ticket," she said. "I leave December twentieth and will return January fifth."

"You're missing New Year's with your little club?" Franklin asked with dramatic—though sincere—shock. She, Six, Devil, and Nora had been thick as thieves since their first day of boarding school in Switzerland at the age of twelve. When Cyn had earned her PhD many years ago, Six had named their group the Doctors Club—Devil with her MD, Nora with her DVM, and Six with her JD rounded out the titles. Now they just referred to themselves as *the club* since it sounded less pretentious, if only a little bit.

But Franklin, being a long-standing member of the board of trustees of the unique boarding school she and her friends had attended, had known them as long as she had, and adored them almost as much as she did. And given that the women were all now thirty-eight, her friends were like daughters to him. Not to mention the fact that, per some secret agreement she wasn't entirely privy to, he also served as the handler for the three of them since they were all foreign intelligence agents for their own governments. Yes, the school they'd attended had been special; who knew a school designed to develop future women intelligence officers operated in a secluded valley in the Alps?

"You are more than welcome to come ring the New Year in and shake that booty with the family, Uncle," Cyn said. "I know you get your freak on after a drink or two." She grinned as she spoke, imagining the look on his face.

"Hyacinth," he said on a breath. "To be sure, I don't have the slightest clue what that even means."

"Sure you don't, Franky," she said, infusing her voice with a Boston accent. She'd been living in the Boston area for twenty years and had an ear for languages. She had the accent down pat and, more to the point, knew it annoyed her uncle.

He sighed again. "Why must you try to bait me? It hasn't worked in all these years. I would think you'd simply accept that it never will."

To be fair, he had a point. *Nothing* riled Uncle Franklin. But still, a girl could dream. "You always praise me for my tenacity, don't eat your words now," she said.

"Hyacinth."

He might not get riled, but he did have a line she didn't wish to cross, and she was close to it now. She set the second Rubik's Cube on her desk and leaned closer to the phone. "I'll think about my future as an agent while I'm stuffing myself full of rich food and drinking far too much."

It wasn't a promise, but since she had zero plans to think about work while on holiday, she had intentionally avoided that word. There was no question her uncle would pick up on her deliberate answer, but she was thirty-eight, shouldn't her life be her own? Sure, when she was younger, the excitement of getting called into a job fed the adrenaline junky in her. But now? She wasn't exactly interested in settling down, but she was getting tired of her government telling her when to jump and how high. Besides, she liked her job—her day job. Teaching archeology at the local university was fun. Some people might bemoan the younger generation, but Cyn found them endlessly entertaining in so many ways.

"You'll regret the drinking part," Franklin said.

A little tension left Cyn's shoulders at Franklin's willingness to drop the subject and she let out a low laugh. "I always do, Franklin. I always do."

CHAPTER ONE

Cyn flicked her wipers on again, clearing a few flakes of the icy January snow from her windshield. She loved almost everything that came with living in Cos Cob, the waterfront community located a little over an hour north of Boston where she and her friends resided. But she did not like it when the snow fell at the precise rate of being just enough to make it difficult to see through her windshield yet not enough that using the wipers had any impact other than to create streaks across the window. Thankfully, she was only a few minutes from home and would soon be out of the elements.

As she turned onto the coastal highway that would lead her to her home five miles up the way, her phone rang. Glancing at the screen on her dash, she smiled when she saw Nora's name.

"Hello, darling," Cyn said, after connecting the call.

"Are you home yet?" Nora asked without preamble. Cyn might have been gone for sixteen days, but there was no need for pleasantries—she and the rest of the club talked nearly every day.

"Five miles," Cyn answered. Nora was the worrier of the group—well, that wasn't exactly right. She was the caretaker of their lot, and she'd wanted to know when Cyn had landed, when she was on her way home, and when she actually arrived.

"Glad you missed the storm this morning," Nora said, obviously deciding to keep Cyn company for the last leg of her journey. "I'm surprised Logan wasn't backed up with delays."

A nasty winter storm had blown into town the night before and blown right on out by ten that morning, leaving eighteen inches of snow in its wake.

"We landed on time, but it took a bit for a gate to open for us," Cyn answered. "It's good to be home."

"Your visit was pleasant?"

Cyn smiled at Nora's question. Raised in Jordan, Nora was the only daughter of a very prominent businessman who had dealings in about every precious commodity there was. Cyn knew for a fact that when Nora visited her family, it was, indeed, "pleasant."

"We ate and drank too much. Daisy pretty much lap-danced her husband every night—they are trying to get pregnant, and she's taken to encouraging his amorous activities to the extremes," Cyn answered, referring to her older sister. "And Ash was convinced I'd made up all the sudoku and crossword puzzles because he was incapable of completing any of them," she said about her brother.

"Did you?"

Cyn grinned in the dark of her car. "Maybe once or twice. He threw me to the wolves with Mum and Dad, so I had to get back at him somehow."

"I take it they are still waiting with bated breath for you to settle down?"

"They are," Cyn confirmed. "You'd think with Daisy married and getting ready to propagate the Steele line that they'd be happy with that. But, of course, they aren't."

"I would think Ash, as the heir, would be the one they'd harass."

Cyn's mind went to thoughts of her brother as she navigated the curvy road north. Occasionally, she caught glimpses of the Atlantic Ocean to her right, but the woods were thick in this part of the state and the vast stretch of water only peeked through in teasing intervals. As to her brother, Ash might be the heir to the family title and the only one to actually be able to carry on the name of Steele—according to the rules of primogeniture—but her parents had long ago given up on him. And with Daisy married, they had, with Ash's encouragement, turned their sights on her—their youngest.

"Yes, well, we know how logical my parents are." They weren't. Not in the least. Alistair and Aurora Steele might be a marquess and marchioness, and might run a not-insignificant business empire, but at home, you'd think they'd stepped right out of a hippie commune. Which was another factor that made their apparent obsession with grandkids so weird. They'd always encouraged their three offspring to live their lives, stand on their own, and be their own people. Yada yada yada. Falling into the cliché role of desperate wannabe grandparents had thrown Cyn, Daisy, and Ash for a loop. Then again, maybe that had been her parents' plan.

"All quiet here?" Cyn asked as she stopped at the stop sign at the intersection of Cos Cob's Main Street and the state highway. To her left, Main Street stretched eight blocks before turning back into a rural road that wound its way west. But those eight blocks were lined with colonial style buildings, housing everything from restaurants and art galleries to the more practical merchants like a pharmacy, food co-op, and bookstore. While her chosen hometown was always charming, with a recent snowfall and Christmas lights still hanging, this time of year was especially delightful.

"Isn't it always?" Nora answered.

Cyn eased forward through the intersection. The roads had been cleared from the earlier snowstorm, but during her first winter in the Northeast, she'd learned about that sneaky little bastard otherwise known as black ice. "You almost sound a little put out by that, Nora-luv. Everything all right?" Cyn replied as she continued north. Her house was the last house within the city limits and was another mile up the road.

Nora hesitated, then sighed. "Everything's fine. I found a litter of abandoned puppies this morning and you know how I get about stuff like that."

Cyn's heart clenched. Nora attracted strays and helpless creatures like other people attracted mosquitos in the summer, and while Cyn had a hard time understanding how someone could dump a litter of puppies, let alone do it in the dead of winter, Nora would feel it ten times more. "Are they going to…?" She didn't want to finish her sentence, but the chances of a helpless litter of puppies surviving unprotected in this weather wasn't high.

"I have them in the warmer. They seem hardy and hopefully they'll make it, but it's too early to tell." That was Nora in a nutshell—she had a bigger heart than the other three of them combined yet still had an innate ability to stay grounded and pragmatic.

"Well, I'll come by to see them. Maybe Auntie Cyn will bring a toy or two."

"There are nine of them. You better bring more than two. Devil and Six brought cozy fleece blankets and extra bottles, so you have some competition in the *favorite auntie* category, too."

"They beat me there on purpose, didn't they?" As she spoke, she passed the turnoff to Six's house and Cyn shot a glare in her direction for good measure.

"Maybe. Probably." Nora chuckled. "You're always the first one to show up with treats for my strays. I guess the only way they could beat you was when you were out of the country."

Cyn gave a dramatic sigh. "I suppose I'll have to live with that. I will come by tomorrow, though, and we'll have a good chin-wag."

"Are you home now?" Nora asked.

"Nearly to my drive. Thanks for keeping me company, luv."

"Anytime. See you tomorrow and sleep well."

"I always do," Cyn replied, then disconnected the call. Less than a minute later, her driveway came into view. The state highway curved to the west, and drivers often mistook her driveway for a road because it continued straight. For that reason, she'd put a bright yellow gate fifteen feet up her drive and had her groundswoman keep an area cleared for people to turn around if they accidentally went straight instead of turning with the highway.

As her wheels transitioned from the pitted and uneven state-maintained road to her recently paved one, the cabin of her car quieted. Hitting a button on her Bluetooth display, the flimsy gate opened. It wouldn't really keep anyone out, and it wasn't meant to—*that* gate was farther up her drive—but it was, generally speaking, enough to let the accidental tourist know that they'd made a wrong turn.

Pulling through as the arm opened, she paused on the other side. Watching in the rearview mirror until the gate latched behind her, she then eased her foot off the brake and continued forward. Her jet-lagged body clock was telling her it wasn't quite yet nine, so she wasn't too tired. That didn't stop her from dreaming of her bed and its big, fluffy down comforter, though, as she drove toward the main gate of her property. The one that was actually intended to keep people out. Or, she supposed, in.

She rounded a bend, and the tops of the wrought-iron structure came into view, bringing with it a familiar feeling of belonging. Her house might be big enough to fit her entire family and then some, but it was home.

Smiling to herself, she let her mind wander in anticipation. Soon, she'd park in her warmed garage, then traipse in through her mudroom. Dan, her personal chef, would have a light meal and a good bottle of wine waiting for her. No doubt, the gas fireplace would be on as well.

Thoughts of having a small bite to eat and a nice glass of wine were dancing in her head when she rounded the last bend before the gate. Finally, it came into full view, all twenty-feet-long-by-twelve-feet-high of it. A utilitarian fence ran the perimeter, but the gate itself was a work of art, literally. A local metal artist had designed and built it for her. Sure, many aspects of her life made her need to be extra cautious about security, but that didn't mean that security had to be ugly.

She smiled as her eyes traced the top lines then fell down the center to the big faux keyhole. She was reaching for the button on her Bluetooth display that would trigger the opening mechanism when something caught her eye. She hesitated, squinting through the windshield. Stopped so close to the gate, her headlights were too high to shed any light on the form propped along the bottom and she couldn't quite discern what it was. Switching off the headlights, she turned her fog lights on, immediately illuminating the ground area.

She stilled and stared.

Then cocked her head and stared some more.

When she'd first seen the form, she'd thought maybe one of her friends had left her something and just hadn't bothered driving all the way to the house to drop it. But as warped as her friends were—well, particularly Six—none of them would have left what she now recognized was waiting for her.

No, her friends might still have the capacity to surprise her, but there was no way in hell they would have left her a dead body.

Made in the USA
Monee, IL
10 July 2022

99420771R00174